KU-153-082

A
DEATH
IN
CALABRIA

A DEATH IN CALABRIA

MICHELE GIUTTARI
Translated by Howard Curtis

ISIS
LARGE PRINT
Oxford

Copyright © Michelle Giuttari, 2009
Translation Copyright © Howard Curtis, 2010

First published in Great Britain 2010
by
Little, Brown
An imprint of the Little, Brown Book Group

Published in Large Print 2011 by ISIS Publishing Ltd.,
7 Centremead, Osney Mead, Oxford OX2 0ES
by arrangement with
Little, Brown Book Group
An Hachette UK Company

All rights reserved

The moral right of the author has been asserted

British Library Cataloguing in Publication Data
Giuttari, Michele, 1950–
    A death in Calabria.
    1. Ferrara, Michele (Fictitious character) - - Fiction.
    2. Police - - Italy - - Fiction.
    3. Mafia - - Fiction.
    4. Calabria (Italy) - - Fiction.
    5. New York (N.Y.) - - Fiction.   **LP**
    6. Detective and mystery stories.
    7. Large type books.
    I. Title
    853.9'2–dc22

        ISBN 978–0–7531–8790–6 (hb)
        ISBN 978–0–7531–8791–3 (pb)

Printed and bound in Great Britain by
T. J. International Ltd., Padstow, Cornwall

To my wife Christa and my sister Rosa

*. . . andragathia est viri virtus adinventiva commu-
nicabilium operum.*
(. . . andragathia is the virtue of a man, whereby
he thinks out profitable works.)

St Thomas Aquinas, *Summa Theologica*, II–II
Quaestio 128, *De partibus fortitudinis*

PART ONE

NEW YORK

Prologue

Saturday, 1 November 2003

Suddenly he heard the creak.

Someone had opened the heavy glass and wrought-iron front door of the building and was coming in.

He took off his glasses and rested them on the shelf of the doorman's booth. In front of him, a few yards away, he saw three police officers in their dark blue uniforms. One was wearing a raincoat. He was taller than the others, with a muscular physique. The doorman looked at them with eyes as dark as ink stains.

They were young, probably between twenty-five and thirty, and were walking past the sign that said ALL VISITORS MUST BE ANNOUNCED.

He waited.

"Good evening," the officer in the raincoat said.

The voice was friendly enough. So was the smile.

"Good evening," the doorman replied, looking at them with great curiosity, anxious to know why they were here. This was something new. In more than thirty years, he'd never seen three police officers entering this building together. Especially not at eight thirty in the evening.

"We're from the 17th precinct," the same officer continued, unbuttoning his coat. "We need to check something."

The doorman nodded, then placed his left hand on a register with the word RESIDENTS on its black cover and with the other put his glasses back on. "Who are you here to see?" he asked.

"Nobody."

"I don't understand . . . I'm the doorman, I need to know who you're here to see, so that I can call up."

"We know you're the doorman. Just behave and everything'll be fine. Don't move!"

This time it was another officer who had spoken. He was shorter than the first man, of average build, with an olive complexion. He had stepped inside the booth. And his tone of voice had been harsh, almost menacing.

The doorman opened his eyes wide in terror. A long-barrelled pistol touched his left side. It was as if an electric shock had coursed through his body: his heart leapt in his chest, and his legs began trembling. His insides turned to ice. Even his lips shook. He was paralysed. He'd only ever seen a gun in cop shows on TV.

"Don't get any bright ideas," the shorter officer hissed in his ear, sitting down next to him on a stool, lowering the pistol and keeping his dark eyes fixed on him.

4

At that moment, there was a noise. The usual creaking. Someone was coming in.

The police officer jumped up, pulled his cap down over his forehead and put the index finger of his right hand on the trigger. But only for a moment. The newcomer was just a boy: no danger.

The elderly doorman was petrified, overcome with a whole mixture of feelings: consternation, incredulity, terror. Unusually for him, he started to pray. Big drops of sweat rolled down his forehead.

The smell of fear was in the air.

The elevator rose quickly. When the door opened on the nineteenth floor and they stepped out, they found themselves alone.

No sound. No voices, not even in the distance. No TV or radio noises. Only silence. The walls of the landing were white and the floor was covered with spotlessly clean blue carpeting. The lighting was dim.

The two officers stopped for a moment, exchanged knowing glances, then set off like athletes along the corridor to their right.

They soon came to the last apartment.

The muscular one pressed the bell. Once only. His companion had a dark complexion and several days' growth of black beard.

They did not have long to wait. A few seconds later, an eye looked out at them through the peephole. After another moment or two, there was a click . . .

The door slowly opened.

It was 8.36p.m. in Manhattan.

CHAPTER
ONE

Madison Avenue is one of the main thoroughfares of Manhattan. Situated between Fifth Avenue and Park Avenue, it is renowned as a street full of fashionable boutiques.

That Saturday evening, it was even more crowded than usual, despite the cold and the rain. The traffic was heavy and the pedestrians, wrapped tightly in their raincoats and overcoats, were hurrying along under their umbrellas, some with their coat collars raised, others with caps pulled down over their ears, and others with scarves around their necks. Many were on their way to Grand Central Terminal.

This wasn't just a normal Saturday.

The previous day had been Halloween, and all night the parade of witches, ghosts, skeletons and other macabre figures had wound through the streets of Greenwich Village. And the following day, Sunday, the 34th New York City Marathon was due to take place.

It was just after 9.25 p.m. that an elderly resident entered the building near the corner of East 42nd Street and Madison Avenue, in midtown Manhattan. It was the kind of apartment building where the rents were astronomical. With his right hand, the man was holding a little dog on a lead. As he walked into the lobby, he glanced towards the doorman's booth, and saw the doorman with his head tilted on to his right shoulder.

What's he up to? the man wondered. *Is he asleep?* Puzzled, he went closer to get a better look. The light from the large crystal chandelier on the lobby ceiling was so bright, he had to screw up his eyes a little.

The sight that greeted him was a harrowing one.

The doorman's cheeks were covered in blood, his eyes were wide open, and his tongue was hanging from his half-open mouth. His uniform was spattered with blood, and there was blood in a bright pool on the marble floor.

He stood there for a few minutes in silence, stunned. Then he raised his left hand to his bony forehead, as if to wipe out the horror of the scene, but at that moment the little dog yanked at the lead, pulling him back into the present. He looked around. There was nobody in sight. He rushed to the elevator, repeating over and over, "Oh, my God!"

The telephone began ringing just as Lieutenant John Reynolds was getting up from his chair to go home.

It was 21:50 according to the digital clock that stood on his tidy desk next to a framed photograph showing the lieutenant with his wife and daughter. It had been a tough day, full of muggings and robberies. Late in the afternoon, a mother had come in to report that her twelve-year-old daughter had been sexually assaulted.

Probably by the same pervert who had been terrorising Manhattan teenagers and their parents for some time now. A difficult case.

He lifted the receiver thinking it was his wife wanting to know when he'd be home. But it wasn't her.

"Lieutenant Reynolds?" The voice was a woman's — the switchboard operator.

"Yes, what is it?"

He listened.

"I'll be right there," he said, and slammed down the receiver. Then he put on his raincoat over his dark suit and hurried out. The expression on his face was a mixture of tiredness and irritation.

Arriving on the scene, he found the place swarming with NYPD patrolmen and detectives who had been alerted after the elderly resident had called 911.

They were talking among themselves about what had happened when Reynolds, still scowling, entered the spacious lobby.

"Here he is," one of the detectives said, immediately breaking away from the group and coming towards him. "Evening, Lieutenant."

"Evening, Mike!"

John Reynolds was head of the detective squad at the 17th precinct. He was a tall, broad-shouldered, hard-faced man, his thinning hair almost completely grey. After thirty years on the job, he knew the criminal world of Manhattan like the palm of his hand. He was fifty-six, the oldest detective still working the streets. Others his age preferred sitting

8

behind a desk giving orders. It was less stressful and you got more sleep. Reynolds was an exceptional investigator, one of the old school. There weren't many of his kind left.

Michael Bernardi, one of the rising stars of the detective squad, was head of homicide. He had been in the Times Square area when the call had gone out, and it had taken him only a few minutes to reach the scene of the crime.

"Any witnesses?" Reynolds asked.

"None so far, apart from the old guy who phoned," Bernardi replied, pointing to a man standing not far from them, talking to a policewoman. Reynolds glanced at him. He was tall, so thin he was verging on the skeletal, and almost bald.

"It could have been a robbery that went wrong," Mike went on. "There are two bullet cases inside the doorman's booth. Small calibre — .22, I think."

"Do we know the name of the victim yet?" Reynolds asked, rubbing his chin with his hand — a habitual gesture of his, almost a nervous tic. No hair grew on that part of his chin, thanks to an old wound received in a shootout with gang members in the Bronx.

"Bill Wells," the policewoman said, approaching the two men with an open notebook in her hands. She was young, with long black hair gathered under her cap and not a trace of make-up on her face. She gave Reynolds a curious look: she knew him only by reputation. "I checked out the name, Lieutenant. No priors. Completely clean."

"Good work, officer."

"Nothing's been touched, Lieutenant," Bernardi said.

"Good. Let's wait for the medical examiner to get here. In the meantime, cordon off the crime scene and make sure no one comes in."

The policewoman moved nimbly away. Reynolds went over to the doorman's booth, slowly walked around the body and stood looking at it for a while. Blood had gushed from the victim's head, transforming his face into a mask.

Then Reynolds had a word with the elderly resident who had discovered the body. The man's voice was so weak that he kept having to ask him to speak up.

"I took my dog out around eight for his usual walk in the park behind the Public Library, just around the corner here . . . Bill was at his post. He smiled at me as usual and waved. When I came back in, just before nine thirty, I found him in that position . . . I'm so sorry . . . He was a good man. I'd known him for years . . . I'm so sorry . . ."

All at once they heard footsteps. Someone was arriving in a hurry. Immediately afterwards they heard a voice. "Who's in charge? I want to speak with your chief!"

Reynolds turned and saw a man in his forties, clearly agitated, wearing dark blue jeans and a striped turtleneck sweater, and, next to him, a teenage boy in a sweatshirt and sneakers. They were just beyond the yellow tape bearing the words POLICE — DO NOT CROSS. Reynolds lifted the tape, ducked under it and walked up to them.

Meanwhile, the members of the Crime Scene Unit had started to check for fingerprints inside and outside the booth and on the panels of a wooden cupboard against the wall containing household items . . .

No stone would be left unturned.

CHAPTER
TWO

"My name's McGrey, and I'm a doctor," the man said excitedly. He indicated the boy. "This is my son Denis. We live on the fourth floor."

Denis looked thirteen, fourteen at the most. He was slim, tall for his age, with fair hair and a pale face. He was staring at Reynolds with his intense blue eyes, perhaps struck by the lieutenant's imposing physical presence, all six and a half feet of him.

"I'm Lieutenant Reynolds, head of the detective squad. Go on."

"My son says he saw a police officer, Lieutenant —"

"Hold on, just calm down. It might be better if we moved away from here." They walked over to the far end of the lobby, next to a large window through which evergreen plants could be seen beneath a glass roof.

"Now," Reynolds said reassuringly, "just calm down and tell me what happened."

"It isn't easy to calm down, Lieutenant."

"Why?"

"I just heard the doorman was killed. It doesn't make sense . . ."

"In what way?"

"My son . . . Denis . . . told me that, when he came home this evening, he saw a police officer inside the doorman's booth, with poor Bill."

"What time was this?"

There was a pause, during which Dr McGrey looked Reynolds straight in the eye. Then he turned to his son and said, "Denis, tell him what you told me."

The boy could hardly wait to speak up. That afternoon, he said, like every Saturday afternoon, he had gone to baseball practice. He wasn't sure what time he had come back. "It might have been around eight thirty."

"Why do you say 'might have been'?"

"I didn't have a watch on. When I go training, I leave my watch at home." He glanced at his father, who nodded.

"And what did you see?" Reynolds asked.

"I came into the building and saw Mr Bill," the boy continued in a determined tone. "He was in his booth, as usual. I think he was sitting down. There was a police officer next to him."

"What was this police officer like?" Reynolds prompted.

At that moment, he heard a baritone voice calling a greeting. It was Robert Cabot, the medical examiner, who had just arrived. Reynolds was relieved to see him. He preferred Cabot to the rest. From the first time they met he had felt an instinctive empathy for him, struck by his straightforward manner and keen intelligence.

"Like the police officers who are here," the boy replied. "He had the same uniform, even the same cap."

"Are you sure he was a police officer, Denis?"

"Absolutely sure. I know what cops look like. I'm not making a mistake."

"Denis wants to join the police, Lieutenant," his father said.

"That's right," Denis said, smiling, revealing the brace on his teeth. "I want to be a detective." His face had become slightly flushed.

"Can you describe this police officer?"

"I only saw him for a second, Lieutenant. I was running because I was late."

His father nodded silently.

"Go on, Denis."

"I'm not sure if I said hi to Bill. Maybe not. I thought he was talking with the police officer."

"Had you ever seen a police officer in the doorman's booth before, Denis?"

"No, never. This was the first time."

"Can you remember anything at all about the officer?"

"No. I think he was standing, because he was taller than Bill."

"Good! That's useful to know." Reynolds put a hand on his shoulder. "See if you can remember any other details like that."

Yes, details! Those details which are always so important in any investigation. At first they might appear insignificant, but as time went by they often turned out to be crucial, perhaps even the key to the whole case.

Denis fell silent.

"Was he white?" Reynolds asked, rubbing his chin.

"Yes, he was, I'm sure of that."

"Young? Old?"

"Young, I think, but I can't be a hundred per cent certain."

"What age would you say?"

"I don't know. But he wasn't old. He wasn't like Bill."

"Beard, moustache?"

"I don't know. I don't think so."

"Do you remember anything else?"

"No."

"Did you see anyone looking suspicious before you entered the building?"

The boy shook his head. "No. No, I didn't."

"Or anything unusual?"

"No. I already said no." With his hand, he began picking at a spot on his right cheek.

"Stop that, Denis," his father said. "You're going to make it bleed."

It was pointless to continue. It would only be a waste of time. And right now every minute was precious.

"I understand, Denis. Just try to think about it a bit more. Dr McGrey, if your son happens to remember anything else, let us know."

"Don't worry, Lieutenant, I will."

"Thanks." Reynolds took his card from his wallet and handed it to him. "All my phone numbers are here. Call me any time."

"Of course. I want to know what happened more than anyone. I'm concerned about my family.

Manhattan just isn't safe. All these policies they've brought in lately don't seem to have done any good. Sure, the streets are cleaner now, they've gotten rid of the vagrants, you don't get stopped on the streets and asked for money like you used to, but there's still plenty of crime. And it's not just at night; something can happen to you any hour of the day. Well, you would know all about that, Lieutenant. Am I right?"

Reynolds made no comment, simply said goodnight to them. Father and son both took the elevator.

As soon as they'd gone, he scanned the lobby, looking for cameras.

There weren't any. That was a pity: CCTV might have confirmed Denis's testimony.

For the moment, they had nothing to go on.

CHAPTER
THREE

It was the medical examiner who provided the first clues.

Robert Cabot looked forty at the most. He was slim, with longish brown hair combed back from his face, a light complexion, and keenly alert eyes. Looking at him without knowing him, you'd be unlikely to guess that this was a man who worked out of the Kings County Hospital mortuary, in daily contact with death. Unlike some of his colleagues in the Medical Examiner's office, he wasn't the kind of person to make cynical wisecracks as an antidote to the more distressing aspects of the job.

He approached the lieutenant with an air of tranquil assurance, still wearing latex gloves and overshoes.

Rigor mortis had not yet set in, he explained, and he had found two bullet holes in the back of the dead man's neck. No doubt about it: this was a homicide.

"How long has he been dead?" Reynolds asked.

"Not long. I'll be able to be more specific after the post mortem."

"Any hypostatic stains?"

"No."

That meant, Reynolds calculated, that death must have occurred four hours earlier at most. Any longer, and the blood, through force of gravity, would have accumulated in the lower parts of the body and filtered through the skin tissue, forming bluish marks, the so-called hypostatic stains.

"Exit wounds?" Reynolds asked.

"No."

"So the bullets are still in the body?"

"That's right. I'll recover them during the post mortem. Then we'll be able to clarify their trajectory and determine the positions of the doorman and his killer when the shots were fired."

"Thank you, Dr Cabot. When are you planning to do the post mortem?"

"Tomorrow morning at ten, I hope. I'll try to get the report to you as soon as possible."

"Detective Bernardi will be there."

"I'll be expecting him," Cabot said, taking off his gloves and raising his arm by way of farewell. Reynolds had never seen him shake anyone's hand — it was as if he feared infection from the contact.

He called Bernardi over and asked him to check around the precincts to see if any police officers had paid a visit to the building that evening. Then he ordered searches of the doorman's booth and the victim's apartment, and assigned officers to go door to door, asking all residents to report to the precinct house as soon as possible, preferably the following morning, to be interviewed. "Anyone who isn't home, leave a card under the door."

The officers dispersed.

In the meantime, the Crime Scene Unit technicians had already finished their work, and now two of them were getting ready to take the body away in a black plastic sack.

The doorman's booth was on the small side.

In his years of service, John Reynolds had come across some which were bigger, and many that were downright squalid. This one had a long wooden counter and a two-door cupboard, also of wood, crammed full of newspapers, magazines and leaflets. A plastic shopping bag in a corner contained the remains of Bill Wells's dinner: a cheeseburger and a sachet of ketchup from the nearby McDonald's. A can and a small Diet Coke bottle, both empty, were in the litter bin, next to a well-preserved mahogany desk. The only item of clothing, a dark grey overcoat, somewhat worn at the elbows, was hanging from a plastic coat hanger. In one of the pockets, the detectives found a bunch of keys, but no wallet. They had hoped it might be there, as it wasn't on the body or on the counter.

"Do we know where he lived?" Reynolds asked Bernardi.

"Yes, Lieutenant. The manager of the building gave me the address. It's in Queens. He lived alone since his wife died ten months ago. I'm on my way there now."

"I'll walk out with you," Reynolds said, joining him.

As soon as they were out on the sidewalk, heavy rain and high winds lashed at their faces. Lightning flashed across the sky at ever decreasing intervals. It was almost midnight and they seemed to be in the second circle of Dante's hell. Only a few reporters had gathered so far. They ignored them.

The atmosphere on the streets of Manhattan was no different than any other night: expectation and excitement for some, a sense of danger, even extreme danger, for others. Behind the façades of its skyscrapers and on its avenues and streets, New York, the city that never sleeps, concealed traps for the unwary. That was how it was. Even on a stormy night like tonight.

The predators were always lying in wait.

CHAPTER
FOUR

Sunday, 2 November

Michael Bernardi was forty-two years old.

The son of Sicilian immigrants, he'd been born, and had always lived, in New York. Of medium height, solidly built, with a dark complexion, short chestnut hair with a sprinkling of grey, and piercing dark eyes, he was tireless and determined in his work, a detective with a secure future in the police department. Always helpful, he was much appreciated, a favourite of the lieutenant and his colleagues. His reports were always clear and detailed. He double-checked everything scrupulously, and never accepted anything at face value. Highly intelligent himself, he had a short fuse when it came to stupidity and arrogance in others.

Now, at the head of a small team of officers, he stood outside the front door of Bill Wells's apartment building. It was located at the end of a dead end street, and they had had to park their cars in a nearby square and cover the last few yards on foot. The area was a decaying one, filled with low-rise housing, factories and potholed streets.

The apartment was on the second floor of a dilapidated brownstone building with deep cracks in the walls and a rusted fire escape. It had been a barracks at one time, but decades of neglect had reduced it to a squalid, unrecognisable state. There was no uniformed doorman here. No security system. No one to give out information at such a late hour.

Before knocking at the door of the apartment, the detectives stood listening for a moment or two. There was no sound from anywhere. But their arrival hadn't gone unnoticed. On entering the building, Bernardi had glanced around and had seen a curtain moving in the dim light of a street lamp. He knocked at the door. Several times. It was no use. One by one, he tried the keys from the bunch found in the overcoat, until at last one of them turned in the lock. Once, twice, three times. The door opened.

"Anyone at home?" he called out, going in with his gun in his hand.

Silence.

He switched on the lights.

There was no corridor. The three small rooms had low ceilings, damp-stained walls, and threadbare carpets. The furniture was sparse and of poor quality. The living room was empty apart from two armchairs and a couch, covered in some synthetic material, presumably to hide wear and tear. But at least the place was clean and tidy.

There was an indescribable air of sadness about the place.

The detectives started searching.

The search was an indispensable routine. It was here that the victim had lived his life, and it was here, among the things that had belonged to him, that they might find a few clues to his death.

They looked everywhere, even in the unlikeliest places.

Experience had taught them that people, especially older people, hid money, jewels and their most valued possessions in their homes, either because they'd stopped trusting banks, or else out of fear.

So they looked in the lavatory cistern, the bag in the vacuum cleaner, the lampshades, the refrigerator, the freezer and — the oldest and commonest hiding place in the world — under the mattress. They didn't find anything anywhere, except in an old dresser in the bedroom. When they opened the four drawers with floral motifs on them, a strong smell of mildew emerged. They were full of linen, socks, sweaters and shirts, some very worn. Here, too, everything was tidy. In the last drawer they discovered a tin box containing photographs of the victim and others, perhaps relatives and friends, along with some yellowed letters and a diary with names and addresses. Buried right at the back were papers relating to an account at a bank in Manhattan. They took everything away with them.

But there was still no trace of a wallet. More than ever, Bernardi was convinced that Bill Wells had been the victim of a petty robbery that had ended as badly as it possibly could: in murder.

He knocked at the door of the apartment opposite Wells's.

The door opened, but only as far as the chain would allow. An elderly man stared out at Bernardi, his angry eyes saying, *Why the fuck are you knocking at my door at this hour?*

Calmly, Bernardi opened his leather wallet and showed the man his badge. "Detective Michael Bernardi," he said.

The man's eyes lingered for a moment on the badge, then moved to Bernardi's face, then back to the badge, for longer this time, as if he wanted to examine it. The chain was still in the same position.

"What's going on?" he asked in a sleepy voice.

"I'd like to ask you a few questions. Can I come in?"

"A few questions? What about?"

The crack in the door widened, but only as far as the length of the chain.

"Your neighbour, Mr Wells, was killed this evening."

Immediately, the man turned pale. At last he took off the chain and opened the door.

"Come in," he said, moving away from the door, a sad expression on his face. "My name's George Brooks."

He had long white hair and a pale, emaciated face. He was wearing only a pair of long woollen underpants with a large hole over the left knee and a sweater that came down to his waist.

"Thank you," Bernardi replied. "I'm sorry we didn't warn you we were coming, but I'll only be a few minutes."

The apartment was freezing cold. Bernardi followed the old man down a narrow corridor past the open door of the bathroom, through which he glimpsed an old-fashioned toilet with a chain, a little washbasin and a pile of linen in a corner, until they came to the small kitchen, which smelled of fried fish. They sat down at a table covered with a stained plastic tablecloth with a floral pattern.

The man told him that his neighbour was a very serious individual, who had often had a faraway look, and a hint of tears, in his eyes of late. "He lost his wife, you know. They loved each other very much. He had no one else in the world."

"Had he had any strange visitors lately?" Bernardi asked. "Did you hear anything suspicious?"

The man shook his head. Two large tears were running down his cheeks. For a few moments, he was silent. Then he started speaking again. "No, nothing at all. He led a quiet life. I can't believe he was murdered."

"You haven't seen or heard anything unusual in the last few days?" Bernardi persisted.

"Nothing, and nobody I don't see every day. The punks, the dealers . . . This isn't exactly the best of neighbourhoods. Well, I'm sure you people know that."

"Thank you. You've been very helpful. I'm sorry to have called on you so late."

As Bernardi rose from his chair, he heard subdued voices and footsteps out on the landing. His colleagues. He had to go. At the door, he turned and handed the man a card. "Don't hesitate to call me if you remember anything."

"I'm sorry I didn't even offer you anything to drink," the man replied, closing the door quietly.

Turning to his men, Bernardi hesitated for a moment, thinking, *What do you know — humanity, in a rat hole like this!*

CHAPTER
FIVE

When John Reynolds got back to the 17th precinct, he immediately gave instructions to his men about the interviews they would be conducting. "Dig," he said, urging them, "and you will find." Then he opened a bottle of water, poured some into a paper cup and took a long gulp.

He occupied the typical head of detectives office space: a large corner office at the end of a long corridor. On one wall hung two big maps of Manhattan, strewn with pins. The first indicated the rapes, assaults and murders reported within the past six months. The second showed the houses, banks and commercial premises robbed during the same period. Next to it was a graph showing the decline in crime statistics. On the left-hand wall just next to the desk was another map, which had been there for a few months now, showing locations for two crimes that were on the increase: rape and sexual assault.

He walked to the window. Large raindrops were beating noisily against the panes. He thought about calling home again.

That morning, when he had left, his wife Linda had had all the symptoms of flu. She was pale, sweating, and shaking like a leaf. When he had last phoned her, at around eight in the evening, she had told him that she had a temperature of 102 degrees and that she had already phoned the doctor. Now he dialled the number again. Linda answered at the fourth ring.

"Hi, darling, did I wake you?"

"No, John, I was in the bathroom."

"Sorry about that. How are you feeling?"

"A little better."

"What did the doctor say?"

"Nothing too serious. Just a bout of flu. I should be up and about in a few days."

Reynolds hesitated before replying. He imagined his wife in her nightdress, the black lace one, his favourite, with her dark hair falling softly over her shoulders.

Linda was a tall, beautiful woman with full hips and blue eyes. Reynolds had always been jealous of the admiring glances she received from other men, although he was sure she was faithful to him — and took pride in the fact.

"Look after yourself, darling," he said at last. "Keep away from draughts."

"Don't worry. When are you coming home?"

"There's been a homicide."

"Where?"

"Here in Manhattan. The doorman of an apartment building was murdered."

"Another murder . . ." There was a kind of exhaustion in her tone, and perhaps something else. He caught the hint of it, and the terrifying thought suddenly struck him: *What if Linda gets so tired of this life that she decides to leave me? What would become of me?*

But it was only a fleeting impression. "Only a little while longer, darling, you know," he hastened to reassure her.

"Let's hope so."

"When I get home, I'll try not to wake you."

"I love you, John."

"I love you too."

Both hung up simultaneously.

Reynolds knew that his career was about to change. His promotion and transfer to a desk job at NYPD headquarters on Park Row, which would allow him to work more sociable hours and to devote more time to himself and Linda, had already been decided.

A reassuring future.

The offices of the detective squad occupied one whole floor.

Homicide was on one side of the corridor, spread over a series of rooms. Each room contained four desks. Rows of metal filing cabinets lined the windowless walls. The last room was Michael Bernardi's office, separated by large windows from the space where his men worked.

The rooms were crowded, the computers switched on, and the telephones were constantly ringing. The chairs in front of the desks were occupied by witnesses, answering questions with an air of boredom, convinced they were only wasting their time. Their answers amounted to little more than the same litany:

The victim was a good man . . . He'd been working there for more than thirty years . . . He was always helpful, always doing little jobs . . . He was a quiet man and didn't go in for gossip . . . He never did anything at all suspicious . . .

There was complete unanimity. No one had heard anything unusual, any gunshots, no one had seen anyone suspicious in the past few days. No one confirmed Denis's story of having seen a police officer in the building.

In separate rooms, the victim's two fellow doormen gave their statements. They mentioned the occasional argument Bill Wells had had with local punks who'd tried to bum a few dollars off him, some of them even threatening violence. "In this town," one of the two men said, "you can be killed for a ten-dollar bill in an old wallet. That's how New York is. It's a violent place. What happened to Bill could have happened to one of us on our shift."

Just before leaving, having given their fingerprints to be compared with those found inside the doorman's booth, they both asked the same question.

"Will you get him?"

"That's what we're trying to do."

"Please find him."

It was almost a prayer.

When the last witness had left the office, Lieutenant Reynolds called his men together.

He listened patiently to all the reports, but nothing he heard sounded particularly useful, though his men had made a thorough search of the area for possible leads. No one had seen anything, not even a suspicious car. It wasn't the first time. In these cases, fear kept mouths firmly shut.

Bernardi, just back from the search of the victim's apartment, stuck his head round the door, and Reynolds motioned him to come in. To the rest of the men, he said, "What are you waiting for? Keep your eyes open. Check all surveillance cameras in the area. We can't afford to waste time. We're dealing with an unpremeditated homicide here. So let's get going!"

Once the men had gone and Reynolds was alone with Bernardi, he grabbed the bottle of water, filled two paper cups and said, "Hold on a moment, Mike." Then he lit yet another cigarette, possibly the last of the day, and took a few drags. Clouds of smoke formed in the air, making it smell even mustier than before.

Bernardi sat down opposite Reynolds and brought him up to date on the search of the victim's apartment and on the answers they'd obtained from the other precincts in New York. No squad car or police officer had been called to the building on Madison that evening. No one from that address had phoned 911 or any of the precincts to request assistance.

Reynolds threw his now empty cup into the waste bin. "So none of the witnesses we've questioned so far has mentioned a police officer. Except Denis . . ."

"I know what you're thinking, Lieutenant. A kid with a vivid imagination, who wants to be a detective . . ."

Reynolds nodded. Then his mind went back to the testimonies of the victim's colleagues, and he mentioned to Bernardi what they had said about Bill Wells's confrontations with neighbourhood punks. At these words, Mike pulled a face, as if to say, *That's it! There's our confirmation!*

They switched out the lights and left the office. Reynolds glanced at his wristwatch. It was 3.50 in the morning on what should have been his day off. He said goodnight to Bernardi, lifted the collar of his raincoat and got into his grey Ford Crown Victoria next to the driver, who had already started the engine. "Take me home," he ordered. "Home" was Battery Park, at the southern tip of Manhattan, on the western side looking towards New Jersey.

And so they drove through the night, in a city now wrapped in a blanket of fog.

CHAPTER
SIX

It was an unusually mild morning for the time of year.

The fog had lifted as suddenly as it had settled. The weak, grey-pink light of dawn had given way to a clear blue sky tinged with gold. The air had been swept clean by the wind from the ocean. But still the usual smog and poisons clung to the façades of the skyscrapers.

It was 8 a.m. and already New Yorkers, tourists and athletes were pouring out on to the streets.

The newspapers carried page after page devoted to the marathon. The murder of the doorman, on the other hand, merited only a few brief mentions on the inside pages, which merely reported that the previous evening, in an apartment building in midtown Manhattan, a doorman named Bill Wells, sixty-one years old, had been shot dead. There were no eyewitnesses, and as yet no indication of the identity of the perpetrator or his motive.

Only the *New York Times* gave the news a little more space.

In the concluding lines of his article, the reporter lingered over a detail ignored by all the other papers:

It appears that, shortly before the murder took place, a resident of the building saw the victim in the company of a police officer inside the doorman's booth. When quizzed about this, the NYPD press office declined to comment. But we have reason to believe that there has been definite corroboration. Is this yet another embarrassment for the NYPD?

Detective Bernardi read the article on the way to Kings County Hospital mortuary. His tired face flushed with anger. He looked for the name of the journalist who had written the piece. It was David Powell, a crime reporter who had a history of coming up with excellent sources, some inside the NYPD itself.

Bernardi folded the newspaper and tossed it angrily onto the pile of papers on the back seat.

"What's the matter, sir?" the driver asked.

"Nothing, Raymond, just the usual press crap."

"Right!"

"Some son of a bitch looking for a scoop and not caring what damage he causes along the way. The stuff he's written shouldn't have been made public yet."

"Journalists are scum, sir. I'm with you there."

"We'll make this one pay sooner or later . . . same goes for whoever it is who's giving him his information."

The driver shook his head. Knowing Bernardi's dogged determination, he was sure that David Powell would be feeling the heat sooner or later. For the rest of their short journey, they spoke little, and soon reached their destination.

After walking down a series of cold corridors, Bernardi took the stairs that led to the basement where post mortems were carried out. In this part of the hospital all the hours of the day were the same, it was a place with no windows, untouched by daylight. Even the smell never changed: that characteristic stench that greeted him now and became even sharper as soon as he walked through the door of the autopsy room.

A shiver went down his spine.

The body lay naked on a stainless steel table in the middle of the room.

An orderly was washing it down with a hose.

The medical examiner, Robert Cabot, standing by a counter with the instruments, had already put on a white coat, green rubber gloves and a mask. His long chestnut hair peeked out from under his cap. He was ready. He and Bernardi exchanged a brief greeting, then Bernardi, too, put on a white coat and mask, omitting only the gloves. Then he stepped closer to the table to observe the post mortem. Although he knew by heart every movement Cabot would make, he was always surprised by the ME's meticulous precision.

Dictating to a tape recorder, Cabot carefully examined the corpse and described its external appearance, then began cutting it open. As he worked, he filled the test tubes on the steel cart beside him with urine, blood and other bodily fluids for subsequent analysis. Finally, he started the circular saw, breaking the grave-like silence with its roar.

He opened the scalp and pulled it back, sawed through the skull vault, and examined the brain. With a long pair of tongs, he extracted two bullets and placed them on a little tray. Bernardi took a few steps forward to get a better look.

Now they were sitting on two visitors' chairs in front of the desk, slowly sipping hot coffee.

"There are a number of significant factors," Robert Cabot said, with the self-satisfied air of someone who is in a position to demonstrate his own skill for the umpteenth time. "Three for certain, I'd say."

Bernardi put his cup down on the desk, and took his ubiquitous notebook and pen from his briefcase. "Go on, Doctor."

"Just a minute!" Cabot said, and drank down the rest of his coffee before proceeding. "First: the time of death. Between eight and ten last night. Give or take a few minutes either way. This can be inferred from the absence of hypostatic stains, from the rectal temperature, and from the fact that his dinner was fully digested. Second: there are no signs of physical attack. Third: the two bullets. They entered behind the ear, went through the cranium, and lodged in the right lower jaw."

Bernardi nodded. The first two factors confirmed what they had already surmised. The third, on the other hand, was new and required further explanation.

As if reading the detective's thoughts, Cabot jumped in before Bernardi had even opened his mouth and said, in an even more professional tone, "The route the bullets took runs from the back to the front, with a slight inclination from top to bottom, which suggests that the victim was sitting when he was shot, and that the killer, at the moment he fired, was in a higher position, probably standing to his left."

Bernardi nodded, pleased with the results.

Cabot handed him two small plastic bags containing the bullets. They were .22 calibre, like the cases discovered on the floor of the doorman's booth. Bernardi put them in his briefcase. Then he asked when the report would be ready.

"In a few days," Cabot replied. "But I've already told you my most significant findings."

"Thanks."

Bernardi closed his notebook, took off his white coat, said goodbye and left. But he didn't go back to the precinct house. On the spur of the moment, he decided to pay a visit to the Crime Scene Unit's ballistics lab.

And there he would learn something unexpected.

Something really unexpected.

The killer's gun had been fitted with a silencer.

The tips of the copper-coated, round-nosed bullets had been found to have semicircular dents, caused by the bullets making contact with one of the metal diaphragms of the silencer which was not perfectly aligned with the axis of the gun barrel.

"A silencer, Lieutenant! They're sure of it. No doubt whatever."

Bernardi had rushed straight from the ballistics lab to the precinct house and was now sitting facing Reynolds, leaning forward with his elbows on the desk.

"This changes everything. The theory that this was an unpremeditated murder by some street punk is starting to look very shaky. We're going to have to think again."

"Are the dents on both bullets?" Reynolds asked.

"Yes, although they aren't perfectly identical, but that's quite normal, according to ballistics. The similarities are significant. Every mark on the two bullets was compared through an optical microscope."

There was a long pause.

The sun, now high, flooded the room and flared off the lieutenant's nameplate.

In an investigation everything could be useful: preliminary reports, interview transcripts, post mortems, expert analyses, sometimes just a routine door to door. But solving the case depended on reading and interpreting the material evidence correctly. Both Reynolds and Bernardi knew how important it was not to rely on intuition alone. What they had just learned was the first piece of concrete evidence they had, the first piece in the jigsaw.

"How about prints?" Reynolds asked, breaking the silence.

"All the prints found at the crime scene belonged to the victim and his colleagues," Bernardi replied.

"No one else?"

"No one else, Lieutenant. Unfortunately."

"And on the bullet cases?"

"No prints on them."

Which meant that the killer must have been wearing gloves when he loaded the gun — a precaution usually taken by hit men.

"So the killer was a professional!" Reynolds said. "Everything we have right now points to that."

The theory of a professional hit was also supported by the weapon: the .22 was the weapon of choice for hit men. It was easy to conceal, and with a silencer it produced no sound other than the noise of the mechanical parts.

But there were details that didn't fit this picture. Why would a professional hit man have killed the doorman at his place of work when there would surely have been other, less risky, opportunities? Why would a hit man take the victim's wallet? And why on earth had the doorman not reacted? Had he known his killer? Did he have a secret life, unknown to his colleagues, the residents of the building, and his neighbours?

That made for a lot of questions. So far, there were no answers.

Bernardi stared down at his notebook. Better to get back to concrete facts. He brought the lieutenant up to date on the cause of death, the supposed time of death, the bullets and their trajectory.

"Mike," Reynolds said when he had finished, "we need to find out more about Bill Wells's past."

Bernardi nodded, although he had his doubts. Having seen the man's apartment, he thought it unlikely that such an anonymous existence could hold any secrets.

"Oh, one more thing, Mike."

"Yes, Lieutenant?"

"The case is yours. You call the shots, but I'd be grateful if you'd keep me informed of what's happening as it happens. You know what I mean." He rubbed his chin with his hand.

Bernardi nodded. "Sure, Lieutenant. I know you like to follow certain cases personally."

John Reynolds smiled — his first smile of the day. As head of the squad, he could supervise and coordinate his detectives' activities without necessarily being involved personally. But everyone at the 17th precinct knew that wasn't how he worked. He had always had a particular interest in homicide — not to mention the fact this would, in all probability, be his last case.

From the street, they could hear shouts and cheers from the marathon spectators. It had been shortly after ten when a cannon shot had given the signal for the race to start from Verrazano Bridge.

Reynolds was about to get up from his chair when the telephone started ringing. It was 1.46 according to the clock on the desk. He was late, he knew. He had promised Linda that he would be home by one. That morning, when he had left, she had been asleep and he had not wanted to wake her. At the third ring he picked up.

But it wasn't his wife.

It was the switchboard.

And he suddenly had to change his plans.

CHAPTER
SEVEN

"Get your coat, Mike," Reynolds said, grim-faced, as soon as he put down the phone.

"Where are we going?"

"Same building as last night. East 42nd Street."

Bernardi did not ask any more questions.

Reynolds grabbed his coat from the stand and put it on, and they went out.

The streets were packed with people cheering on the runners. The atmosphere was festive and chaotic. The driver turned from East 51st Street on to Lexington Avenue. Although he had his siren on, it took him nearly ten minutes to drive nine blocks.

"It'll be like this till the last runners have crossed the finishing line," he said. "The whole route, all the way to Central Park. It's like this every year."

"Yes," Reynolds replied. "Today's a special day, but not for us."

When they finally reached East 42nd Street, the driver double-parked and let them out.

Reynolds looked around. There wasn't a single journalist about. The sidewalk had already been cordoned off. An officer lifted the tape and let them pass. As they made their way into the building there was a disturbing silence in the lobby. The elevator took them up to the nineteenth floor. The police sergeant who was standing outside the door of the last apartment at the end of the corridor came to meet them.

"What happened?" Reynolds asked.

"A massacre."

"What?"

"Six bodies, in there." He pointed to the door, which was standing wide open. "It's a mess."

"Did you find the door open?" Reynolds asked.

"Yes, but there are no signs of forced entry."

"You mean it was left like this?"

"No."

"What, then?"

"She opened the door with her key," the officer said, indicating a young woman at the other end of the corridor.

Reynolds looked at her for a moment. She was a pretty girl, wearing a pair of tight-fitting jeans with a low waist, a black leather coat, and shiny high-heeled boots. She had dark chestnut hair, cut fashionably short. She was sitting, and next to her a police officer was taking notes.

"Who is she?" Reynolds asked.

"The niece of the guy who owns the apartment. She was the one who phoned 911. She already gave a statement, but she seemed pretty vague."

"What did she say?"

"That she let herself into the apartment with her key, saw a body and was so scared, she ran straight out again."

42

"What's her name?"

"Maria Pre . . . Just a minute, it's an Italian name." The officer looked through the notebook he had in his hand. "Prestipino, that's it, Lieutenant. Prestipino."

"Thanks."

"Do you want to speak to her?"

"No, I want to take a look inside the apartment first." Then, as if he hadn't understood correctly, he asked, "You did say six bodies?"

The officer looked at him. "That's right, Lieutenant. Five men, one woman. All adults."

"Who are they?"

"Right now, we don't know. One of them could be the owner of the apartment. They seem to be Italians, apart from two of them, the man in the hallway and the woman in the dining room."

"OK, I need gloves and overshoes. We can't afford to waste time on this one."

The officer took the things out of a small case and handed them to him.

"Mike," Reynolds said, putting on the latex gloves, "find out who's available and get them over here."

Bernardi nodded.

Reynolds walked in through the open door.

Alone.

An unmistakable smell, sickly and nauseating, different from any other, immediately hit him so strongly that his breath died in his throat.

The stench of death.

The first thing he noticed was the card his men had slipped under the door the previous evening. Then he saw the body near the door, and the dried brown blood. Everything looked cold, frozen.

He took a deep breath and walked on. The door to the dining room was wide open. He went in. The stench struck him again like a wave, even more fetid and nauseating than before. He looked around. The room was large and filled with light. The rays of the sun, filtering through the windows with the curtains pulled back, made it even brighter. In addition, the crystal chandelier on the ceiling was still lit.

There was a couch against one wall, with a large flat-screen TV above it. It was switched on, and an Italian programme was showing. Against another wall were two armchairs with green cushions that matched the colour of the display cabinet facing them. Above the armchairs, a large oil painting. Slowly, he moved.

And saw more corpses.

Two sat with their torsos thrown across the table, which was elegantly laid with trays of food in the middle. Two more, including the woman, lay on the marble floor. A bottle of red wine had fallen to the floor and smashed into a thousand pieces. The walls were riddled with holes and spattered with blood, now dry. There was more blood on the furniture. He noticed the many cartridge cases strewn on the ground. They were all small calibre: .22.

He knelt to get a better look at the bodies. The faces were horribly disfigured. They had multiple bullet wounds and appeared to have been shot at point-blank range, judging by the brain matter spattered everywhere. He lingered for a while, studying the positions and the bloodstains.

An act of homicidal madness had transformed this room into a slaughterhouse.

Reynolds had smelled something even sicklier and more unpleasant. He cast his mind back to one of his first cases, right here in Manhattan, almost twenty years earlier. It had been 16 December 1985. Around 6p.m., in a street filled with people doing their Christmas shopping, Paul Castellano, the most powerful Mafia boss of the time, was shot dead, along with his driver and right-hand man, just as they had been about to enter a steakhouse. It had been a horrific sight: their bodies had been riddled with bullets. What he saw now demonstrated the same ferocity on the part of the killers. But were the killers the same?

The old Mafia, Cosa Nostra, had been dead and buried since the death of the last godfather, John Gotti, and had been supplanted by the Chinese triads, the Japanese yakuza, the Colombians, the Jamaicans, and — most vicious of all — the Russians. Where it existed at all, it had been relegated to a minor role.

Reynolds dismissed these images and proceeded with caution. He still had not seen the sixth corpse. He found it in another room, clearly a kind of den, at the end of the long corridor. Here too, the door was open. The body was lying on the floor behind the desk, the legs slightly splayed. The face, tilted to one side, was almost unrecognisable. The left eye had been blotted out by a bullet that must have gone through the eyeball and the brain.

It was immediately obvious to Reynolds that the victim must have been standing when he had been hit and that his killer would have been facing him. The shots to the head were a clear signature: it had been a Mafia-style execution, right here in a Manhattan apartment.

Two other details caught his attention.

One was that the dead man was wearing, on his left wrist, a gold Rolex encrusted with diamonds. It must have cost a fortune!

The second was the pistol on the floor beside the body. It was a 7.65. Next to it, a cartridge case of the same calibre. It appeared that the victim had managed to fire a single shot before he died.

Reynolds turned to the desk, a valuable antique. On it stood two photographs in silver frames. He looked at them, first one, then the other. It took him a moment or two to realise that they showed the same man at two different times in his life, but in the same setting, with a small mountain church in the background. There was a definite resemblance, he saw, between the man in the photographs and the victim. Then he noticed an oil painting on the wall: a landscape. In the foreground of the painting was a little church, perhaps the same one as in the photographs. Next, his eyes were drawn to a bookcase, the lower part of which had doors, and they were wide open. He crouched to look inside: a safe, with its door ajar. It was empty. He spent a few moments staring into the void, then at the digital combination pad, as if examining it.

In the other rooms, everything seemed clean and tidy. It was possible the killer, or killers, hadn't even been in them. Reynolds thought over what he had seen: this was a luxury apartment, and the owner must have had a lot of money, there was no doubt about that. He looked for signs of a struggle, but found none. There was no way these had been chance killings. The victims had been specifically targeted. The killer, or more likely, the killers had entered the apartment and apparently taken away the contents of the safe.

"Mike," he said to Bernardi as soon as he was back in the corridor, "we need to check out the hospitals as soon as possible."

His colleague looked at him questioningly. "Why?"

"There's a gun next to one of the bodies, a 7.65 calibre, and a cartridge case. The victim must have had time to fire a shot."

"I'll get right on it, Lieutenant."

"Now let's leave the Crime Scene Unit to its work. When that's over, I want a thorough search, and I want you to deal with that personally, Mike. Oh, and phone the Assistant DA, he's going to want to know about this."

"Sure thing, Lieutenant," Bernardi said. "This has all the marks of a mob hit."

Reynolds paused, then said, "We need to know all we can about the owner of the apartment."

"Yesterday one body, now six more."

The voice was unmistakable.

Reynolds turned, grim-faced. It was Cabot again. He hadn't yet finished his shift. He'd often joked about the medical examiner's deep baritone with Bernardi, but right now he was finding it really irritating. He would have liked to plug his ears, but instead he nodded a curt greeting. He watched as Cabot walked towards the forensics team, who had started combing through the apartment. Some were taking photographs from every angle to record the position of the bodies, some were spreading argentoratum powder to detect prints invisible to the naked eye, others were using vacuum cleaners to pick up fibres and hair, others were taking samples of blood from the floor . . . The usual routine.

The uniformed officer who had been talking to Maria Prestipino approached Reynolds and held out some sheets of paper. "The owner of the apartment was a man named Rocco Fedeli," he said. "This is everything we have on him."

Reynolds started to read. Rocco Fedeli had recently celebrated his fortieth birthday. He had been born on 20 August 1963, in a small village in Calabria, San Piero d'Aspromonte, and had come to New York in 1986 on business. According to police records, he was an entrepreneur, the owner of a company distributing Italian food products in New York State. He also owned an Italian restaurant on the Upper East Side, near Central Park, and a three-star hotel, the Jonio, in Little Italy. He had no criminal record, and had never had any problems with the Internal Revenue Service. Someone quite unremarkable, so far as the authorities were concerned; one of the many Italians who had made their fortune in America.

He folded the papers and passed them to Bernardi, who had just rejoined him. "This is all we have on the owner of the apartment. He seems clean. I've certainly never seen the name before."

"Yesterday, a doorman shot dead with a gun equipped with a silencer. Today, six people murdered in an apartment. All in the same building, and the work of professionals. There has to be a connection, Lieutenant."

"I'm thinking the same thing, Mike. It can't be a coincidence."

"I made the call. Assistant DA Morrison will be here soon."

"Thanks, Mike."

From the other end of the corridor came the sound of someone sobbing. The two men turned to investigate.

"It might have been twelve, or twelve thirty at the latest, when I decided to come here."

Maria Prestipino was answering the lieutenant's questions. He had sat down on a chair next to hers. She was crying, her arms hugging her chest and a vague look in her eyes. So far she had said nothing new, merely repeating what she had told the uniformed officer. In her right hand, she clutched a paper handkerchief, which she raised to her eyes from time to time.

"What made you come here?" Reynolds asked.

"My parents and I had an appointment with my uncle at one o'clock. We were supposed to meet at his restaurant near Central Park, and I tried to phone him to tell him that Mom and Dad would be a little late, but there was no reply. I tried his cellphone, too, and couldn't get through."

Her voice was low, imbued with a deep sadness, and her face was as white as a sheet. She was silent for a few moments.

"What did you do then?" Reynolds prompted, looking her straight in the eyes: they were remarkably dark, though swollen with crying at the moment.

"I started to get worried. I thought something had happened, but then I told myself I was being silly."

"Why?"

"My uncle doesn't live alone."

"Is he married?"

"No, he lives with his domestic staff."

"Why did you have an appointment near Central Park?"

"I was going to meet my other uncles. And also to see the marathon, as we do every year." There was a catch in her voice as she said this.

"Your other uncles?" Reynolds asked.

"Yes, they arrived from Italy yesterday."

"What did you do then?"

"There was nothing I could do."

"I mean, what did you do when you got here?" Reynolds asked.

"I rang the bell, but no one opened. I got more worried." At this point, she burst out crying again. She wiped her tears slowly, sighed, and said in a thin voice, "I saw him there on the floor in the entrance . . ." She was still sobbing softly.

"It's all right . . ." Reynolds stood up, went closer to her and stroked her back. "It's all right, Miss Prestipino. When you say 'him', who do you mean?"

"The man who worked for him. He helped in the apartment and was also his driver, and his wife cleaned and cooked. She was a really good cook."

"How long had they been working here?"

"More than ten years, even before they were married."

"Were they Italian?"

"No, Puerto Rican."

Reynolds thought it best not to continue with his questioning for the moment. Maria Prestipino had turned even paler and now looked as though she might faint. She asked permission and got up to go to the bathroom, accompanied by a woman police officer. While they waited, Detective Bernardi sat updating his notes.

When Maria returned and sat down, Reynolds picked up where he had left off. "So you rang the bell and no one came to answer the door. Is that right?"

The young woman nodded, without looking up.

"So what did you do?"

"I opened the door. My uncle had given me a set of keys . . . For when he was away from New York . . ." She was about to break down again.

"It's all right. Tell me, did the door look as if it had been forced?"

"No. As I said, I opened it with my key, the way I always do." She fell silent for a few moments. Her eyes were tearing up more than ever and with her left hand she was twisting the fringe which came down over her forehead.

He asked her if she had touched anything, and she said no. She had stopped in the entrance, she said, at the sight of the body and the blood. First she had phoned her parents, then she called 911.

Reynolds asked her if she felt up to coming into the apartment with him and identifying the bodies.

"No, I can't. Please. Once was enough. Please don't make me!" She lifted her right thumb to her mouth and began to bite the nail, in an obvious state of agitation.

"All right, there's no need for you to go in. But can you just tell us if your uncle kept any photographs on his desk?"

"Why are you asking me that?" There was a tightness in her throat as she spoke.

"I'd just like to know."

"He has two photographs of himself in front of the shrine of the Madonna of Aspromonte. Like all our family, he's very religious. One of those photographs was taken when he was only eighteen."

Reynolds did not press her. She'd more or less told him what he wanted to know: that the body in the den was indeed that of Rocco Fedeli.

There was a long pause.

In response to further questions, Maria Prestipino said that she had seen her uncle for the last time the previous Friday, when they had had lunch together in his restaurant and had arranged to meet today.

"Thank you, Miss Prestipino. I'm going to have to ask you to come down to the precinct house with your parents as soon as possible to make a statement."

"All right, I'll be there, and so will my parents." A little colour had come back into her face.

As he said goodbye to her, Reynolds noticed that her hands were red and moist and that her nails, although well cared for, were unpolished. He was walking away, followed by Bernardi, when he suddenly turned.

"By the way, Miss Prestipino," he asked, "do you work with your uncle?"

"No. I'm a student. I'm in my last year of college."

"What are you studying?"

"Law. I attend Columbia Law School."

As the two detectives were walking away, she bent and took her cellphone from her shoulder bag. It had been ringing for a few moments; the ring tone was Celine Dion's "My Heart Will Go On". Reynolds and Bernardi heard her reply, "Darling, thank God it's you!"

And her face lit up.

When Reynolds entered the apartment for the second time, Bernardi followed him.

In the den, someone was talking. They saw two members of the CSU bending over the body. The Assistant DA was next to them, saying something.

Ted Morrison was fifty-five years old, a short, bald man with a thin moustache and a paunch that made a bulge in his jacket. He was wearing a light grey suit. As coordinator of the special unit in organised crime, he was an expert in the field. The two detectives approached and greeted him.

"When I got here," Morrison asked, with his usual cordial air, "I saw you talking to a young woman in the corridor. I didn't want to disturb you. Who was she?"

"The niece of the man who owned the apartment." Reynolds gestured towards the body. "That guy . . ."

"What's his name?"

"Rocco Fedeli. An Italian, from Calabria."

"Can't say I've ever heard the name. Does he belong to one of the families?"

"Not as far as we know." Reynolds told him what he had learned from the files.

"A complete unknown, then!" Morrison commented.

The two detectives nodded.

"And the others?"

"We still have to identify them, but they all seem to be Italians, apart from the man in the entrance and the woman. They're both Puerto Ricans who worked for Fedeli."

"And the others?" Morrison asked again.

"Two of the men might be Rocco Fedeli's brothers; the other man we really don't know anything about. At least, not from what Fedeli's niece told me."

"Well, Lieutenant," Morrison said, "my advice is that you should ask the Organised Crime Control Bureau for help. This could be big."

"I think you're right. In fact, I don't think we have any choice."

"The FBI too," Morrison continued. "We all need to work as a team on this. NYPD, the Manhattan DA's office, and the Feds."

The two detectives exchanged looks and nodded.

"I'll contact them as soon as I can, if they haven't already been informed," Reynolds replied. Deep down, he'd have preferred not to contact them at all. He wasn't crazy about the Feds. He didn't like the way everything was always so hush-hush with them, and he particularly couldn't stand the way they swaggered around as if they were God's gift to law enforcement. He liked to work with his own detective squad, and that was that.

"Great!" Morrison said.

In the meantime, Bernardi had switched his attention to two of the CSU people, who were busy doing paraffin tests. He went closer and took a look at the exhibits that had already been photographed and filmed: the gun, the 7.65 cartridge case, and the many .22 calibre cartridge cases. The latter particularly interested him. He went back to Reynolds and whispered in his ear, "They're .22s, just like the bullets that killed the doorman."

Reynolds nodded and was about to reply that he had already noticed this when the oldest of the technicians motioned him over. "We just found the 7.65 calibre bullet under the bookcase. It had ricocheted off the wall and ended up near the corner. And the licence number of the gun has been filed away."

Reynolds asked the men to check the safe, in particular for fingerprints.

"We'll do that last," they replied, looking at Morrison, who wandered over to the safe.

At that moment, a detective put his head in at the door and announced, "Lieutenant, the Prestipinos have arrived."

"I'm John Reynolds, head of the detective squad," the lieutenant said, heading towards them. "Mr Prestipino, perhaps you could come with me so we can get on with the identification."

"I'll go," the woman said, stepping forward. "I'm Rocco Fedeli's sister. My name is Angela Prestipino."

She was a short, sturdy woman in her early forties, her thick black shoulder-length hair slightly tinged with white. Her intense brown eyes gave a certain brightness to her face, which was devoid of make-up. She was wearing a black woollen suit, the jacket of which was single-breasted, and — the one touch of femininity — a pair of gold earrings.

Reynolds looked at her, surprised. "All right, follow me!"

They both put on paper overshoes and entered the apartment. Without any hesitation, Angela Prestipino identified the victims.

In the entrance she identified the Puerto Rican man, and in the dining room the bodies of her brothers, Domenico and Salvatore, as well as that of her cousin Nicola, who for years had managed the Hotel Jonio for her brother Rocco.

She then identified the maid, and, finally, the corpse in the den: her brother Rocco.

Reynolds found it impossible to gauge the woman's frame of mind as she did this. She was as impenetrable as a locked safe. Several times, he looked her in the eyes, but he couldn't see in them any of the grief he might have expected. In his entire career, he had never seen a woman identify the bodies of her own relatives with such detachment. Angela Prestipino was unlike any other woman he had met. She was unique.

"You'll need to come down to the precinct house."

"I'll follow you," was all she said in reply.

"Your husband and daughter will have to come, too."

Angela Prestipino nodded her head slightly. "They'll come."

She lapsed into icy silence.

"Lieutenant, is it true there's been a multiple slaying?"

"Who found the bodies?"

"What can you tell us?"

"Have you arrested anyone?"

Always the same questions. The barrage started as soon as Reynolds left the building with his hands buried inside the pockets of his raincoat.

The sidewalks were swarming with people. TV vans, with satellite dishes on their roofs, were blocking the traffic, causing a long tailback of cars.

The reporters had gathered in little groups, as if they had come for an impromptu press conference. As soon as they saw him, they descended on him like vultures, some with cameramen in tow, waving big microphones with various TV and radio station logos in front of his mouth. And yet they all knew him, and ought therefore to have known that they stood no chance of getting any information from him.

In fact, his first reply was, "No comment." Then, as he quickly walked away, he added, "I can confirm that a number of people have been killed, but that's all I'm able to say at the moment. As soon as we have anything we can release, the press office will let you know." He reached the car and opened the door, the reporters still in pursuit.

"Did you find anything useful in the apartment?" a woman reporter asked as he was about to get in, placing the microphone directly under his chin. "Is it true they're Italians? Was it the Mafia?"

He did not reply, but irritably slammed the door shut. The driver set off with a squeal of tyres, leaving the cameramen to film the back of the car until it turned on to Madison Avenue.

It was 5.40p.m.

Evening was slowly falling over the city.

The last marathon runners had already passed the finishing line in Central Park and the crowds were dispersing.

Life was getting back to normal.

But not for everyone.

CHAPTER
EIGHT

Less than an hour later, Angela Prestipino was sitting in a waiting room in the 17th precinct.

She was leafing through a magazine she had chosen from the pile on the table, the least dog-eared one she could find. Suddenly, her eyes fell on a feature about the new routes being used in the international drug trade. She was engrossed in her reading when she heard her name being called. Discarding the magazine, she got to her feet.

Reynolds had just put down the phone. He had made two calls immediately after getting back: the first to the precinct captain, the other to the press office.

As she sat down, Angela Prestipino glanced around the office, then put her hands together on her lap, looked at Reynolds and waited patiently for him to speak.

Reynolds, very conscious of her scrutiny, immediately began asking questions, starting with general ones.

It was 7.45 p.m. For the record, the woman provided her name and address, and stated, still with the same self-control, that she was married to Alfredo Prestipino and that they had one daughter, Maria.

"You've already met her, Lieutenant," she said. "We don't have any other children." She explained that in the 1980s they had left their birthplace in Calabria and had emigrated to America, along with her brother Rocco.

"There was no work for anyone in Calabria. And my husband didn't have anyone to keep him there. His parents died in a road accident when he was two years old."

Reynolds continued asking questions, as tactfully and respectfully as possible.

"When did you last see your brother Rocco?" he asked, looking closely at her. It was his turn to study her.

"The day before yesterday, Friday. We had dinner together."

"Did you notice anything different about him, anything unusual?"

"No. My brother was a quiet man, a calm man. He was no different than usual."

"Did he live with a woman?"

"No. He lived alone, apart from the husband and wife who worked for him."

"As far as you're aware, was he having any particular problems?"

"No. I would have known. I wasn't just his sister, I was his friend, his confidante. We were very close."

"So you have no idea who might have had a motive for killing him?"

"No. But whoever it was should burn in hell!" Her tone was curt, her eyes hard.

60

"And when did you last see your other brothers?"

"Last summer, when we visited our village in Italy."

"What line of business are they in?"

"The same as my father."

"And what's that?"

"They're farmers."

"Were they here on business?"

"No. They came to see us. We made them promise when we said goodbye after our last visit."

Silence fell.

Reynolds tried to put his thoughts in some kind of order. He had worked out a very specific strategy for handling the investigation, and every question he had asked so far had been in line with that. He decided the time had come to adopt a more direct approach.

"Did your brother have any friends who were, perhaps, a little disreputable?"

The woman took her time answering. She looked directly at him with eyes that were like ice and a malicious sneer on her lips.

"How dare you, Lieutenant!" she said at last. "My brother had many friends, but not the kind you're referring to. Rocco was a hard worker. All he cared about was his family. Me. Our mother!" She spoke with the pent-up fury of a volcano ready to explode.

"That's all right, Mrs Prestipino. I understand. There's no need to get angry. We have to ask these questions. It's part of our job."

"I know, Lieutenant."

"One last question and we're done, at least for tonight."

"Go on."

"How do you explain your brothers' death?"

"Are *you* asking *me*, Lieutenant?"

"Someone must have had a reason to kill them. Don't you think so?"

"Surely it's up to you to find the reason. I don't have the slightest idea. I already told you. Rocco was a quiet man, a hard worker, just like my other brothers. Whoever killed them will have to pay . . . The Madonna will punish them."

As she spoke, she took out a necklace from inside her blouse; at the end of the chain was a small medallion bearing a sacred image. She lifted it to her lips and kissed it several times.

John Reynolds watched her intently, more convinced than ever that she was different from any other woman he had ever met. He would have liked to know what image it was, but did not ask her. The one thing he was sure of was that he had never seen anything like this in his career.

He had always been guided by his intuition — the one thing no good police officer could do without — but this time it was no help.

"Then how do you explain these murders?"

"I think they were killed in error. It was a case of mistaken identity. That's the only thing I can imagine."

Her voice was still emotionless, but on her face Reynolds read a clear message: *If you don't believe me, that's your problem. Now stop all this and let me go.*

Reynolds realised it would be a waste of time to insist. "We're done for now," he said, "but I need you to remain available. We may have to speak to you again."

It was 8.10p.m. Angela Prestipino asked, with barely a change in her tone, when the bodies of her three brothers would be handed over to her.

"When the judge authorises it," Reynolds replied.

"We have to take them home, to their village."

"I understand. You'll have to wait a few days. We need to do post mortems. The law requires it in cases like this."

"I know. I just hope the law doesn't forget . . ."

She was about to say, *That we are Italians — and, what's more, Calabrians.*

But she stopped herself.

She left the room, and, as she did so, she put her necklace back inside her blouse with a loving gesture.

Reynolds immediately asked for her husband to be brought in.

Passing him in the corridor, Angela Prestipino had time to throw him a silent message, which he caught without hesitation.

Alfredo Prestipino was short and thin, with brown eyes and sparse, greying hair, and looked older than his forty-two years. He had a dark complexion, as if he spent most of his time sunbathing. He was exactly the way an American would imagine a southern Italian looked.

He spoke quietly, his voice little more than a sigh. He seemed to stoop on his chair, sitting with his head tilted and his chin propped on his slightly unsteady hands, as if he were lost in thought.

He added nothing to what his wife and daughter had already declared.

Then it was the turn of Maria Prestipino, but she was interviewed by another detective in Bernardi's team.

She confirmed the statement she had given earlier. Only now her expression had changed. Reynolds, who saw her passing in the corridor with her head held high, almost proudly, had difficulty in recognising her.

Someone was knocking at the door of the office.

Reynolds had been gazing nostalgically at the photograph of his daughter taken when she was a teenager. Now she was married to a lawyer and lived in Miami. He was looking forward to celebrating Christmas with her.

The knock at the door plunged him back into reality. It was Bernardi.

"Sit down, Mike. Any new developments?"

"Yes," Mike replied, sitting down on the same chair where Alfredo Prestipino had been sitting a few minutes earlier. His face looked drawn. The burden of responsibility was weighing heavily on him. Years of hard work and sacrifice could all go to hell if he screwed up on this one, especially now that his dream of taking Reynolds' place seemed about to be realised. To think that, before this case had come along, everything had been going so smoothly!

"Cabot's examined the bodies. He reckons the victims had been dead for several hours. They were almost certainly killed last night."

Reynolds nodded.

"Each victim was shot several times," Bernardi continued, consulting the notebook in front of him. "Apart from the man in the entrance hall, who had only one bullet to the head."

"How many wounds on the other victims?"

"A lot. This was a real execution. Forty-eight cartridge cases have been recovered, and there were quite a few bullets lodged in the walls and floor."

Ghastly images of the bodies flashed across Reynolds' mind.

"How about your search?" he asked. "What did you find?"

They had taken away a substantial amount of material, Bernardi told him, all of it presumably connected with Rocco Fedeli's business activities: diaries, notebooks, video cassettes, cellphones and photographs. He added that they had discovered another safe, this one in the bedroom.

"Where was it? What was in it?"

"It was behind a large painting. There were a lot of papers in it, also mainly financial. Right at the back was an envelope full of photographs. They're all in black and white, and they're yellow with age."

"Photographs of what?"

"The same people. A boy and a girl, shown in various places: a house, a square, in the mountains. The boy's definitely Rocco Fedeli, not much more than a teenager, just as he is in one of the two photos on the desk. In some of the photos, you can see the same church in the background."

"The same church that's in the painting?"

"Yes."

"And who's the girl?"

"Apparently not his sister."

"A girlfriend?"

"Could be."

"Has the apartment been sealed?"

"Of course."

"Good."

The clock on the wall said 9.30.

Bernardi sat behind a desk piled high with papers, rereading the reports, hoping desperately to make some sense of these murders.

He was exhausted.

He stood up, went to the window and looked out at the street. He saw a few uniformed officers leaving the precinct house for home and some getting into their patrol cars to head back to their beats. Soon the city would be transformed, as it was every night, into a maelstrom of emergency calls.

He returned to his desk, lit a cigar and took a couple of puffs. He started reading again, but soon broke off and stood up. He started walking up and down the room. Something was stirring in his mind.

At 10p.m., his men came in and the meeting started. It was cold in the office, and they huddled side by side in their wind-breakers. The oldest of them, a grey-haired, round-faced man, was the first to speak. He reported that no one had been admitted to any of the hospitals with gunshot wounds.

"You can drop that, the bullet's been found," said Bernardi, checking his notebook. Damn it, he'd forgotten to tell his men!

Another man confirmed that the two brothers, Domenico and Salvatore Fedeli, had landed at JFK late on Saturday morning on an Alitalia flight direct from Milan. According to the form they had filled in on the plane, their brother Rocco's hotel, the Jonio, was their place of residence in New York.

Bernardi concluded by summarising the situation to date. There were no real clues, and they were still no closer to finding a motive for the murders. There was only one thing they knew for sure: the six people in the apartment had been killed around the same time as Bill Wells. That was the second major piece in the jigsaw.

"So we're dealing with seven murders, not six," Bernardi said. "You'll need to check all security cameras in the area, and to question all store owners and employees in the vicinity of the building. And I don't want any leaks. The media are hovering like vultures. Let's get going on this. The Feds will be muscling in on our turf very soon." All the faces in the room fell. Having to share any success they might achieve wasn't an encouraging prospect.

He looked from one to another, as if to say, *We're in the shit, so let's get this show on the road.*

The detectives filed out, just as they had come in.

Alone once more, Bernardi began drafting an initial report for Ted Morrison. It was only a few pages, summarising the facts and what they had found so far and, most importantly, asking for authorisation to tap the phones of Angela Prestipino, the restaurant and the Hotel Jonio.

New developments weren't long in coming.

They came from an unexpected source.

And they came in person.

Reynolds was drumming his fingers on the desk when Peter Murray, the head of ballistics, and Frank Porter, head of the detective squad at the 101st precinct in Queens, appeared in the doorway of his office. Porter was carrying a file.

Surprised by this unexpected visit, he pushed back his chair and got to his feet to greet them.

"What brings you two here?" he asked. His curiosity was aroused, especially as he had seen Porter smiling broadly.

"Ballistics just killed two birds with one stone," Murray said, also smiling.

"Make yourselves at home," Reynolds replied, leading them into a little side room, where they sat down. Frank Porter laid the file on the table.

"Lieutenant Reynolds," Murray said, "we've come up with something on the gun found next to Rocco Fedeli's body: it was used in a homicide."

"What homicide?"

Murray explained that, thanks to the Integrated Ballistic Identification System, they had been able to establish that the cartridge case and the bullet had come from a 7.65 calibre Beretta used in a homicide the previous year. He added that the bullet had the same helical dents as the barrel of the gun. It was a signature as unmistakable as a fingerprint. The cases, too, when compared, showed identical marks of percussion, extraction and expulsion.

Good news at last! Reynolds thought. "Who was the victim of this homicide?" he asked.

"A woman who owned a real estate agency in Manhattan," Frank Porter said. "She was killed in her apartment in Queens in April 2002."

"And how did the case pan out?"

"Well, we never found the perpetrator," Porter replied, still smiling, "but at least we now know who owned the gun."

"But we don't know when Rocco Fedeli came into possession of it," Reynolds objected. "Between that homicide and the ones on Madison, a year and a half has gone by. Fedeli might have gotten hold of the gun some time after April 2002."

"Sure, but given what we know now, the case could be reopened, even though Rocco Fedeli's dead. Plus, that investigation last year could be useful to you."

"True. Mind if I take a look at the file?"

"Sure, that's why I brought it. I'll leave it with you."

"Thanks. Did Rocco Fedeli's name come up at the time?"

"No."

"We have something else for you," Murray cut in.

"What?"

Murray explained that they had managed to discover the serial number of the gun by applying an acid that accentuated the rough areas of the metal where the numbers had been stamped. The weapon had been acquired in a gun store in Manhattan in 1990, and the man who bought it had reported it stolen when his house was robbed in 2002, one week before the homicide.

"You'll find a copy of the report in the file," Porter said.

Murray handed Reynolds an envelope. "Here's our preliminary report. This has all the results we've obtained so far, including the examination of the .22 calibre cases and bullets."

Reynolds saw them out and then opened the envelope. It contained, as Murray had indicated, the results obtained from the .22 calibre bullets and cases found at the scene of the crime. There were no positive matches with anything in records, but it was clear that in the apartment, as in the doorman's booth, shots had been fired from weapons equipped with silencers.

The envelope also contained the results of checks run through the FBI's Fingerprint Identification System, to which all police departments throughout the country had access. None of the victims' fingerprints were on the database, which meant they were all clean. None of them had criminal records.

The incontrovertible fact, though, was that there was a link between the two crimes aside from their having happened at about the same time: both had involved silencers.

Then he started looking through the file on the April 2002 homicide. The first document, a few pages long, was a summary of the basic facts of the crime, information on the victim, and the results of the phone taps and interviews. As he read, Reynolds felt the blood quicken in his veins. The door had shown no signs of forced entry and no one, apart from the cleaning woman, had keys. The investigators had surmised that the victim knew her killer. The cleaner had a cast-iron alibi and had immediately been taken off the list of possible suspects.

Reynolds pushed his chair back and went to get himself a drink. He needed some water and a cup of coffee before going on.

When he resumed going through the file, he found a pile of duty reports and handwritten notes: the sort of things that always got left at the bottom of a file, which could sometimes provide useful leads if you knew what to look for.

Next he studied a series of 6 × 4 photographs taken inside the victim's apartment. Everything seemed tidy, except in the bedroom. He lingered over the photographs of the body. It was lying on the floor, beside the half-unmade bed. From the chest up it was hidden by the bed. The victim, Susan George, was thirty-five, a slim, attractive blonde. She had been shot four times: twice in the chest, once in the right shoulder, and once in the head.

Then he read through the notes on the interviews — nothing helpful — a chronology of the victim's last days — nothing special — and, finally, a few press cuttings

— nothing new. The investigation had focused on Susan George's ex-husband, from whom she had been separated for years, but it had turned out that on the day of the murder he had been in Brazil on business. The woman's private life had also been probed to identify possible lovers, but they had drawn a blank there, too.

Reynolds leaned back in his chair. He closed the file. Could there be something linking the crimes?

The whole scope of the investigation was widening.

"Drugs are what makes the world go round these days. The killers could have been coke heads."

The comment came from a member of the drugs squad. He and Bernardi were in the corridor, drinking coffee, when they heard a telephone ringing from Bernardi's office. Bernardi rushed in and grabbed the phone.

"Seventeenth precinct, Detective Bernardi."

"Michelino?"

"Who's that?"

"Salvatore, your uncle from Italy. What time is it over there?"

"This isn't a good line, Uncle," Bernardi replied in his shaky Italian. "It's eleven twenty at night. Has something happened?"

"No, I just wanted to know what's going on over there. I'm here in the bar with some friends and we just heard the five o'clock news on TV. They said there was a massacre . . . Everyone here is shocked . . ."

"Massacre? What do you mean?"

"All those murders, Michelino. It's like the days of Al Capone . . . You know what I'm talking about."

"Yes, I do. That's why I'm very busy at the moment, Uncle . . ."

"Be careful, don't take too many risks, they're animals . . ."

"What?"

"Wild animals — no, worse than that . . ."

"Take it easy, Uncle. How are you all? How's my aunt? How's Mario?"

"Fine, the usual life, the usual diseases of old age. We sent you a package, with salami, chestnuts, sundried tomatoes —"

"Thanks, I'll phone you when it arrives. I hope to see you on my vacation next summer."

"Is that a promise?"

"Yes, I'm coming to Sicily."

"Then I'll see you soon," his uncle said by way of conclusion.

"Yes, soon, I'll see you soon," Bernardi was saying, but his uncle had already hung up. He slowly put down the receiver.

His mind went back to the first trip he'd made to his parents' birthplace, Piazza Armenia, when he was barely seven. He remembered cycling with his little cousin Mario, Uncle Salvatore's son, down a long, narrow lane. That plunge into the past troubled him. It was as if the daily course of his life had become that lane.

The phone rang again. This time, it was Reynolds asking him to come to his office for an update.

CHAPTER
NINE

Monday, 3 November

The news exploded on to the front pages like a bomb.

All the newspapers implied that these were Mafia killings. Some speculated that a new gang war had broken out and predicted more deaths to come. Inevitably, they all linked the murder of the doorman to those on the nineteenth floor.

The *New York Post* headline screamed: BLOODY SUNDAY: MAFIA SLAYINGS IN MANHATTAN.

It was the kind of headline usually reserved for wars or national and international disasters. That was the way of the world.

Under the headline, there was a photograph of the entrance to the building on East 42nd Street.

The Italian media, too, led with the "Mafia slayings" in New York. The angle adopted by their correspondents, as well as by the leading news agencies, was that this had indeed been a Mafia-style execution.

It was a few minutes to seven and already the pink and blue hues of dawn had filtered into the room.

John Reynolds was still in bed, in a half-waking state, when the telephone rang on the night table. He slowly opened his eyes, picked up the receiver and said in a flat voice, "Hello?"

"Lieutenant Reynolds?"

"This is he."

"Dick Moore, FBI. Did I wake you?"

"No, go on."

"We've been brought in on the Fedeli case and I need to meet with you. When do you think you could get here?"

"Where?"

"Federal Plaza."

"I could drop by sometime this morning."

"It might be best if you came as soon as possible. We'd like to start immediately. We're waiting for you, Lieutenant."

"All right."

"And bring all the documents with you, including any reports from the Crime Scene Unit."

"I'll have to swing by my office first."

"Thanks."

Reynolds put the phone down, wrinkling his nose as if he could smell something unpleasant. He lay for a while longer in bed, then, as soon as he heard his wife muttering, he got up.

"Linda, you're right," he said as he walked towards the bathroom. "I really hope this will be my last case."

"Let's hope so. But this isn't the first time you've said that. At your age, you should be thinking about slowing down . . ."

"No, this time it's going to happen. The transfer is really only a matter of days away."

She sighed and rubbed her forehead. It was still hot. The fever had not completely subsided yet even though her temperature had gone down.

"Your daughter is grown up now, she's already married. And she's seen so little of you in all these years. What you have — what *we* have — isn't a life . . ."

"We'll go and see her for Christmas."

"Let's hope so. Christmas, at least!"

"Darling, we'll soon have a normal life. I promise."

He brought her breakfast in bed: a steaming cup of coffee and a couple of brioches. Then he kissed her warmly on the lips, said goodbye and left.

At work, John Reynolds had a reputation for being tough and uncompromising. But he was a man who knew when and how to show his feelings.

The Jacob K. Javits Federal Building at 26 Federal Plaza in Lower Manhattan is more than forty storeys high. John Reynolds got out of the car and paused beside the low wall where the name of the building is displayed on a plaque. Tired and heavy-lidded from lack of sleep, he took a last drag of his cigarette and flung it away irritably.

An agent was waiting for him in the marble-floored lobby. He led him to a row of elevators. They rode up to the FBI's New York field office on the twenty-third floor in silence. Leaving the elevator, they walked down a long corridor lined with offices until they came to the conference room. The agent opened the door and stood aside to let him in.

A group of agents were sitting around an oval walnut table, lit by ceiling lights. There was one woman, and she was wearing a white blouse and dark pants suit. The men were severely dressed in grey business suits, matching ties and white shirts.

With one exception.

Next to this one exception, Reynolds recognised the FBI's assistant director for New York, Dick Moore. He was sitting at the centre of the table with a colour photograph of President George W. Bush behind him. Reynolds needed only a quick glance to recognise the woman, too. Her name was Mary Cook. Before joining the FBI, she had been a detective in the homicide squad, the youngest at the time.

"Lieutenant Reynolds, good to see you again," Moore said, standing and walking towards him with his hand held out and a polite smile on his thin, intelligent face.

Dick Moore was forty-five years old. He was over six feet tall, light-skinned, and of regular build. His most prominent features were his aquiline nose and his receding hairline. He was as punctilious in his relations with his colleagues as he was in his dress.

Reynolds shook his hand. "Same here," he replied. But he felt a curious sense of foreboding.

"Let me introduce my colleagues," said Moore, leading him round the table. Then they sat down and Reynolds took the documents from his leather briefcase.

"Maybe you could start by giving us a summary of the case," Moore said.

"Of course," Reynolds replied, biting his lower lip and rubbing his chin with his hand.

For the next half hour, he gave an account of the homicides and the progress of the investigation to date, including the interviews with Rocco Fedeli's family and the details relating to the Beretta found next to his body. Dick Moore and his colleagues listened attentively.

"So you didn't learn much from Fedeli's family," Moore commented when he had finished. "But that filed-down licence number on the gun clearly suggests an organised crime connection."

"I agree."

"And how about your search of the apartment?"

"We took away a lot of material. My men are examining it now."

"Who's in charge?"

"Detective Michael Bernardi."

"Anything else?"

"Yes. There are two safes in the apartment. One of them contained a number of documents."

"Interesting!" Moore said, turning to the agent sitting next to him, who looked absolutely at ease in sweater and jeans. This was Bill Hampton, head of the Criminal Investigative Division of the Organised Crime Section.

Then Moore turned back to Reynolds. "And what do we have so far from the labs?"

Reynolds went through the ballistics results. Everyone continued following his words intently.

"It seems pretty obvious to me we're dealing with professionals," Moore remarked when he had finished.

Reynolds nodded.

"Now it's my turn to tell you something," Moore went on.

There followed a few moments' silence. Reynolds waited for Moore to continue. He had only one concern: were the Feds going to take over his investigation?

Right then, he'd have bet his life on it.

Dick Moore cleared his throat. "Rocco Fedeli has been known to us for some time," he said.

A heavy silence fell over the room. Reynolds gave Moore a questioning look. Seeing this, Moore said, "I understand your concern, Lieutenant. Let me say right away that I think it only fitting that my office cooperate with your squad. Those are the DA's instructions. We've already been in contact with Assistant DA Morrison —"

"— who was at the crime scene yesterday," Reynolds cut in, anticipating him. If what Moore was offering was simple cooperation, then that was fine by him. He already had more than enough problems to deal with in his precinct, starting with the string of assaults on young girls. The Feds would be able to take some of the burden off his men: thanks to laws passed since 9/11, they now had wider investigative powers.

"I know," Moore said. "We exchanged a few theories." He fell silent for a moment and sipped at his drink. Then he examined a few sheets of paper on the table in front of him.

No one spoke.

"Lieutenant," Moore resumed, "I think we need to be clear about our respective roles from the start, to avoid any possible ambiguity."

Reynolds gave him another questioning look and shifted uneasily on his chair. His mind was racing. Their respective roles? That sounded ominous . . .

"Your detective squad will continue to run the investigation," Moore went on. "You can assure your men of that, especially Detective Bernardi."

Reynolds nodded. At last his face seemed to relax.

Suddenly a giant screen on the wall lit up.

Moore raised his right hand, and one of the agents brought up the first images: two very well-dressed men at JFK Airport, both carrying suitcases in their right hands.

The agent froze the image, and Moore said, "These men arrived in New York two months ago and met with Rocco Fedeli." He ordered the agent to resume the slideshow.

More images of the two men appeared, showing them at different times on the same day — the date and time was displayed in the bottom right-hand corner of each image — and always in the company of Rocco Fedeli.

"Did they come here specifically to meet with Fedeli?" Reynolds asked, perhaps only to get explicit confirmation of what he already suspected.

"Yes."

"Why?"

"Drugs, we suspect."

"Who are the two men?"

"Mafiosi. Here's a copy of what he have."

Moore handed Reynolds a thick file with the name Rocco Fedeli on the cover, and below it, written with a red marker in block capitals, the word: SUSPECT.

Reynolds was about to open it, but Moore headed him off. "You'll be able to read it at leisure in your office. This copy is yours to take away. You'll find everything in there, including why we first started to take an interest in Fedeli."

"I'll have a look at it as soon as I get back to my office."

"Good. The important thing now is to establish a plan of action. I think it'd be a good idea to divide up the tasks."

Reynolds nodded.

"Getting back to the murders," Moore went on, "one thing seems certain to me: this was a Mafia execution, possibly a settling of scores. The question is, which organisation was responsible? Have you any ideas yet, Lieutenant?"

"Not really. At this point I'd rather read your documents first."

"In any case, it'd be good to take a long hard look at Rocco Fedeli and his activities, which are probably only a cover. And to find out all we can about the sister and the families of the other victims."

"My men have phone taps on Fedeli's sister, his restaurant and hotel."

"Excellent," Moore said. "We'll be doing a few phone taps as well."

The Feds certainly wouldn't meet any objection from the judges, who had become more malleable since the resurgence of terrorism. You didn't even need reasonable cause any more to get authorisation for phone taps: you just had to show that your investigation conformed with Federal law. Everything had become much easier.

In conclusion, Moore suggested they meet again over the next few days, or even the next few hours.

Reynolds put the Rocco Fedeli file in his briefcase, gestured in farewell and left the room, thus sparing himself the usual FBI smiles and handshakes.

The agents trooped out one by one. As they did so, Dick Moore motioned to Bill Hampton to come with him to his office.

When they got there, he immediately closed the door.

A large sheet of paper lay rolled up and secured by a rubber band at the back of the desk drawer. Moore took it out as carefully as if it were a religious relic and handed it to his colleague.

Bill Hampton was nearly six feet tall, with an athletic build and longish black hair. He looked more like a rock star or Tony Montana in *Scarface* than an FBI agent. But what was most striking about him were his round eyes, usually hidden behind dark glasses, which gave the impression of capturing the tiniest detail, even the most apparently insignificant.

"Read it," Moore said, visibly tense.

Bill Hampton had witnessed Moore handling a lot of difficult situations lately, but he had never seen him look so worried. The first thing he noticed when he looked at the paper was that it was a confidential document. At the top, in the middle of the page, he read:

Transcript of a telephone call
received 1 November — Classified

Persons involved: Assistant Director Moore — Mr X.

Mr X: Director Moore?

Moore: Yes. Who is this?

Mr X: You may not know me personally, but I consider myself your friend.

Moore: I see. Go on.

Mr X: Some hit men have arrived in the city. There's going to be a lot of blood spilt.

Moore: Who are they?

Mr X: I don't know . . . Not yet, anyway . . . Don't ask too much of me.

Moore: I need to know who they are.

Mr X: And I repeat, I don't know, but I can tell you for certain that there's going to be a bloodbath . . . Very soon . . . In a matter of hours, not days.

Moore: Where?

Mr X: In Manhattan.

Moore: Where in Manhattan?

Mr X: In an apartment, that's all I know.

Moore: Won't you tell me who you are?

Mr X: Not for the moment. But you know me indirectly.
Moore: What do you mean?
Mr X: You helped a relative of mine.
Moore: Who?
Mr X: I can't tell you any more for the moment. But you have to take this warning seriously.
The line goes dead.
Mr X does not phone again.
The call was made at 17.12 on 1 November from a public telephone in Grand Central Terminal.

Bill Hampton raised his eyes from the sheet of paper and looked at his chief.

"Well, Bill," Moore said, as if anticipating what Hampton was about to say, "I didn't take the warning seriously. That's why I haven't talked about this to anyone."

"We get so many anonymous tip-offs, sir."

"True, but unfortunately, this one turned out to be genuine. Just a few hours later, there was a mass homicide in an apartment in Manhattan, where we would never have expected something like this to happen. It can't be a coincidence, Bill. This caller knew what he was talking about."

Moore was unusually grim-faced. It was as if he was watching his career ambitions dissolve in front of his eyes.

"You weren't to know, sir," Hampton said, encouragingly.

"What's done is done, Bill, but now, we have to identify this guy."

"How do we do that?"

"I know it isn't going to be easy. Grand Central is like an airport, especially at that time of day. And let's not forget, this was the day before the marathon. But we have to do everything we can."

"Provided he was telling the truth, sir."

"Well, he was right about the homicides!"

"Let's hope he calls again."

"Let's hope so," Moore agreed.

"Did he have any kind of accent?" Hampton asked.

"Not that I could detect. If he's foreign, he must have lived here a long time. And the voice didn't sound young. I'll play you the recording."

There was a tape recorder on the desk, next to the telephone. Moore pressed the *Play* button.

Hampton concentrated on every word. "You're right, it's someone who lives here, there's no accent. I'd like to hear it one more time, though."

Moore rewound the tape and played it again.

"The closest I can get is that it's probably a Brooklyn accent."

Moore had thought of that, too. The caller did indeed seem to have the typical nasal accent of Brooklyn. But he didn't want to send the tape to the lab for voice analysis. If it became known that he had received that call, a fissure would open up beneath his feet, and soon it would swallow him whole.

Hampton asked him why he had recorded the conversation.

"I got suspicious when the switchboard operator told me the man refused to give his name or to speak to anyone but me."

"Right. Did he phone 911?"

"No, he called the agency number directly. But please, Bill, let's keep this between ourselves."

Moore instructed him to investigate the call personally, checking out the relatives of all witnesses they were currently working with in the hope of finding a match. He also cautioned Hampton to go easy with the men of the 17th precinct detective squad. "The case is ours now, but these cops have good sources and we have to keep them onside."

"Of course, sir," Hampton replied, passing his hand through his hair. "You can rest easy."

CHAPTER
TEN

The weather, which had been mild at first, had already started to deteriorate by late morning.

Dick Moore parked his car in the garage and took the elevator, still obsessing about the call he had received on the afternoon of 1 November. He was angry with himself: how could he have been so negligent?

He lived in a smart apartment near Columbus Circle, with a view of Central Park. Whenever he could, he went jogging in the park to keep in shape and relieve the stress of his job.

Entering the apartment, he placed his briefcase on the console table in the entrance, taking care not to knock the marble Adonis. At that moment, he was startled by an air-shattering clap of thunder, which sounded like a bomb exploding. He went into the bedroom, took off his jacket, and put his 9mm Glock, still in its holster, in the drawer of the night table.

He walked to the corner bar in the living room, pausing at one of the two large windows: the monument to Christopher Columbus, erected by Italian-Americans to commemorate the four hundredth anniversary of his great voyage, was almost invisible in the thick mist. Turning, his eyes came to rest on the copy of Roy Lichtenstein's *In the Car* on the wall behind the couch. It showed a man at the wheel of a car and, sitting next to him, a woman with long blonde hair, wearing a leopard-skin coat. The painting was suddenly illumined by a flash of lightning. A few moments later, there came another clap of thunder.

With his right hand, his fingers tapered like a pianist's, he picked up a crystal glass with a gilded rim. He poured himself two fingers of scotch, squirted a little soda in it, and drank. Then, exhausted and still tense, he collapsed on to the white leather couch.

The calm, relaxed atmosphere of his home had no effect on his mood.

He switched on the TV, and tuned to CNN just as a news bulletin was starting. The main item was the murders on Madison. The anchor summarised the known facts in very general terms, emphasising the lack of progress in apprehending those responsible. There was a clip of Police Commissioner Ronald Jones, in his usual dark grey suit, speaking to camera in a determined voice: "We're putting all we have into this investigation. This case is going to be solved quickly . . ."

The bulletin switched back to the anchor, who moved on to the next item. "There was another suicide attack in Baghdad this morning . . ."

Moore pressed the red button on the remote and the screen went black. The news from Iraq was always the same these days.

Just then, he heard the door open, followed by footsteps. Slowly he turned. It was his wife, Jenny, a tall, slim woman with delicate features and short blonde hair, who bore a vague resemblance to Sharon Stone. In her hand she was still holding the lead of their Labrador, Sam. The dog immediately ran to him, wagging its tail.

Jenny came up to him, stroked his cheek and gave him a kiss: he could smell her perfume. "Dick, we have to hurry, we're expected at Paul's and the weather's not looking too good. We need to get going before the sky falls on our heads!" Then, seeing his grim, anxious expression, she asked, "What's the matter? What are you doing with that glass of whisky in your hand?"

He put the whisky down on the low glass table and slowly got to his feet. "It's been a hell of a day," he replied. It was all he needed to say.

"God, you work harder than a beat cop! You're assistant director of the FBI, damn it, you should be able to take it easy once in a while." She stroked his cheek again, and for a moment she gazed at him with those blue eyes of hers, which for him glittered brighter than any jewel. "Now let's get ready," she said, smiling. "Let's go out and enjoy ourselves. You know my policy on your problems at work: they don't come through our front door."

He returned her smile and headed resignedly for the bathroom.

In a Starbucks near the corner of Park Row and Broadway, Bill Hampton was sitting at a table with his colleague Mary Cook, who for three years had been his partner in private life as well as at work. They were drinking macchiato from large paper cups and discussing the Fedeli case.

Mary Cook was slim, with the long legs of a model. She was certainly a very attractive woman, with medium-length blonde hair and clear, penetrating eyes. At only thirty-two, she was rising rapidly through the ranks of the FBI, where she worked more regular hours than when she had been in homicide. And along with professional success, she had also found love.

"What did Moore want?" she asked, finishing her coffee and putting the cup down on the table.

"Nothing special. He's just worried about this case. He thinks there could be more murders. Maybe he's right."

"If it was the Mafia, then definitely. For some reason we don't know, the balance of power has changed."

"I agree, Mary. Anyway, Moore gave me a free hand. There's no time to lose."

"I can't wait, darling!"

"Do you miss homicide?"

"Don't even joke about it, Bill." Her expression turned grave. "The only thing I miss is you. I'm sure you're going to be really tied up with this case. More than I'll be . . ."

"Let's get back to work," he said, and they left the coffee bar and made their way back to Federal Plaza in the pouring rain.

At the 17th precinct, Bernardi was in Lieutenant Reynolds' office.

He had just finished reading the file on Rocco Fedeli which Reynolds had handed over to him on his return from 26 Federal Plaza.

"Interesting?" Reynolds asked.

"Yes, very interesting."

"So, tell me all about it, Mike."

"From the beginning?"

"Yes."

The two Mafiosi from Palermo, Bernardi explained, had stayed at Rocco Fedeli's hotel, and had met with him several times, either alone or with others. Some of these other men were known to the Feds from old investigations into the international drug trade. He was about to show Reynolds the photographs contained in the file, but Reynolds stopped him.

"You can skip the photos, Mike. I already saw them during the meeting. Just tell me, when did these guys arrive?"

"In September. They stayed for ten days."

"Do their names mean anything to you?"

"No, nothing."

"And the others? The ones already known to the Feds?"

"Those I do know, Lieutenant. Some were linked to the Pizza Connection case."

Reynolds recalled the major police operation back in the early 1980s which had led to the dismantling of an Italian-American drugs network.

"But why were the Feds trailing these Sicilians in the first place?"

"They'd had a tip-off from the police in Palermo They'd been tapping their phones as known Mafiosi and learned that they were coming to New York."

"OK. But were there phone taps here, too?"

"I was just coming to that, Lieutenant. There were. There's even a report with today's date on it."

"What does it say?"

Bernardi took a sheet from the file. "It says that yesterday morning there were several attempts to call Fedeli's landline from a phone registered to Alfredo Prestipino of Brooklyn. None of them were answered."

"So the niece was telling the truth," Reynolds said. "She was, but her mother wasn't. I'm sure Angela Prestipino knows more than she's willing to tell us. You should've seen her when I interviewed her, Mike. She kept looking at me as if she was sizing me up." These words were accompanied by his usual rubbing of the chin.

"A strange woman, eh?"

"Never seen anyone quite like her."

Then Bernardi suggested they needed to find out more about what phone taps the Feds had set up and what they had discovered. "They have to put all their cards on the table. There aren't even any actual transcripts of conversations in the file."

"Of course. You're right, Mike. This time, they have to put all their cards on the table."

Bernardi went on to say that Rocco Fedeli had been in contact with Calabrians in Canada, members of the

92

Siderno Group, who, according to a report from the Royal Canadian Mounted Police, were involved in the drugs trade in association with the Colombians. The Colombians themselves were currently in negotiation with a Russian Mafioso to acquire arms, helicopters and even a submarine.

"A submarine?"

"That's what it says, Lieutenant."

"Are you trying to tell me they're planning to use submarines to transport cocaine?"

"Anything's possible. You know as well as I do, these people are always one step ahead compared with us." Bernardi smiled sardonically as he got up to leave. "And they always think of everything."

When Bernardi had gone, Reynolds started pacing up and down the room. He needed to stretch his legs and think over what he had just heard, especially about the phone taps.

Suddenly a thought struck him.

What if they had been illegal?

CHAPTER
ELEVEN

Tuesday, 4 November

The murders were still front-page news.

It was now generally accepted that these had been Mafia executions, perhaps a settling of scores between rival organisations, vying for control of the drug market in New York. A few in-depth articles attacked the authorities, including the politicians, for lowering their guard in the fight against organised crime in the rush to prevent further terrorist attacks in the wake of 9/11. The mayor, Bruce Field, came under particular fire for the lack of security in Manhattan. The public were starting to demand more effective measures.

Dick Moore was sitting at his desk. He felt strange, vaguely depressed.

That morning, before leaving home, he had quarrelled with his wife. Jenny had given him an ultimatum: either you change your way of life or I go.

The telephone call that came through the moment he entered his office had done nothing to lighten his mood. *There's trouble brewing*, he had thought, looking at the flashing light on the phone, which indicated that his boss, FBI Director Joe Brook, was on the line from Washington. He had lifted the receiver even before sitting down. Joe Brook was a sharp dresser who spent his days shut up in his office telephoning the heads of the local field offices and urging them to get results. And he was an early riser.

He had given Moore a real dressing down.

"People here are getting stirred up about this," he had begun, in a resolute tone. "I tell you, they aren't happy."

Moore could imagine him sitting back in a leather armchair in his huge, tidy office, with all the newspapers open on his desk.

"They aren't happy at all," Brook went on. "They want results on these homicides. They say you're wasting time up there in New York. We shouldn't be having problems with the Mafia these days, we shouldn't even be thinking about the Mafia, instead of which —"

"Wasting time?" Moore had cut in, his face turning red with anger. "My men are working around the clock on this. So are the detectives of the 17th precinct. You call that wasting time?"

Not to mention my domestic problems, he would have liked to add.

"I'm just telling you what people have told me. They want immediate results . . . It's understandable. With this terrorist thing going on, we can't afford to be fighting on another front right now, one that's taking us back twenty, thirty years. There have been seven victims in twenty-four hours, and all in Manhattan. It may not even be over yet."

"We'll continue to put everything we have into it," Moore promised. There was no point in arguing with Joe Brook. It was better to agree with him.

"And the media are having a field day. We have to give them something, and as soon as possible. I'm expecting results." Without giving Moore time to reply, he hung up.

This really wasn't a good time for the Feds. After all the mistakes they had made before and since 9/11, they needed results to restore credibility.

The day had begun badly for Dick Moore and was getting worse. It never rains but it pours.

And still he couldn't imagine what was in store for him.

Lieutenant Reynolds had received a similar phone call that morning. He had had to endure a lecture from the captain of his precinct, another early riser. In the kind of high-handed tone he wouldn't have used even to a rookie, he had snapped, "The Commissioner's like a bear with a sore head . . . He wants results . . . Don't disappoint me." As if that was not enough, he had urged him to look into the case of a famous English lawyer, on vacation in New York, who had been wounded in a street robbery two evenings before. The news was all over the British media.

The day was taking a nasty turn. Reynolds felt tense and his nerves were on edge.

Not that it was anything other than a typical New York day. The athletes were all gone, and so were the vast majority of the tourists who had come from all over the world to watch them.

But New York never changed. It was always ready to welcome you, to lift you up — or drag you down if you didn't come up to its expectations. It was like a proud woman with two faces, one beautiful, the other terrifying.

It was just after nine in the morning when Moore's phone rang again.

He picked up the receiver and said "Hello?" He was hoping it would be Jenny, calling to apologise for storming out on him. She knew he was crazy about her, he adored her, and their quarrels always hurt him a lot.

Unfortunately it wasn't Jenny. When he said "Hello?" and heard in reply, "Am I speaking with Assistant Director Moore?" he immediately recognised the voice. He pressed the *Play* button on his recorder.

"This is he," he replied, keeping his voice under control.

"You see, I was right!"

"I know who you are and I want to meet with you."

"That isn't possible, at least not for the moment. What you need to do right now is to go to St Paul's Chapel. I've left something there for you."

"Whereabouts?"

"Go to the bell in the cemetery, in back of the church. Look in the garland that's been put on the pedestal."

"But —"

The line had gone dead. It was clear the anonymous caller liked calling the shots.

"Son of a bitch!" Moore muttered. He sat there motionless for a moment with the receiver in his hand, then replaced it and pressed the *Stop* button. He wound back the tape and listened to the call. Once, twice. He scrutinised every word, but it was no use. He hadn't the faintest idea of the man's identity. Even though he knew the place well, he memorised the directions he had been given, Then, taking the Glock from his desk drawer and slipping it into his shoulder holster so that it was covered by his jacket, he put on his coat and almost ran out the door. Alone.

He didn't hear his cellphone ringing.

He didn't have far to go.

Just fifteen minutes on foot, walking at normal speed.

St Paul's Chapel is the oldest church in Manhattan. It was to this chapel, close enough to the Twin Towers that it was a miracle it was untouched, that the first 9/11 casualties were taken. It wasn't long before it became a place of pilgrimage, which made it the ideal spot to leave a message — and to make sure that it was picked up by the right person.

As he walked, Moore kept wondering what exactly the anonymous caller wanted from him. Tip-offs were invariably motivated by self-interest, and were usually offered in the hope of getting money in exchange.

When he got to the chapel, he saw a long line of people by the railings, waiting their turn in religious awe and looking at the messages and the photographs of those who had disappeared on 11 September.

He passed the queue and made his way down the left-hand side between the benches and the beginning of the little cemetery.

The treetops were wreathed in mist and even the graves seemed blurred in outline.

Reaching the rear of the chapel he stopped for a moment to look at Ground Zero opposite, a huge empty space still reeking of innocent blood. Then he turned his gaze to the large bell, with the sign saying BELL OF HOPE. It was on a large stone pedestal directly facing the rear door of the chapel, almost in the centre of the cemetery, and was there as a memorial to the victims.

Propped on the pedestal was a garland of white and red flowers.

There was no one nearby. The visitors were all inside, praying or reading the pieces of paper fixed to the walls, each of them bearing the name of someone who had disappeared in the attack, mementoes left by relatives and friends so that the victims should not be forgotten.

Discreetly, Moore approached the bell. As he advanced, he kept his hand on the grip of the Glock. He had not ruled out the possibility that the mystery man was luring him into a trap. It would have been the perfect place for it.

Reaching the pedestal, he kneeled, pretending to tie a shoelace, and took a last glance around. Then he looked inside the garland and saw a little plastic envelope. There seemed to be something in it. He slipped on a latex glove, deftly grabbed the envelope and popped it into a specimen bag, which he then placed in the inner pocket of his coat.

He took another quick glance around. He couldn't see anything suspicious. And yet he was sure someone was watching him, perhaps from the other side of the street, beyond the iron railings around the cemetery. He made his way back into the chapel through the rear door, passing under the flags that hung from the ceiling and the cloths with their patterns of stars, flowers and trees and the words HOPE and PEACE FOR YOU, stitched by adolescent hands. Keeping to the left-hand side, where there were fewer people, he walked the entire length of the chapel until he came to the altar, which was at the entrance — in other words, at the opposite end to the traditional church layout. Glancing at the small group standing in front of the pew where George Washington had sat and prayed, he sidestepped the visitors who were coming in and exited through the main door.

He turned on to Fulton Street and continued as far as Church Street before stopping for a moment in front of the Millennium Hilton to gaze at the construction site where once the Twin Towers had risen majestically. Then he walked the outer perimeter of the chapel, but could see nothing suspicious and no one behaving in a way that attracted his attention. He carried on slowly along Church Street until at last he felt it safe to lower his guard — although he knew the game had only just started — and allow himself a cup of coffee and a doughnut. Then he headed for Worth Street.

Less than an hour after leaving Federal Plaza, he was back in his office.

It was a cat-and-mouse game.

But which of them was the cat and which the mouse?

Moore took off his coat, sat down at his desk and took a deep breath. He put on a new pair of latex gloves, then took the envelope out of the little specimen bag and opened it. It contained a letter, probably written on a computer. It was addressed to him.

Assistant Director Moore

Thank you for coming. Don't waste time trying to find out who I am. I think you've already wasted a lot of time, perhaps too much. When the time is right, you will understand who I am or, if the conditions are favourable, I'll be the one to identify myself. Don't worry. I know very well how generous you are to those who help you.

I want you to take what I'm writing very seriously. Don't disregard it, the way you did last time. I think you know what I mean.

The killings were ordered by the Italians, but not only the Italians, to punish Rocco Fedeli, a traitor, a man of dishonour.

They say revenge is a dish best served cold, don't they?

Fedeli had got his hands on a considerable quantity of cocaine which failed to reach its intended destination.

You know, Moore, when there's too much money, people go crazy, they destroy the delicate balance of things, they forget commitments they've made, old vows they've taken.

Take a good look at the material found in Fedeli's apartment. Don't forget the photographs. You could learn a lot from them.

One thing I can tell you is that the cocaine was being carried on ships leaving Colombia, bound for Italian ports via the Straits of Gibraltar. The drugs were hidden beneath the water line.

Investigate those journeys and you will discover who killed Fedeli and why.

By the way, you won't find the people who actually killed him. It's too late for that now — others have dealt with them. But I may be able to tell you something else about that over the next few days.

One word of advice: don't waste time looking for fingerprints on this paper, I took every precaution. And don't waste time trying to figure out who my relative is, because he doesn't exist. He was just a trick to reel you in, but he turned out to be useless, given what happened.

But now you really have to get cracking, and when the time is right you'll have a chance to show me your gratitude.

I almost forgot. The ships from Colombia left from the port of Turbo and were sailing under Japanese or Ecuadorian flags. This is an important clue.

One more thing: there were three million dollars in the safe!

Now it's up to you.

Good luck!

The bastard! Moore thought when he had finished reading. *The fucking bastard!* He knew too many things, too many details. Were they true? But he'd been right about the killings.

He read the letter again. Then again. He felt as though he was missing something, but couldn't see what.

He made a couple of photocopies, underlined some words on one of them and transcribed them into a notebook:

Italians, but not only Italians . . .
A traitor, revenge, old vows . . .
Colombia, Turbo, Japanese or Ecuadorian flags
Safe, three million dollars . . .

And then:

Don't forget the photographs. You could learn a lot from them . . .

Which photographs? How could they help him to solve the case?

He read the letter once more. Then he put it away in the top drawer of his desk. As soon as possible he would send it to the CSU lab: perhaps the precautions the stranger said he had taken had not been sufficient and some fingerprints remained.

Finally he closed his notebook and called Bill Hampton.

His voice cold and tense, he summoned Bill to his office.

"What's happened, sir?" Bill Hampton asked as he entered the room.

Moore's tone of voice had alerted him to the possibility that some significant development had come up. He found Moore standing behind the desk, looking angry.

"Read this!" he said, handing him one of the photocopies.

Bill Hampton sat down on one of the visitors' chairs. Silence descended over the room.

"How did this get here, sir?" he asked when he had finished reading.

"The son of a bitch phoned again and told me where to go . . . Saint Paul's Chapel." He switched on the tape recorder and played him the conversation.

"No doubt about it, sir, it's him. I recognise the voice. And I'm sure now the accent is Brooklyn."

Moore nodded.

"He sounds like someone who knows what he's talking about, sir."

"How far have you got with tracking him down?"

"I've been checking the phone records of Grand Central Terminal, but haven't found anything useful so far." From his face, it didn't seem he was likely to succeed.

"Bill, I think this letter is pointing us in one direction. It's time you took a trip to Italy. What we've learned to date needs corroboration, and I can't see anywhere else we'll find it."

Bill Hampton nodded. "I think you're right, sir. Italy is where the answers are."

"OK, Bill. Contact Detective Bernardi. He may want to go with you."

"I'll do it today, sir."

"All right. And keep me posted."

"Sure."

Bill Hampton went out.

The prospect of a trip to Italy was one that appealed to him. His one regret was that Mary Cook wouldn't be able to go. There was no question of asking Moore: the assistant director didn't even like his agents living together, let alone travelling abroad together on official business, especially such a long way . . .

PART TWO

MISSION TO ITALY

CHAPTER
TWELVE

Friday, 7 November

Three days later.

It was just before ten in the morning when a blue luxury sedan belonging to the US State Department entered the car park of the DIA, Italy's Anti-Mafia Investigation Department, in Rome's Via di Priscilla, just off the noisy Via Salaria.

The DIA, established in 1991, had its headquarters in the architectural complex known as Il Cenacolo. Built near the Catacombs of Priscilla at the end of the 1920s for the order of Our Lady of the Cenacle, Il Cenacolo now housed both the DIA and the Police Training School.

Part of the large garden had been given over to the DIA's motor pool and parking for the staff; there was no admittance for the general public. The high surrounding wall was equipped with sophisticated surveillance cameras and other security devices. The place was a fortress.

Inside the sedan were FBI Special Agent Bill Hampton, Detective Michael Bernardi and Bob Holley, the FBI's legal officer at the US Embassy. Holley, a short, plump man of fifty, had been working in Rome for a couple of years and had managed to establish an excellent relationship with the upper echelons of the Italian police.

Hampton and Bernardi, having arrived at Fiumicino Airport the previous evening on a direct flight from New York, were already over their jetlag. After a delicious dinner at the restaurant La Fontana, not far from the famous Via Veneto, they had spent the night in Embassy accommodation. During the car journey, they had sung the praises of Roman cuisine. The *bucatini all'a-matriciana* and the suckling lamb *al forno* with a side dish of artichokes *alla romana* had quickly won them over — not to mention the copious antipasti: buffalo *mozzarelline*, aubergine and roasted peppers, Calabrian olives, meatballs, dried peppers in oil.

A smartly dressed plain-clothes officer was waiting for them outside the front door of the small red building. He greeted them and immediately led them to the office of Director of Investigations Michele Ferrara.

Bob Holley, who already knew Ferrara, made the introductions.

"Chief Superintendent Ferrara, these are my colleagues from New York . . ."

"Pleased to meet you. Welcome to Rome. Bernardi? That's an Italian name."

"Yes, my parents are Sicilian. But I was born and brought up in the States."

Ferrara smiled. His face was framed by thick dark hair, greying now at the sides.

"My colleague Detective Bernardi speaks Italian quite well, Chief Superintendent," Holley said. "But when it comes to work, he prefers to speak in English."

"That's fine with me. There are shades of meaning in any language, and in our line of work, it's important that we all understand one another."

The office could not be described as austere. There was an area for Ferrara's desk, a lounge area, and an area where Ferrara held meetings with his team. A large window looked out on a quiet, well-tended inner garden. One wall displayed the insignia of various European police forces, commendations for successful operations, and commemorative plaques for fallen officers.

Ferrara ordered four coffees from the bar, and while they waited for them they talked about terrorism. A few days earlier, on 4 November, there had been two terrorist acts: one in Rome, the other in Viterbo. In the first, an explosive device had gone off in a video case delivered to a Carabinieri barracks. The commanding officer who opened the package had suffered serious injuries to his hands and face. A second device, made of the same explosive, had been found at the post office in Viterbo. Nobody had claimed responsibility for either attack.

"So is this some kind of new wave of Italian terrorism?" Holley asked.

"It's not real terrorism," Ferrara said, taking a Mezzo Toscano cigar from a brown leather case and holding it, unlit, between the fingers of his right hand. "Real terrorists always claim responsibility. It's always been that way. There were letter bombs last month, too, in Rome and Sardinia, but they have nothing to do with the Red Brigades."

"What's it all about, then?"

"The strategy of tension, Mr Holley."

"Ah-hah!"

"I think you know what I mean. Italy is the country that invented the strategy of tension, and it's also a country where people feel nostalgic for the good old days, the old revolutionary struggles . . . But once we get started on that subject, we'll never stop."

"Then let's change the subject and talk about cooking," Holley proposed with a smile. "My colleagues have been appreciating your cuisine." He glanced across at Bill Hampton.

"I'm pleased to hear it," Ferrara said. "And I'd be happy to invite you out to dinner while you're here."

"Thank you," Hampton said, and at that moment his eyes fell on a silver trophy on a low table, bearing the inscription:

To Chief Superintendent Michele Ferrara.
With deep respect and sincere friendship.
His colleagues in the Squadra Mobile of Florence.
Florence, 10 July 2002

"It's a memento from my men in Florence," Ferrara said, noticing his interest.

Chief Superintendent Michele Ferrara had been replaced as head of the *Squadra Mobile* in Florence by his deputy, Francesco Rizzo.

After the bomb attack that had taken place on the morning of 1 October 2001, he had had to leave Florence for "security reasons". That was the official explanation, and it was consistent with the career path of a public official who had been very successful in the Tuscan capital. Ferrara, though, suspected that there was another reason: his presence at Police Headquarters in Florence had become a nuisance to some people. And he could no longer count on the support of his friend, Deputy Prosecutor Anna Giulietti, who had been killed in a Mafia attack a few days after the one that had targeted him.

When he had read the telegram informing him that he was being transferred to Rome, his first thought had been that it was a kind of punishment from the State Police Department. Of course, being the loyal officer that he was, he had obeyed unhesitatingly, as he had always done. Ultimately, he knew that, whereas men change over time, institutions always stay the same, and he had sworn loyalty to the State, not to men. In his heart, though, he still hoped that he would be able to return to Florence when the supposed "security reasons" had faded from memory.

His transfer had taken him to the capital, where he had a small service apartment in Il Cenacolo, but he lived with one foot in Florence and one in Rome.

His German-born wife Petra had followed him. To make the new apartment welcoming, she had hung the walls with paintings and photographs of their past. She thought it was important that they have happy memories of their life together constantly in front of them. In Rome, Petra had also been able to realise a long-term dream of hers, finding a job on the editorial team of a leading women's magazine. In the morning, though, before going out, she continued to prepare her usual copious and very German breakfast: a breakfast which, as had been the case in Michele's other postings, was often the only meal husband and wife managed to eat together. At weekends, when they could, they went to their apartment in Florence, where Petra patiently and lovingly tended the flowers she kept in the part of the terrace she had transformed into a greenhouse. She never gave up on the idea that one day they would go back there for good.

After coffee, Bob Holley launched into a full account of the murders in Manhattan, some of the details of which were known to Ferrara. It took him just over half an hour.

"It certainly bears the hallmarks of a Mafia killing," Ferrara said when Holley had finished. "And the perpetrators in this case, or rather those who sent them, could well belong to the Sici —" He broke off and corrected himself. "— Italian Mafia. What do you know about Rocco Fedeli?"

"Only what the Bureau has communicated to the police in Palermo and, since the murders, to Italian Interpol: that he probably had links with organised

114

crime. He owned a gun with its licence number filed off."

Bill Hampton took a copy of the file on Rocco Fedeli from his briefcase and handed it to Ferrara.

"It's all here, Chief Superintendent," Holley said. "This copy's for you."

"Thank you."

"But these Calabrians," Bill Hampton asked, "are they still the same Mafia we're familiar with?"

"They're a bit different. Relations between the Sicilian Cosa Nostra and the Calabrian Mafia — the so-called 'Ndrangheta — have always been good, ever since they got together to traffic contraband cigarettes, back in the sixties."

"So in what way are they different?"

Ferrara went into detail about the 'Ndrangheta, which he described as the most dangerous criminal organisation in Italy. Over recent years, they had acquired an almost absolute monopoly over the European cocaine market. Globalisation had affected crime, too, and the 'Ndrangheta had developed its own strategy, spreading its field of operations first to the rest of southern Italy and then to the outside world: Australia, Canada, the United States, Germany, Spain . . .

"We pointed out the danger they represent in our last report to Parliament," Ferrara said.

Bill Hampton was looking at him, intrigued.

The 'Ndrangheta, Ferrara continued, was no longer entirely structured around families deeply entrenched in their native territories, but now consisted of

115

interdependent groups with a top echelon over and above the individual *'ndrine*.

"*'Ndrine?*" Bill Hampton cut in.

"*'Ndrine*. It's a synonym for 'gang'. It's actually a Calabrian dialect word deriving from ancient Greek. In Greek, it means an upright man, a man who doesn't bend. In 'Ndrangheta circles it indicates a family controlling an entire village or an entire city neighbourhood."

Agent Hampton nodded.

Bob Holley remarked that he had participated in a conference in Reggio Calabria about the 'Ndrangheta. "They're a world power these days!" he commented.

"Yes, they are. For example, right now we're cooperating with the Royal Canadian Mounted Police on an investigation into the Siderno Group, a Canadian branch of the 'Ndrangheta."

At this point, Bill Hampton mentioned that the FBI had contacted the RCMP to check up on Rocco Fedeli's links with figures in the Siderno Group.

Ferrara nodded. For more than a decade the Siderno Group had been running the drugs trade in Canada in cahoots with the Colombians.

"I'm curious about one thing, Chief Superintendent," Detective Bernardi said — the first time he had spoken.

"Go ahead, Detective."

"What does 'Ndrangheta mean?"

Ferrara explained that it was not even an Italian word, and was generally only used by investigators, crime reporters and criminologists. The organisation's own members preferred to talk about "societies" or "families".

"If it isn't Italian, where does the word come from?" Bernardi asked.

"Again, it's derived from a Greek word — *andragathia*, meaning the virtue of being able to take advantage of events. From that, it's come to mean a grouping of valiant men."

Bernardi shook his head ruefully.

"If the 'Ndrangheta are behind the murders in New York," Ferrara said, "then we're dealing with something new."

"Why?" Hampton asked.

"Because it would be the first time the 'Ndrangheta have operated abroad in such an open manner."

"There's always a first time!" Holley said. "Maybe they wanted to send a message."

"Who to?" Ferrara asked.

"If we knew the answer to that question," Hampton said with a slight smile, "we'd be a lot nearer to solving this case."

"Did Rocco Fedeli have a criminal record in Italy?" Holley asked.

"We can check that right now," Ferrara said, standing up and walking over to his desk.

He bent over the computer and tapped out the name Rocco Fedeli and his date of birth.

"Yes, he has a few priors, from the beginning of the eighties: attempted extortion, illegal possession and transportation of explosives. Arrested, released, tried in his absence, acquitted for lack of evidence."

"Why 'in his absence'?" Bill Hampton asked.

"He simply didn't show up at his trial. But tell me, how's the investigation going at your end?"

Holley took a memo from the brown leather case that accompanied him everywhere. It contained the information on the murders and on Rocco Fedeli which Dick Moore had gleaned from the mystery caller's letter, without making any reference to the phone calls or to his own involvement, which he still preferred to keep secret. Holley handed it to Ferrara, who flicked through it quickly, then proposed another meeting, expanded to include the heads of the *Squadre Mobili* of Palermo and Reggio Calabria and the director of the SCO, the Central Operational Service. Teamwork was always useful.

The Americans agreed that they would meet again at four o'clock the following afternoon, in the same place. Ferrara shook hands with them and repeated his invitation to dinner, and the three of them left the room with smiles on their faces.

Alone now, Ferrara took off his jacket, loosened his tie, and collapsed into his chair. He sat back and closed his eyes for a moment. The first questions were running through his mind. Why had the 'Ndrangheta, who had always maintained a low profile, decided to raise their game? What were they planning to do now, after such an unprecedented settling of scores? Because that was what it must have been — a settling of scores.

Finally he lit his cigar and took a long drag. The room filled with the acrid odour, and clouds of smoke wafted up towards the ceiling.

CHAPTER
THIRTEEN

Saturday, 8 November New York, 9a.m.

Dick Moore was sitting at his desk, trying to
reconstruct Rocco Fedeli's past, however distant. The
illegal possession and transportation of explosives and
the gun with the filed-off licence number both
suggested connections with organised crime. Moore
put on his gold-framed glasses and started reading the
ballistics report and the preliminary post-mortem
findings on the six victims.

As they had suspected from the start, Rocco Fedeli
and his guests and domestic staff had been killed at
about the same time as the doorman. This was shown
by the rigidity of the muscles (rigor mortis), the
stabilisation of the hypostatic stains (livor mortis), and
the lack of food in the victims' stomachs, duodenums
and jejunums.

But the findings also indicated something else: the
Puerto Rican man had suffered a — non-fatal —
trauma to the skull, probably caused by a blow with the
grip of a pistol. This suggested that the killers had
knocked him out as soon as he had opened the door to
them, and killed him later, probably before leaving the

120

apartment. The ballistics report contained significant data on the trajectories of the bullets: the other victims of the massacre had been shot by at least two people firing from opposite sides of the room, first from a distance, then at close range.

The facts were clear. Moore took a piece of paper and began writing.

The killers, at least three of them, enter the building. One stays in the doorman's booth to keep an eye on the doorman. The others go up to the nineteenth floor. There, they don't need to force the door, but are admitted, perhaps because they're recognized or they're considered above suspicion. The Puerto Rican who works there opens the door and is knocked out with the grip of a gun. They then enter the dining room and surprise the victims, who have not yet started to eat. They fire at them from different positions, then move in closer to finish them off. Then they go into the den, where they find Rocco Fedeli. He has time to fire one shot before he, too, is killed. The killers open the safe (or find it open?), take the contents and go. Before leaving the apartment, they kill the Puerto Rican, presumably because he has recognized them, or could be a potential witness.

Moore stopped. What had the anonymous caller told him? *Take a good look at the material found in Fedeli's apartment. Don't forget the photographs. You could learn a lot from them.*

It was time he paid a visit to the scene of the crime.

He phoned Lieutenant Reynolds and arranged to meet him on the nineteenth floor.

An officer removed the seals and they went in. The smell of death still hung in the air.

Followed by Reynolds, Moore began inspecting the rooms. On the dining-room floor and the study floor there were still chalk outlines where the bodies had fallen. Moore focused his attention on the paintings and photographs, examining them one by one. The paintings seemed to be originals, and were all signed. Apart from one painting of a small church in the mountains.

"This is the only one that's unsigned," Moore said out loud.

From the desk, Reynolds picked up the photograph showing Rocco Fedeli beside a church, and held it out to him. "It's the same church as in this photograph, don't you think?"

"Yes," Moore replied. "Why are they so interested in that church? Strange people, these Italians . . ."

"The niece said it's the church of a Madonna that her uncle and all the family are very devoted to. It must be in Calabria."

Moore was lost in thought for a few minutes, then ordered his men to take away both the photograph and the painting.

122

Situated on the Ionian side of the province of Reggio Calabria, San Piero d'Aspromonte nestled in the foothills of the Aspromonte, one of the principal mountain ranges in the region, extending as far as its southern tip. With a population of just over a thousand, a high percentage of them members of the 'Ndrangheta and an equally high percentage unemployed, it was not very different from countless other Calabrian villages.

Crumbling houses, apparently long abandoned. Non-existent house numbers. Narrow, neglected streets. It certainly didn't give the appearance of a wealthy community, and the statistics bore out the impression of poverty. With an annual per capita income of just under five thousand euros, San Piero d'Aspromonte was among the poorest municipalities in Italy. No cinema, no theatre, no hotel, no street with shop windows displaying designer goods, just a few bars, the church, the pharmacy, the Carabinieri barracks.

Appearances, of course, can be deceptive. And perhaps even deliberate. It seemed unlikely that there would be much more than petty crime in these alleys, where even by six o'clock in the evening it was pitch black. It certainly did not seem the kind of place where a Mafia-style organisation could possibly flourish.

At ten in the morning that Saturday, the funeral of the four victims began in the parish church. As soon as the NYPD had completed the formalities, the bodies had been handed over to the family, and they had finally landed in Italy the previous evening. News of their arrival had spread throughout the region, and the church was packed with people paying their last respects. It was so crowded that some people had to remain outside on the steps or in the square. The mahogany coffins were lined up in the central nave.

The women, dressed all in black, formed separate groups from the men. None of them wore a trace of make-up, and almost all of them were clutching handkerchiefs. The oldest among them threaded rosaries through their fingers and prayed under their breaths, grief etched on their wrinkled faces. A small group huddled around the next of kin. The mother of the Fedeli brothers was easily distinguished: an old lady who was clearly even more grief-stricken than the others. In one fell swoop, she had lost her three sons. Now there was only Angela left, and she'd be going back to New York in a few days. The one consolation was that, at least until her strength abandoned her, she could go to the family chapel every day, lay flowers and pray.

Angela sat next to her in the front pew, holding her mother's thin hand in hers and staring straight ahead at the coffins. She, too, was dressed all in black. The silk shawl round her neck left uncovered the small gold chain with the sacred image. Unlike most of the women, she was not wearing a veil. And there was something else that distinguished her from the others: her behaviour. Not only was she not crying, she was very composed. It was unusual, even unnatural, given the situation. But to anyone who knew the customs of the area and could interpret gestures, it was

124

immediately clear that she would be the one to take over as head of the family.

Most of the men had remained outside. Among those standing in the little square was Francesco Puglisi, known as Ciccio the Knife, a nickname he had been given as a small child because of the thin knife he always carried in his pocket.

He had just turned sixty. Short and thin, he had very white hair and a rugged, olive-coloured face with deep-set sky-blue eyes. For the occasion he had put on a black corduroy suit and a waistcoat with a gold watch chain hanging from the pocket. On his head was the traditional cloth cap, also black. He held a stick in his right hand, to support himself on his unsteady legs.

Francesco Puglisi, Don Ciccio, was the undisputed boss of the 'ndrina of San Piero d'Aspromonte. He was surrounded by his most trusted men, and everyone bowed to him as if he were a sultan.

When the crowd began to disperse, he was approached by Antonio Russo, an ambitious local boss, who was always very smartly dressed. Today he was wearing a white shirt, a dark grey suit and a matching silk tie. The two men walked a few yards away from the crowd.

"Don Ciccio," Russo said, "please accept my sincerest condolences."

"Thank you, 'Ntoni. And thank you for coming."

"It was my duty, Don Ciccio. I'm really sorry about what happened. You know how fond I was of Rocco."

"He was one of the best in the family. I was pleased when he agreed to move to New York for me." Don Ciccio's voice seemed to crack, perhaps with grief.

"I know, Don Ciccio. Remember, I'm always at your disposal."

"I thank you with all my heart, 'Ntoni."

"For anything at all." He emphasised the word *anything*.

Don Ciccio was silent for a few moments, and when he spoke again there was bitterness in his tone. "This kind of thing never used to happen! It's all the fault of global ... What do you people call it? Oh yes, globalisation!"

"I know what you must be feeling, Don Ciccio, but everything has its price." Russo looked him straight in the eye.

"And we're the ones who are paying it! But let's not talk any more about that, it's too late now."

Francesco Puglisi knew he had lost. Deep down, he had known it for a long time, ever since, at the annual meeting in Aspromonte in 1986, some of the bosses, including Antonio Russo's father, had established a new strategy for the 'Ndrangheta. Don Ciccio had not agreed with assigning so much importance to the international drug trade, but he had been forced to fall in line. And it wasn't only drugs: the 'Ndrangheta had also developed an interest in the traffic in toxic waste and radioactive material. Don Ciccio was still allowed a few kidnappings for ransom, but outside the region, and so he had decided to launder the income from the kidnappings by investing in Europe and the United States.

"As you wish, Don Ciccio. Don't forget I'm entirely at your disposal."

"Thank you. We must meet."

"Not this evening, if that's all right with you."

That evening, Antonio Russo had something else he had to do.

Alone again, Don Ciccio was next approached by Rocco Fedeli's brother-in-law, Alfredo Prestipino.

"Alfredo, I need to talk to you later."

"Whenever you wish, Don Ciccio."

"My house, after the funeral."

"I'll be there, Don Ciccio."

For a few moments, Antonio Russo stopped to watch the two men. Something struck him as odd. He looked on as Don Ciccio walked away with unsteady steps and entered the bar that looked out on the little square. Alfredo Prestipino, meanwhile, had made his way through the crowd and was entering the church. Antonio Russo continued watching him. Something wasn't right.

CHAPTER
FOURTEEN

At 4p.m. they were all there.

The conference room at DIA headquarters was on the ground floor, in the wing furthest from the offices. It was a quiet place. On the walls were the insignia of the world's leading investigative agencies and a few paintings. A large framed black and white photograph showed the two anti-Mafia magistrates, Giovanni Falcone and Paolo Borsellino, murdered by Cosa Nostra in 1992.

Michele Ferrara sat down at the head of the solid walnut table, with the heads of the *Squadre Mobili* of Palermo and Reggio Calabria on one side and, on the other, Chief Superintendent Stefano Carracci, director of the Special Operational Service, the SCO. The Americans took their places opposite.

Stefano Carracci coordinated the activities of the *Squadre Mobili* in all the cities of Italy. A contemporary of Ferrara, he was a tall, sturdy man with thick fair hair. Unlike Ferrari, he was on good terms with Armando Guaschelli, the head of the state police.

Ferrara made the introductions, and explained the reason for the presence of his American colleagues. After a brief pause, just long enough to catch his breath and clear his throat, he continued, "One lead in the case points to Italy, and I'd like to ask the legal adviser of the US Embassy, Mr Holley, to present it."

"Thank you, Chief Superintendent Ferrara."

All eyes turned to him.

Bob Holley distributed photocopies of the FBI memo, and said, "Assistant Director Moore believes this information is reliable. He is confident that we will receive all due cooperation from the Italian police, from your sections in particular. He would like to thank you for that right now."

They all nodded, then silence fell over the room as they read the memo, some of them for the second time. The one who showed the most interest was the head of the *Squadra Mobile* of Reggio Calabria, Lorenzo Bruni. A tall, athletic-looking man of thirty-nine, with jet-black hair and a dark complexion, he had been running the *Squadra Mobile* for more than two years, having risen though the ranks, and was currently one of the few people in the state police with an expert knowledge of the 'Ndrangheta.

Ferrara was aware of this, and when they had all finished reading he turned to him. "What do you think, Chief Superintendent Bruni?"

"This memo is more interesting than it may appear at first sight. Fascinating, in fact."

In a calm, professional tone, he reported that an investigation currently being carried out by the Reggio Calabria operations centre of the DIA had revealed links between members of the 'Ndrangheta and Colombian drug dealers.

The silence that followed was broken by Carracci.

"We know there are a few gangs who work with the Colombians," he said, with the air of somebody who knows everything about everything. "But there's no evidence that drugs are transported in the way described in this memo."

"But at least it's a starting point," Ferrara said. "This man Fedeli may provide the key to breaking open any trafficking operation he may have been involved in and which may have led to his murder."

He proposed setting up a task force, based at the Reggio Calabria operations centre of the DIA.

They all agreed, including the Americans. Only Carracci appeared to waver.

"I need to speak to the head of the state police," he said, "before I can authorise personnel from the *Squadra Mobile* and the SCO to be part of this task force." His tone was curt, brooking no debate.

A dubious expression appeared on Ferrara's face, but he said nothing, merely nodded grimly.

There followed a long silence.

"I understand what you're saying, Chief Superintendent Carracci," he said at last, "but I'd ask you to give me an answer as soon as possible."

Though he could not understand Carracci's reservations, it would not do to appear too negative in front of their American guests.

That evening, Ferrara and the Americans had dinner at Dal Bolognese in the Piazza del Popolo. It was the most heavily booked restaurant in Rome, but they always managed to find a table for Ferrara. It was a relaxed evening, and the Americans were impressed with the excellent cuisine. The first course of home-made pasta — tortelloni with sour cheese and spinach and tagliatelle *al tartufo* — was enough to make them forget all about the investigation.

When Ferrara got back to his service apartment, he was holding a package in his right hand.

Petra was lying on the sofa. She was wearing a turquoise tracksuit, the kind of thing she tended to wear at home. With her blonde hair gathered in a ponytail, she was reading a German novel. In the background, he could hear the voice of Vasco Rossi, a singer-songwriter she liked a lot.

Michele kissed her on her lips and then, with a boyish smile, handed her the package.

"For me?" Petra asked.

"Open it."

Petra gave him a knowing smile and unwrapped the package. She had guessed what it contained: a large slice of St Honoré cake! It wasn't the first time Ferrara, coming home from a working lunch or dinner, had brought her dessert. He knew how much she liked it.

Petra got up and headed to the kitchen to fetch a small plate and a fork. In the meantime, Ferrara went to the bedroom to take off his suit, but above all his tie, which, after a long day's work, tended to make him feel as if he was being slowly strangled.

They sat down next to one another on the sofa.

Petra was savouring her cake.

"You know what I think, darling?" he said, sipping a glass of Slyrs whisky, a Bavarian speciality produced in limited quantities. It was a gift from a close friend of theirs in Germany, and he allowed himself a glass only on special occasions.

This was one of them.

"What, Michele?" Petra asked, always very sensitive to her husband's moods.

"I'm afraid I may have to go to Calabria."

Her hand, holding the fork, stopped suddenly in mid-air. "What?"

Petra had very pleasant memories of the Calabrians, especially their neighbours, about whom she thought often. She remembered the morning they had moved out, their neighbours looking on from their windows with tears in their eyes. At the same time, she was convinced that it was dangerous for her husband to return to such a high-risk place, where he had had such a difficult time — a time she had shared.

Like Sicily, Calabria was a beautiful, fascinating region, an amazing place to live — but not for a policeman, especially not one who was always on the front line. "If you'd been a teacher, we'd have been able to stay there," Petra would say every time the subject came up.

"What?" she repeated, putting the plate down on the coffee table.

"There's an ongoing investigation with the Americans. I may have to go there to coordinate it."

Petra said nothing more, nor did she ask for details. She was accustomed to not asking him questions about

132

his work, having refrained from asking him any in all these years. But she could not conceal her anxiety.

Vasco Rossi's voice was still resonating through the room.

"But, Michele, if you're working with the Americans, why don't you go to America?"

"That hasn't been ruled out, Petra. I may end up having to go to New York. If that happens, then I'd like you to come with me."

"Why?"

"Because I don't want you to do what you did when I was in South America."

Petra screwed up her eyes, as if remembering. That terrible time was still vivid in her mind: Michele away and her at home alone, eating her heart out with a thousand thoughts going through her mind!

"Do you think I could?" she asked.

"Of course. It wouldn't have to be like that time in Peru . . . when the phone in my hotel room never stopped ringing because you were worried. No, you'll come too."

"OK, as long as my boss will let me go. But promise me you won't go to Calabria. I'm afraid."

"If I can possibly avoid it, I will, I promise."

Petra looked at her husband, moved closer to him and gave him a long, passionate kiss. Her green eyes were even brighter than usual. She picked up the plate again. Michele continued sipping his whisky, lit a Mezzo Toscano cigar, and started thinking.

What intrigued him was that the 'Ndrangheta was no longer the organisation he had known in the early eighties. They were operating at an international level now, and that was a whole new ballgame.

Meanwhile, on the stereo, Vasco Rossi was singing "We're Alone".

He took a last gulp of whisky, put down the glass and extinguished his cigar in the ashtray, even though he had only smoked half of it. Then he stood up and went to the bedroom, soon to be followed by Petra.

That night Ferrara thought several times about Carracci's objections. He recognised the signals: Carracci hadn't trusted him when he was in charge of the *Squadra Mobile* of Florence, and he still didn't. Nor did Armando Guaschelli, the head of the state police. And the feeling was mutual, particularly where Guaschelli was concerned. The image of the man's shark-like smile, the last time the two men had met at the Ministry, was still engraved on his mind. It was the smile of a man who wasn't merely petty-minded but treacherous and vindictive too.

Eventually he fell fast asleep, with one arm over his wife's shoulder. But he did not dream.

That night, the god Hermes left him alone.

Antonio Russo had inherited from his father, who had died a few years earlier, the leadership of the *'ndrina* of Castellanza, a small village on the Tyrrhenian side of the province of Reggio Calabria. He was not yet forty and was already widely considered a rising star, both intelligent and tough. He was of medium build and height, with a dark complexion and sparse chestnut hair.

That same night Antonio Russo got into his big Mercedes with its Catania plates, parked outside his farmhouse. The house was a large two-storey stone building with a wide portico, dating from the eighteenth century, which had once been an oil mill. The first floor, which had been completely refurbished, contained the bedrooms, each with an en-suite bathroom. The ground floor, on the other hand, had been left in its rough state, and comprised a large living room and a vast kitchen. There were outbuildings on either side, used as storehouses, and extensive olive and citrus groves. On the left-hand side there was an enclosure for the horses. Everything was monitored by high-definition security cameras.

He had a briefcase with him. He opened it. Inside was a cloned satellite phone, home-made by a young engineer in Milan, an electronics expert. Following the usual procedure, he inserted a coded number. When that number appeared on the screen, he pressed the delete key, then dialled the number of a foreign mobile phone and pressed the star key. After a couple of rings there was an answer at the other end.

"Hi, 'Ntoni, how are you?"

"Not too good."

"Oh!"

"In fact, not good at all. And you?"

"Not good either. I heard."

"Ah!"

"You know they want their money, 'Ntoni."

"I know, no one gives anything for nothing."

"'Ntoni, it's a serious problem."

"Yes, yes. But how was I to know . . . You understand?"

"I do, but I'm not so sure about the others. The problem that occurred . . ."

"Yes. I know, I know."

"We have to meet, 'Ntoni."

"I'll send someone."

"No," the other man replied in a resolute tone. "You and I have to meet."

"I can't come to see you, and you know why."

"We'll meet in Spain, then, 'Ntoni. Usual place."

"All right. When?"

"Tuesday evening. The eleventh."

"Fine."

"And you'll bring what we need?"

"I will."

"'Bye, 'Ntoni."

"'Bye."

Both men hung up simultaneously.

It was five minutes to midnight.

CHAPTER
FIFTEEN

Sunday, 9 November

Don Ciccio Puglisi and his wife were in their dining room.

In the middle of the table, spread with a pure linen table-cloth with embroidered edges, were two crystal carafes, one containing clear spring water, the other red wine. Glasses, plates and cutlery had been neatly laid out, and displayed in the middle on a silver tray was a good-quality bone china coffee set.

Their house was on the edge of the village, a large but outwardly modest one-storey detached villa. It was surrounded by olive groves and there was also a vegetable garden for seasonal produce. The nearest houses were a hundred yards away. But that did not affect security. Quite the contrary. Don Ciccio's most loyal associates lived in the area, as did various relatives, including relatives by marriage, who always kept their eyes and ears open.

That Sunday the Puglisis were not alone.

The mayor, Franco Giardina, and his wife Vanna were dining with them. The food was excellent: highly seasoned lasagne *al forno* followed by kid cooked slowly over an open fire and served with potatoes.

The atmosphere was intimate and relaxed.

Don Ciccio and Franco Giardina were old friends. They had been constant companions when they were young men, frequenting the best-known restaurants in Reggio Calabria, always in the company of different women. Don Ciccio was almost always the one who took out his wallet and paid. Even then he had had a lot of money.

Franco Giardina had been mayor for a number of years, and was certain to continue as mayor well into the future. At least as long as Don Ciccio was still alive.

Now Don Ciccio and the mayor were discussing the latest events over steaming cups of coffee and slices of mimosa cake brought by friends.

The tone was calm.

"Rocco's death is a terrible loss for the Fedeli family," Franco Giardina said. He was a short, plump man, someone who liked his food, to judge by his appearance.

"You're right, Franco . . . A terrible loss."

"A good son . . ."

"He was . . . Or he used to be . . ." He raised his hand, as if to summon a past that was now over and done with.

"Why do you say 'used to be', Ciccio?"

"I'm old now, maybe I don't express myself correctly. Let's have a nice game of cards."

They settled down to a game of *tressette*.

"What are you doing?" Franco reprimanded him after a while, looking at the card his opponent had just thrown down on the table. A mistake like that was completely out of character.

"I'm sorry, I don't know where my head is today."

It was true: Don Ciccio's mind was on other things.

Meanwhile, the women were gossiping in the kitchen. Grazia and Vanna were also lifelong friends. They had grown up together and both had realised their dream of marrying a man of honour. Grazia was short and slim, with dyed black hair gathered in a huge bun on the top of her head, the same hairstyle she had always had — her attempt, perhaps, to appear a little taller. She was wearing a pearl necklace. The pearls were genuine, and she only wore them on special occasions. Unlike her friend, she wore no makeup.

"Did you see how dignified Angela was in church? She wasn't even wearing a veil . . ."

It was Vanna, her contemporary, who was speaking. She, too, was short, and somewhat overweight: a perfect match for her husband! Her hair was completely white. She was wearing matching diamonds: ring, necklace, earrings. She was helping out in the kitchen, taking the plates Grazia had just rinsed under the tap and putting them in the dishwasher.

"Of course, Angela is a woman of honour," Grazia replied. "Didn't you know that? I wasn't surprised by anything. I've known her since she was a babe in arms . . . Just like you . . ."

"She didn't shed a single tear! I mean . . . Three brothers . . ."

139

"What do you mean? Don't you know that weeping for the dead is a waste of tears? When you talk like that, I don't recognise you any more . . ."

Vanna nodded approvingly.

It was possible that Angela Fedeli was trying to wipe out the cliché of the 'Ndrangheta woman who stood on the sidelines and said nothing. Perhaps she would become a major player on a level with the men, taking over leadership of the 'ndrina. A woman of respect.

Vanna and Grazia changed the subject and started gossiping about mutual friends in the village. They always did the same whenever they met, and they met almost every Sunday, sometimes at Grazia's house, sometimes at Vanna's.

In the meantime, the men continued their game of tressette.

It was a gorgeous day, and the sun flooded the sky with its limpid, serene light.

Alitalia Flight Z1155 from Rome Fiumicino began its descent. After a few minutes, the blue of the sea could be seen through the windows. Then the plane flew low over the Sicilian coast and the city of Messina, which looked so small, you could see the whole of it at a glance. It crossed the straits, heading straight for the airport at Reggio Calabria.

The airport is situated between the sea and the hills. Not an ideal position, especially when the sirocco is blowing hard from Africa. At such times, it can be very difficult for planes to land and passengers feel they are on a roller-coaster. When landing becomes impossible, aircraft are diverted to the nearest airports: Catania or Lamezia Terme. But the sight that greets the traveller is remarkable.

Today, the Sicilian coast looked transparent, and Etna was majestic with its peak covered in snow. When it is inactive, the volcano is like an old man who has fallen asleep, but when it suddenly awakes it becomes like a fiery-eyed demon, with incandescent lava pouring from its mouth: a dazzling spectacle, but a source of terror to the inhabitants of the nearby villages.

As they came in to land at Reggio Calabria airport, the passengers could make out the houses, almost all of them seemingly half finished, devoid of external decoration, as if construction was still in progress. But those who were familiar with the region knew they had been that way for a long time, and would stay like that a lot longer. Unauthorised building was a routine occurrence in the city, an almost physical need in an area with a high rate of organised crime.

The plane, which was almost an hour late, at last taxied towards the landing gate. When it came to a halt, the travellers had to walk to the terminal exit. Among them were the Americans, two DIA officers from Rome and Stefano Carracci. Carracci had obtained permission from Armando Guaschelli for his men to be part of the task force, on condition that he himself coordinate it and communicate every significant development direct to the secretariat of the Department of Public Security.

However reluctantly, Ferrara had accepted Guaschelli's condition in the interest of avoiding rifts which might create a bad impression on their American colleagues. He himself had decided to remain in his office in Rome, keeping in touch with his men by telephone.

The small group were picked up and driven in two cars to the DIA's Operations Centre, a short distance away. On this at least, Guaschelli had yielded. The task force would be based there.

The Operations Centre was in a detached building on the outskirts of the city. It was close to the beach, and some distance from any other buildings, although not quite far enough to avoid prying eyes and ears. Here, even the walls did not provide the requisite security.

Outside the front entrance of the building, the director of the Centre, Felice Trimarchi, was waiting for them. He was a colonel in the Carabinieri, a tall, imposing man of sixty, who had been decorated for his many DIA operations, first against the Sicilians, then against the Calabrians.

"Glad to have you with us," he said to each of the men as he introduced himself and shook their hand.

His grip was firm, the grip of a man accustomed to command.

New York

It was almost seven in the morning when Dick Moore took the call. That Sunday, he was due to leave for Vermont, where he and his wife would be spending a few days together. They went there every year in the fall, when nature produced one of its most beautiful spectacles, carpeting the roads and meadows and maple woods with leaves in every shade of yellow, orange, red and brown. It was an extraordinary display of colour, a unique work of art.

Lifting the receiver, he did not yet know that his plans would have to change. It was the switchboard operator from his office, telling him that there was someone on the line who insisted that he had something urgent to tell him, something he could tell only him.

"What's his name?"

"He wouldn't say, but he asked me to mention St Paul's Chapel."

"Put him on . . . Hello?"

"It's me."

"Yes."

"On the road from Mount Cisco, where they hold the rally, there's something that'll interest you."

"What is it?"

"Go and find out."

"Where exactly? It's a long road!"

"Go along it for a few miles. There's a side road, a dead end, where you'll find something that'll interest you."

"Look, you're going too far this time," Moore said, in a tone that was both irritable and as cold as steel. "I'm tired of this game."

"Don't say that. You need to understand. You know, nothing in life goes the way we'd like it to. That's all I can do right now."

"Don't you think —"

He heard a click. The other man had hung up.

Moore stared expressionlessly at the receiver for a while, then muttered, "Fucking son of a bitch," and put it down. After a few moments he picked it up again and dialled the number of his office.

"Do we know where that last call came from?" he asked.

"Yes, a public phone booth in Brooklyn."

"Thanks."

"Shall I send a car to check it out, Director?"

"Yes," he replied, although he did not sound convinced. He knew perfectly well that the phone call had been very short and that it was very unlikely whoever had made it was still around.

Carracci was going over the facts.

It was 5p.m. and the meeting at the DIA's Operations Centre in Reggio Calabria had only just got under way. Also present were two captains of the Carabinieri with a great deal of experience of places and people connected with the 'Ndrangheta, and vivid recall of their past activities.

One of the two now spoke up. He was Captain Pasquale Foti, forty-four years old, a man of regular build and dark complexion. His hair was dark, too, cut short in the military style. He said he had been told by a Mafioso who had turned State's evidence that the cocaine arrived from Colombia by sea, hidden beneath the water line.

"Excuse me, I don't understand," Carracci said, in a tone both sceptical and curious. "Where exactly is the cocaine hidden?"

"In the rudder space. To get to it from the interior of the ship, you have to open a trapdoor. From the outside you need divers."

"I see," Carracci replied, sounding unconvinced and thinking to himself that this was all bullshit. He shook his head slightly and continued looking at Foti with a certain scepticism.

"The drugs are in containers," Foti continued, "which are tied to the hull with synthetic fibre rope." He stopped for a moment to take a sip of water, while the Americans exchanged a few comments. Perhaps they, too, were thinking this was all bullshit.

Foti resumed. He explained that the cocaine, having been broken down into loaves, was placed in plastic canisters.

"What kind?" Carracci asked.

"Like the inner tubes in coaches and tractors."

"And how are they removed?"

"By divers."

This was a new technique in the experience of the Italian anti-drug authorities — if it existed, and wasn't just some fantasy dreamed up by Foti's Mafia informant.

Carracci waited until Foti had finished and then, making an effort to conceal his true feelings, asked, "Can we speak to this person? Maybe he can give us more details."

"He's being kept incommunicado, we don't even know where," Colonel Trimarchi said. "We'd need authorisation from the Prosecutor's Department to see him."

"In that case, I wonder if it's worth it," Carracci said.

"We can get a request to the prosecutor today."

"Today's Sunday, Colonel."

"No problem. We can reach him at home. He's always available."

Trimarchi's eyes seemed to be saying, *Here in Calabria, there are no days off, and no one ever rests.*

It was only now, even though they had come to the end of the meeting, that Carracci handed the colonel a copy of the order from the Ministry of the Interior authorising the setting up of the task force. To Trimarchi it seemed another example of unfounded police suspicions where the Carabinieri were concerned.

CHAPTER
SIXTEEN

New York

Sitting in the passenger seat of the white Chevrolet Impala, Dick Moore lit yet another cigarette. It was the third one since the driver had come to pick him up from his apartment just before eight. Or maybe it was the fourth — he was losing count. He took a deep drag. Anxiety was etched on his face. His whole body was tingling with pins and needles as if in response to the state of his nerves. The deep grooves in his cheeks made his mouth more pronounced. He thought again of his altercation with Jenny. She had not forgiven him for wrecking the prospect of three days of freedom, three days that were now lost for ever. He thought again of the telephone call, the surprise awaiting him.

One sentence in particular continued ringing in his head: *You know, nothing in life goes the way we'd like it to . . . you know, nothing in life goes the way we'd like it to . . . you know, nothing in life goes the way we'd like it to . . .*

He couldn't get the words out of his mind. It was becoming an obsession. One more element in a perverted game.

You know, nothing in life goes the way we'd like it to . . .

What exactly had the caller meant? He couldn't figure it out. It was a real mystery. Perhaps he would find the answer now, when he located what he was looking for.

The roads were still half deserted. They came to the start of the narrow, dusty road out of Mt Kisco, where the Turkey Tour Rally was held every year. During the rally, spectators lined the route, cheering and taking photographs. He ordered the driver to stop for a moment, opened the road map, and spread it on his lap. Then he said, "Drive on, but slowly." They set off again. They stopped at the corner of every side road and peered down it as far as they could. Some of the longer ones they turned on to and explored in their entirety. But there was nothing to be seen. Just trees and dust. Not a soul about. But that wasn't surprising. It was a road that only came alive once a year. After a little more than a mile, they turned on to yet another side road. After about a hundred yards, the vegetation grew thicker. Beyond a bend, they at last saw something: the burned-out shell of a car. A four-door sedan, now completely black.

Moore took his cellphone from the inside pocket of his jacket and called the office. There was no doubt in his mind: this car was what the mystery caller had wanted him to find.

Was it because it had been used by whoever committed the murders on Madison? Or was it a red herring? What exactly was the son of a bitch playing at?

Was he trying to take advantage of the new balance of power in the underworld? Or was he hoping to get money from the FBI's secret funds? The theories were piling up in Moore's mind.

The Crime Scene Unit arrived, along with a team from the FBI. They examined the inside of the car and found nothing. There were shoe prints nearby, as well as wheel tracks, probably made by a motorcycle. They set about taking casts.

Moore threw a last glance at the shell of the car, then ordered the driver to take him back to the office. He would wait there until the man contacted him.

He hoped he wouldn't have to wait too long.

Italy, 11.30p.m.

The place was safe, well camouflaged and inaccessible. Not many people were ever admitted. And only in special circumstances. Like now.

Antonio Russo had summoned his most loyal associates. It was a habit he had got into of late, whenever he had to leave the area for a few days.

The air was cold, sharp and damp. Not a single star in the sky. Silence all around. Even the large mastiff crouching on the ground seemed to respect it. Thick banks of fog had been descending for hours, covering the surroundings like a pall. Sporadically, gusts of wind would disperse them, revealing a few of the orange trees in the grove outside the farmhouse.

The four of them were in a cramped space in the basement. They were sitting in a circle on bamboo stools with their caps on their laps in the dim light of a naked bulb hanging from the ceiling.

"They're fucking us around," Antonio Russo began angrily, scratching his temples. His eyes were bloodshot, his expression tense. He was wearing a burgundy woollen smoking jacket and blue cashmere trousers.

His loyal associates looked at him with intense curiosity, anxious to know why they had been summoned.

"They've put together a task force and are planning to give us a hard time, just so they can look good to the Americans. So expect to have your houses searched and your belongings confiscated. Expect to be kept under surveillance. The worst of it is that it'll jeopardise relations with our Colombian friends . . ."

He was really furious. He leapt to his feet and began pacing nervously. Then, approaching a small table, he poured some cognac into a glass so violently that it spilled over the brim. He lifted it to his lips and drank it all down in one go. It tasted bitter in his mouth.

His three associates were leaning forward, wide-eyed, hanging on his every word, their lined faces lacking their usual self-confidence. No one spoke. They knew that their boss's sources had always proved reliable. They sipped their cognac in silence.

"I don't want to see a repeat of what happened in the eighties and nineties," Antonio Russo went on, "when the police and the Carabinieri flooded our territory to put a stop to the kidnappings. I've already sent a message to the person concerned . . . I told him there's a risk that the peace we've had for the past few years may be shattered. And you all know what that means."

The men nodded. They knew exactly what he meant. They all had vivid memories of those years when they had been forced to go to ground, either in their homes or in safe refuges, for days on end.

"I'm leaving for Spain. That's why I wanted to let you know that things might change overnight. You must be on the alert, prepared for whatever may happen, and standing by for my calls. Don't say anything yet to the foot soldiers, but please keep an even closer eye on them than usual."

The three nodded again.

"There's something else I need to talk to you about. A matter that needs to be resolved as soon as possible."

Nobody breathed. Their expressions were unequivocal: again, they knew perfectly well what he was referring to.

New York, 6p.m.

He hadn't called!

He hadn't left a message!

Dick Moore was shaking his head from side to side.

He had finished going through the list of calls.

He had gone through it again and again.

Again and again . . .

Nothing.

He hadn't found the call that mattered most to him.

Now, in his office, with his face in his hands and his elbows on his knees, Moore was thinking back over that morning. A long, deep sigh escaped his lips. His intuition had let him down. The day had brought no further word. The mystery caller had retreated back into the shadows. Obviously he was craftier than Moore had thought.

His phone calls home had gone unanswered. He wasn't surprised: during their quarrel, Jenny had threatened to leave him. She had said that kind of thing before, of course, but this time it had been more than a threat.

He wasn't alone at headquarters. The few agents on duty were busy writing reports on the burned-out car and consulting records to ascertain if it had been reported stolen. The telephone rang. Before picking up, he switched on the tape recorder. He was sure it was him.

But it wasn't. It was a member of the Crime Scene Unit.

"It was a taxi," the man announced. "That's right, a taxi."

He read out the licence number and the name of the owner, who lived in Brooklyn.

"Ah-hah!"

"It was stolen."

"When?"

"On the morning of the first of November."

"Where?"

"In the Bronx."

"When was it reported stolen?"

"The same morning."

"Have you found anything useful?"

"Unfortunately nothing significant yet. There's hardly anything left of it, barely even a scrap of upholstery."

"How about near the car? Any prints?"

"Yes, shoe prints, definitely a man's. And the tracks of a motorcycle, starting where the shoe prints trail off."

"Any results yet on those?"

"A few. The shoe prints are nearly three feet apart."

"Meaning what?"

"Meaning the guy was probably in a hurry . . . or at any rate was moving fast. We've sent all the findings to the crime lab in Washington. They may be able to identify the make and model of the motorcyle."

"That's going to take time!"

"A few days, if we're lucky."

Instead of hanging up, he immediately called Bill Hampton. It was almost one in the morning in Italy, but his colleague answered at the first ring of his cellphone.

"Bill, they found a taxi." He brought him up to date on the latest developments, and told him he would shortly be e-mailing the inventory of what had been found in Rocco Fedeli's apartment.

"Try to find out what church that is, Bill. It must have had a special significance to the victim. The Italians should be able to help you."

"Yes, sir."

153

Bill Hampton then told Moore about the confidential information Foti had obtained from his Mafia informant.

"That confirms what was written in the letter!" Moore said, before hanging up.

The news provoked a wave of optimism in him. So the mystery caller knew one of the ways cocaine was transported to Italy. That meant he was someone on the inside.

He went to the window, and looked down at the street and the traffic. It was as busy out there as ever. He checked the time: 7.05p.m. Since the mystery caller still hadn't phoned, there was nothing to do but go home.

All kinds of ideas were whirling around in his head.

Sam, who was always waiting for him behind the door, wasn't there to greet him today.

A bad sign.

What he found, prominently displayed on the console table in the hall, was a note.

It was short and to the point.

I've left, and I've taken Sam with me.

He stood there, breathless, sweating. He felt as though a door had been slammed in his face. He had expected it, but actually experiencing it was another matter. The emptiness was devastating.

CHAPTER
SEVENTEEN

Monday, 10 November

They were waiting for him.

The atmosphere in the room was calm but oppressive.

It had been a long wait.

Captain Foti, Carracci and Detective Bernardi, who had arrived from Reggio Calabria that morning, were in Ferrara's office, ready to meet the informer Annunziato Spina.

Spina entered stiffly, accompanied by two officers from the witness protection squad. He was fifty-five years old, short and very thin, with smooth, dyed black hair and a moustache. His small, bright eyes could not keep still, but darted all over. He sniffed, as if in the grip of a perennial cold. He was chewing a sweet. For some months, he had been in the programme reserved for those who have turned State's evidence. There were a number of criminal proceedings pending against him: one at the court in Rome for international drug trafficking and money laundering, others in Reggio Calabria for criminal conspiracy relating to the traffic in arms and drugs.

His eyes fell on Ferrara. "How nice to see you again," he said in a fairly sardonic tone. "Have you changed cities?" Spina was an old acquaintance of Ferrara's. The latter had arrested him years earlier during a drug investigation that had encompassed both Florence and Milan.

"I've been transferred," Ferrara replied curtly, motioning him to a chair in front of the desk.

Annunziato Spina sat down, crossed his legs, and placed his bony hands on his corduroy trousers. Then he looked at Foti, who was sitting next to Ferrara.

"Hey, what is this? Tell me, Chief Superintendent. There must be a reason why you've brought me here." His tone was now decidedly provocative.

"Yes, there is a reason," Ferrara replied. "A very specific reason." Very calmly, he told him why he had been summoned. When he had finished, Annunziato Spina gave Captain Foti a piercing look, then pursed his lips and swallowed the sweet he had been chewing. His teeth remained clenched for a few moments. He felt betrayed.

Foti ignored him.

"So," Ferrara said, breaking a silence that had become unbearable, "can you tell us anything about drugs transported on ships coming from Colombia and bound for Italian ports?"

"Of course I can tell you something. Why, did you think I couldn't?" His eyes kept darting from Ferrara to Foti and back.

"And what about the drugs being hidden beneath the water line? What can you tell us about that?"

Impatiently, Spina said that he had already talked about this to Captain Foti in the strictest confidence.

"Now tell us," Ferrara said.

"If I really have to . . . A while back, I saw the cocaine being packed and hidden on a ship going to Italy. Later, I supervised the divers who removed it."

"Where was this organisation based?" Ferrara asked.

"In Colombia, in a forest. There was a warehouse where the drugs were stored. Big piles of them like sacks of corn."

A smile at last appeared on his face. His eyes shone with a new, more intense light. They moved several times from Ferrara's face to Foti's and back again, like a pendulum.

"Where exactly was this warehouse?" Ferrara insisted.

"I told you. In a forest."

"But where?"

"Near the town of Turbo."

Ferrara exchanged a brief knowing look with Detective Bernardi.

"And then?"

"Then I went to Turbo . . . It's a big port, very noisy, just like Naples . . . That was where I saw them hiding the drugs on the ship."

"What did they do exactly? I need you to be as specific as possible."

Suddenly talkative, Spina told them how he and a group of Colombians had gone out to the ship at night on a motor boat. Two divers had gone down several times and tied the inner tubes containing the drugs to the ship with synthetic fibre ropes.

"Did they have accomplices on the ship?" Ferrara asked.

"No, none of the crew knew anything about it."

"I don't quite understand."

"The organisation had a few customs officers in its pocket. It was a no-risk operation."

"Where was the ship bound for?"

"It was supposed to arrive in a port in Liguria, but then there was some snag and it ended up on the southern cape of the Istrian peninsula."

Ferrara and Bernardi again exchanged knowing glances.

"What was the ship's official cargo?"

"Bananas."

"And whose drugs were they?"

"Mine. I had them removed by a pair of divers at night. That's the charge I'm up for at the court in Rome."

He emphasised the word *mine*. Perhaps to shift responsibility from anyone else. He was a traitor, a snitch, but in his mind he was still a man of honour.

"Are you aware of any other methods used to transport drugs?"

"I know of another one, but I've never actually seen it."

"Can you tell us what it is?"

"Yes, I heard about cocaine being carried in containers with blocks of granite from Brazil, bound for Salerno and Naples."

"Who was it intended for?"

"I don't know."

"The Colombians, your suppliers, who were they?" Ferrara asked.

"I only ever knew my contact. He lived in Rome and was arrested in the same police operation as me. They tracked him down to a house in Ostia."

Captain Foti looked at Ferrara and nodded.

"One last question."

"All right."

"How were the payments made to the Colombians?"

"In dollars. I exchanged lire for dollars in Milan and then gave them to an emissary of theirs, usually in Spain or in Switzerland . . . Have we finished, Chief Superintendent? . . . At last! Can I go?"

He was about to stand up.

"Sit down, we haven't finished yet. I have another question . . . about money laundering."

"At least let me smoke a cigarette, have a coffee, drink some water," he said, moistening his dry lips.

"All right, let's take a break," Ferrara said. "We'll start again in half an hour."

They were sitting in the same places, but the atmosphere was more relaxed now.

"So," Ferrara said, "what can you tell us about money laundering?"

"I found out that some of the others were going to Switzerland to make payments into an account at a subsidiary of a Panamanian bank."

"What account?" Foti said. "Can you be more specific?"

"No, I can't, Captain. I don't know anything . . . I don't know . . . anything." His tone was tense again.

"Calm down, Spina," Ferrara said. "The calmer you are, the easier it is for us to understand you."

"All right, but as long as it's about things I know. I'm not going to make anything up."

"This really is the last question."

Spina looked at him, visibly annoyed. He had never imagined they'd want so much from him.

"Of the Calabrians involved in the drugs trade with the Colombians, who's the top dog these days?" Ferrara asked in a curt tone, convinced that the time had come to go straight to the heart of the matter. "I'm sure you know, so why not tell us?"

Annunziato Spina fell silent, his lips curled in a bitter sneer. He'd had enough of playing the snitch. What he had told them already was water under the bridge. They shouldn't expect any more from him.

Ferrara and Foti exchanged an imperceptible sign of understanding. As good investigators, they knew you often obtained more by being indirect.

"Annunziato," Foti said, "you can't do this. You're supposed to be cooperating with us, and you have to answer, even in a simple interview like this. In fact, with all the more reason in an interview like this, because what you say here won't be used in any legal procedure, but only to help us with our investigations. We're not under any obligation to inform the public prosecutor."

"What do you mean?" Spina asked, frowning.

160

"I mean that nothing you tell us now can be used against you in court. It's strictly confidential."

"I don't believe that . . . I know all about your confidentiality." He smiled slightly. "But all right, all right. I'm going to give you a name . . . off the record . . ."

"Completely off the record," Foti said, encouragingly. "Go ahead."

"Antonio Russo."

"Antonio Russo from Castellanza?"

"That's the man, Captain. They call him Don 'Ntoni. He's the son of Giuseppe Russo, who died a couple of years ago. The father was a real 'Ndranghetista."

"And the son?"

"Even more of an 'Ndranghetista than the father. He's the man in charge of the cocaine trade, and not only in Italy. When the other organisations, including Cosa Nostra, have something big going down and need help, he's the one they turn to."

There was a pause.

The captain knew that Antonio Russo was suspected of drug trafficking, but had no idea that he was so important internationally. The phone taps had never suggested that degree of involvement.

To break the silence, Ferrara asked, "Did you ever meet Rocco Fedeli?"

"Who's he?"

"He's from San Piero d'Aspromonte, too. Or at least he was. He's been murdered."

Spina looked surprised. "No. Never met him. And I didn't know he'd been murdered, until you just told me."

"So you don't know if there was ever any connection between this Russo and Rocco Fedeli?"

"No."

"Is there anything else you can tell us about Antonio Russo?"

Annunziato Spina thought a moment before replying. Then he said, "He's someone who might have been underestimated in the past, but he always had good contacts." He glanced at Ferrara, and raised a hand to his forehead.

"And who might these 'contacts' be?" Ferrara asked.

"How should I know? Now you're asking too much of me. You're overestimating me."

"We're grateful to you, Spina," Foti cut in. "Now we really have finished."

At last something concrete, Ferrara thought as Spina went out, accompanied by two officers.

Only Carracci showed no reaction. For the whole meeting he had maintained a frozen indifference, sitting a little apart from the others in an armchair in the lounge area of Ferrara's office, as if what Spina was telling them did not really interest him.

Was it because the word "contacts" still hung in the air?

"He's free, Chief Superintendent Carracci, just knock and go in."

Armando Guaschelli's private secretary knew the superintendent well and knew how good his relations were with her superior. He was one of the boss's blue-eyed boys. He was never kept waiting, not even for a few minutes.

Less than an hour after the meeting at the DIA, Carracci was on the second floor of the Interior Ministry.

He knocked and went in. Guaschelli looked up from the papers on his desk. As soon as he saw who it was, a big smile spread over his face, and he stood up and went to greet him. He was only a little over five feet tall, a height that often surprised those who met him: *How did they ever hire him? He must have had connections!*

"What a pleasure to see you, Stefano. Let's sit here." He indicated the long black sofa by the window, from where there was a view of the Piazza del Viminale. They sat down side by side. "So, what do you have to tell me?"

His tone, as usual, was confidential, almost familiar.

Carracci told him how the investigation was going.

"Stefano, I want you to follow the case personally, I repeat, *personally*. Don't let that Chief Superintendent's man take over on this. You know who I mean — Ferrara. We've had more than enough trouble from him in the past." He placed his arm on Carracci's shoulder.

Carracci nodded. "Don't worry, I'll see to it."

Carracci was one of the few people who didn't call Guaschelli "sir".

He told him about the meeting with Annunziato Spina. Guaschelli abruptly changed expression. He had a gaunt, pale face, a chain smoker's face.

"I want you to keep me informed about this Russo," he said in a resolute tone. "I need to know every development. Including anything you hear about these 'contacts'. Or about any other Mafia snitches. You know I have to watch my back with the minister . . ."

"Of course."

"Stefano, we have to avoid the usual nasty rumours, the usual fuss about nothing. These snitches aren't to be trusted." Guaschelli clearly knew a thing or two — or even quite a lot — about snitches. He leaned towards Carracci and whispered something in his ear.

"Yes, of course," Carracci said. "You can rely on me."

"Now go back to Calabria."

"I'll take the first plane tomorrow morning."

They embraced by way of farewell.

As Carracci passed the private secretary, she looked at him and screwed up her eyes knowingly.

New York

Dick Moore was staring up at Frederick Warren Allen's three statues depicting Law, Truth and Equity on the pediment above the ten granite Corinthian columns. The pediment itself bore the words of George Washington: *The true administration of justice is the firmest pillar of good government.*

164

It was just before noon and he was outside the New York State Supreme Court at 60 Centre Street. He had an appointment with Ted Morrison. Moving his eyes down from the pediment, he saw him walking beneath the columns and coming down the steps. He waved and came towards him.

"Hi, Dick. Punctual as ever."

They shook hands warmly.

"So, what do you have for me?" They had already started walking towards the little garden opposite.

"What I have is a burned-out taxi. Believed to be connected to the homicides on Madison."

"Any proof of the connection?" Morrison asked dubiously.

Moore hesitated a moment, as if uncertain. He wondered if he should mention the anonymous calls, and decided against it. This might not be the right moment. Maybe it would never be the right moment.

"It's just a hunch, but based on confidential information received by the Bureau," he replied in a resolute tone.

"I get it: you have a source! I hope it's reliable and you soon hit your target."

Moore looked him straight in the eyes, neutrally, without nodding.

"But remember," Morrison said, "getting close to the target is not the same as hitting it bang in the middle."

Moore nodded. "It's still too early to draw conclusions, but we should have a clearer idea very soon." He preferred to stick to generalities. He hadn't the slightest intention of hinting at the subtle game he was playing with the mystery caller.

"Good. I have confidence in the Bureau. This morning I phoned the national anti-Mafia prosecutor in Italy. He assured me of his full support for your men and the DIA in Rome. He told me they're already working together, in Calabria."

"Thanks, Ted. That's good to know." He reported what he had heard from Hampton.

"What can you tell me about Rocco Fedeli?" Morrison asked.

"We're working with the cops. We should soon have a fuller picture of his activities, and we're also taking another look at the Susan George murder."

"Has the material you removed from the apartment proved useful?"

"They're still looking at it. I think it may be of great use."

"And the safe?"

"According to our source, there should have been a lot of money in it," Moore replied, spontaneously.

"Are you sure?"

"I think so, our source is reliable."

"If he knows that much, he must know a lot more!" Morrison commented.

Moore nodded.

"Let's go eat something, Dick," Morrison suggested.

They headed in the direction of Elizabeth Street, with its many Chinese restaurants.

The gym was the size of a warehouse.

It had a very high ceiling, from which the plaster was peeling. The walls were permeated with different

166

smells, but one predominated: sweat. Right now, there were about thirty young men in the gym, mostly African-Americans, all of them regulars, some warming up, some fighting, their bodies well protected.

One muscular young man was engaged in a training bout with a dark-skinned, grey-haired man. He was kicking his opponent repeatedly in the legs and chest and on the head with all the force of an ancient gladiator, while the grey-haired man urged him to hit even harder. The bout finished with the ritual bow and the young man headed for the changing rooms, while his opponent remained at the edge of the ring.

It was two in the afternoon, in Brooklyn.

Lieutenant Reynolds had watched the bout. There were several reasons why he was here. The discovery of the burned-out cab, the fact that the driver was from Brooklyn, the anonymous call to Moore from a public phone booth in Brooklyn . . . Brooklyn had changed a lot in the last few years, from a dormitory borough to the true heart of New York. Organised crime had taken over in a big way, and a lot of that was Italian. Italians had gradually abandoned Little Italy, with the continual spread of the adjacent neighbourhood of Chinatown.

He approached the grey-haired man, and they shook hands. The man had a grip of steel.

"What are you doing in these parts, John?" he asked.

His name was Rusty Sheridan.

He was a veteran of the Marines, and a martial arts expert. On each forearm, pumped up by physical exercise, he had a large tattoo: on the right, a dragon, and on the left, barbed wire and a few words. A souvenir of the war, perhaps.

He had been eighteen in 1967 when he had volunteered to go to Vietnam and fight in what had seemed to him, as it had to a lot of young men, a just war. There he had discovered the other side of the coin: unimaginably violent reprisals, massacres of women and children, murders among his fellow soldiers, all the fear and cruelty and madness of that terrible conflict. On returning home he had been decorated and had joined the police. He had taken part in peace demonstrations, screaming at the top of his voice, "Put an end to this insane war!" It was all very topical again, given what was happening in Iraq.

"I'm here on business," Reynolds said, rubbing his chin with his hand.

"What are you working on?"

"A tricky case. We found a burned-out vehicle on the road where they hold the rally. A taxi, stolen in the Bronx, but the owner lives here."

Sheridan took off his protection and wiped his face and neck with a towel, which he then placed around his shoulders. "I understand," he said. "You want to find out about the Brooklyn gangs. It won't be easy. These guys are tough cookies, and they're smart, too. They don't let anyone get close. And besides, that road is no man's land. You should know that." There was sarcasm in these last words, which he made no attempt to conceal.

Reynolds chose to ignore it. "I know. That's why I came to see you."

"You also know they know my past. I'd have even more customers here if I wasn't an ex-cop."

"That's the risk we have to take," Reynolds replied with a smile.

Sheridan returned the smile. "You, maybe, not me, not any more." Then he was silent for a few moments. He grabbed the towel and again rubbed his face and neck with it. It might have been Reynolds' request for help that had made him sweat.

"OK, John, I'll see what I can do. If I find out anything, I'll get in touch." It was as if he could feel the police uniform on his skin. He wrung out the towel with both hands.

"I knew I could count on you," Reynolds said. "You've always been a good friend." It was an allusion to the many tip-offs Sheridan had given him in the past.

They hugged, and Reynolds walked away with the smell of sweat on him. At the door, he turned back to look at Sheridan. His friend had already jumped into the ring again, ready for the next bout.

The love of his life! Reynolds thought.

It was true: these days Rusty Sheridan lived only for his gym.

The name wasn't new to him. From the first moment he'd heard it, he'd had a vague feeling he'd come across it before, but somehow couldn't place it.

When?

Where?

Who had he heard use it?

He was in bed, his mind in turmoil.

Beside him, Petra was reading the libretto of Bizet's *Carmen*.

Suddenly, there was a glimmer of light.

He recalled an episode from his past, a past he had tried to forget, to leave behind him for ever. Images that had lain buried for years, of an encounter with a young man in very particular circumstances, began parading in front of his eyes.

It was the beginning of the 1980s. He had been based at Police Headquarters in Reggio Calabria, dealing mainly with kidnappings: the latest source of income for the 'Ndrangheta.

He remembered every detail. He had been searching a farm belonging to a suspect when he had slipped like a sack of potatoes in a cold, dirty pool of mud and fallen to the ground. Two gentle hands helped him to his feet. He turned and saw a young man. One of the suspect's sons. Thin, with an honest face. He was not smiling, but had an expression of genuine regret. No smile. Carefully, with a sponge dipped in water, he wiped Ferrara's camouflage fatigues, getting the worst of the mud off. "I'm sorry," he murmured a number of times . . .

Ferrara could still smell the mixture of hay, manure and goats that hung in the air.

Petra had fallen asleep. But he was still wide awake.

He remembered that face perfectly. And the voice, too. It was in his office, the door was open.

"Can I say hello, Chief Superintendent?"

He had looked up and seen a young man carrying some sheets of paper, smiling at him. He did not recognise him at first.

"Of course you can say hello."

The young man came in, still smiling. "What is it, Chief Superintendent, don't you remember me? That fall brought you luck, Chief Superintendent. Now I'm going to prison, but I didn't do what's written in these papers."

Ferrara remembered the fall, although he found it hard to recall the young man. The face wasn't so honest any more. It was a face that had lived. "I thank you for what you did then," he said. "You can mention it to the prosecutor when you are questioned." As the young man left Ferrara's office, two of Ferrara's men had handcuffed him and led him away.

CHAPTER
EIGHTEEN

Tuesday, 11 November

Ferrara woke up. He looked at the time. It was 5.45.

The lamp on the bedside table was still on. He switched it off.

Next to him, Petra was still in a deep sleep and did not hear him. He looked at her for a moment: her half-open lips, her hair spread over the pillow. He delicately stroked her cheek.

Then he got out of bed. He did not wait for breakfast. He wanted to get to the office early. He left the apartment without making a noise.

The offices were still empty at this hour. Even the bar on the ground floor was closed. He got a coffee from the machine. Carrying a plastic cup, he walked to his room and immediately got down to work.

He took out the files from his past. It was time to rummage in his memories. The files were carefully arranged by year and place of posting. He started looking for the documents relating to the police operation that had led him to search that farm.

As he looked through, he found a letter he had received in the eighties. The vague memory of it had come back to him as soon as he had woken up. It was still there, at the back of his mind. He couldn't remember the sender. Perhaps there hadn't been any indication of one. But the contents, yes, he remembered those. A threat. A genuine threat. The last he had received, before leaving Calabria.

It was in the file relating to the year 1987, along with other documents: reports, notes, carefully folded press cuttings — articles about himself — and photographs of places and people. And two white envelopes edged in black. On them, an unsteady hand had written: *Chief Superintendent Ferrara — Police Headquarters, Via Santa Caterina — Reggio Calabria.*

The first envelope was postmarked 10.10.87 and the second 29.10.87, both posted in Reggio Calabria itself. He opened them. They were both empty, just the way he had received them at the time, sixteen years earlier: he remembered them well. He read the report he had sent to the Commissioner, in which he had concluded: *I attach two of the many black-edged envelopes I periodically receive, clearly meant as death threats. Unfortunately, I cannot attach the threatening telephone calls, naturally anonymous, which I also receive.*

He continued searching.

His eyes now fell on a photocopy of a handwritten letter. This one wasn't completely anonymous. The initials A.R. appeared at the bottom of the page.

He read it.

. . . I don't want to play the victim, but I intend to do all I can, to use every means possible, even unlawful ones, to expose the offences committed by you and your squad to frame me for a crime I did not commit. A simple reading of the trial documents would be sufficient to realise the slapdash nature of the investigation into my case. For the crimes with which I have soiled my hands, I have paid my debts to justice, but I have absolutely no intention of serving time for what other people have done.

Dear Chief Superintendent, please make every effort to ensure that truth wins out, or it will mean that the responsibility for whatever may happen will not be mine alone.

He could not take his eyes off that sheet of paper. And a current of adrenaline went through him. Another threat. With an abrupt gesture, he put the letter away. Then he went further back in the files. In the one for 1985, he finally found the report he was looking for. It referred to Operation Farmhouse: the raid on the property of Giuseppe Russo of Castellanza. He read through it at the speed of a Ferrari. The fall . . . the name of the owner's son . . . Antonio . . . Antonio Russo. There it was. He was sure of it now. It was as if a powerful beacon had been lit in his mind.

It was the same Antonio Russo that Annunziato Spina had talked about. He carefully folded all the documents, closed the files and put them back in their places.

174

Daylight, filtering through the windows, struck his mind as a sign of victory.

Darling, I'm at the office. Everything's fine.

The note was in full view on the table in the kitchen. Petra read it as soon as she entered.

When she had woken up and found that her husband was not beside her, she had become anxious. The note seemed to reassure her for a moment.

Then, pensively, she grabbed the receiver and dialled her husband's mobile number.

"How are you?" she asked when she heard his voice.

"Fine. Why?"

"You went out without telling me."

"You were sleeping like an angel, Petra. I knew you didn't have to go to work this morning. Your first appointment is at midday."

"That's right, I have a business lunch. But you could have woken me for breakfast."

"I've already had it."

"Where?"

"Here, in the office."

"Coffee?"

"Yes."

"And you call that breakfast?"

"You're right, of course."

"What time did you leave?"

"Six o'clock."

"Is something wrong?" She prayed to herself that he would answer no.

"No. I needed to find a file in the office."

"About the Calabrians?"

"Yes."

"Are we going to the theatre this evening if I don't work late?"

"Of course."

"Love you."

"Love you too."

Petra put the phone down. She felt a shudder go through her and held her breath. She was afraid he was going away.

Lost in thought, she forgot to make breakfast.

She couldn't stand this 'Ndrangheta business. It seemed to her that she had gone back in time, to those terrible years in the 1980s when her husband would be woken in the middle of the night to rush to the scene of a murder, a kidnapping, or a bomb attack.

No, she really didn't like to relive those times.

And she decided that this evening she would broach the subject.

"Sit down!"

Captain Foti and Detective Bernardi entered and the door closed behind them. They had come back from Rome on the first morning flight, together with Carracci.

It was three o'clock on a damp rainy afternoon, and a meeting was about to start at the DIA centre in Reggio Calabria. Waiting for them were Captain Trimarchi, Bill Hampton, Bob Holley and the head of the *Squadra Mobile*, Bruni.

"Any news from the capital?" Trimarchi asked.

"Yes, good news," Foti replied, handing him a transcript of the interview with Annunziato Spina.

"We'll need to check with the harbour authorities about ships arriving from Turbo with cargos of bananas," Trimarchi said when he had finished reading. "Then I'd say it'd be a good idea to tap the phones of the victims' relatives."

They all agreed.

"Any other ideas?" he asked.

"Even if we don't find any direct link," Foti said, taking back the transcript, "it could be useful to put a tap on Antonio Russo's phones."

Detective Bernardi nodded his approval.

"It's worth a try, even if only for a few days," Trimarchi agreed.

At that moment, someone knocked at the door.

"Come in!"

Stefano Carracci put his head round the door and then came in, a steaming paper cup in his hand. The room filled with the aroma of hot chocolate.

"Hello!" he said. He looked around and his face clouded over. They had not expected him, even though it was a meeting of the task force.

"So what do you think, Chief Superintendent Carracci?" Trimarchi asked.

"About what?"

"About this Antonio Russo. Should we tap his phones or not?"

"I suppose we could do that," he replied casually, almost as if he was not really interested. But he could feel the blood rushing to his head. His hand shook and a few drops of chocolate spilt on his trousers. Irritably, he put the cup down on the floor and tried to dry them with a sheet of paper. "We could try, anyway," he added in a weak voice, holding his hand against his trousers.

"Is there a problem with that?" Trimarchi asked.

"No, no, it's fine. I'll take them to the laundry."

"I think you misunderstood me. I was referring to the phone tap."

"Oh, yes! No problem. Except that these Mafiosi never discuss business over the phone. They're too clever for that. It's usually a waste of time."

"We know that, of course, but sometimes they drop their guard. Just a few words can tell us a lot. And it's useful to know who they're in contact with."

"All right, Colonel," Carracci replied, indifferently.

"Good," Trimarchi said, obviously annoyed. "So let's divide up the tasks."

They decided that Captain Foti and his team would keep an eye on Antonio Russo's activities, including those on his home territory, and that the officers of the DIA would remain at the centre, listening in to the tapped phones. As for the men of the *Squadra Mobile* of Reggio Calabria and the SCO, they would handle the surveillance operation in San Piero d'Aspromonte, as well as checking with the harbour authorities.

"Do you people have — I don't know what you call it — we call it 'sneak and peek'?" Bill Hampton asked, looking to Holley for help.

"Under US law," Holley explained, "the FBI can search a house when the occupants are out, reserving the right to inform them only when the investigation can no longer be compromised." This was one of the exceptional measures introduced in the Patriot Act, the law approved after 9/11, which widened the FBI's powers in the fight against terrorism.

"No," Carracci replied. "We don't have that here. We can enter premises under false pretences, but only in major investigations, and only to place bugs without the occupants' knowledge. But it always has to be authorised by a public prosecutor."

The Americans nodded. They had that same option, but sneak and peek was something different and gave them greater autonomy.

We're not in America here, the colonel thought, *and fortunately we haven't had a 9/11!*

"Any developments at your end?" Trimarchi asked, turning to Bruni.

"We didn't find much on Rocco Fedeli either at headquarters or at the police station in Siderno. Just a few documents going back to the 1980s. Nothing we don't already know."

"Any links with Antonio Russo?"

"Nothing."

"Hasn't he ever been stopped at a roadblock?"

Bruni shook his head.

"How about the other victims?" Trimarchi asked.

"Nothing there either. None of them had criminal records. All we found were official papers, like passport application forms."

"What shall we call this operation?"

Several ideas were put forward, but Foti's prevailed. Operation Orange Blossom.

The orange blossom is the scented flower of the bergamot plant, whose most favourable habitat is the narrow strip of land between Villa San Giovanni and Monasterace, bordered on one side by the furthest foothills of the Aspromonte, and on the other by the Ionian and Tyrrhenian Seas. It was here that San Piero d'Aspromonte was located.

Yes, a powerful earthquake had been reported in America, but the epicentre seemed to be located here in Calabria, where the earth was fragrant, not only with the smell of the sea and the scent of orange blossom, but also with the blood of many victims.

Some time later, the Americans again came to Trimarchi's office.

Bill Hampton was holding a small bundle of photographs in his hand.

"Colonel, my colleagues would like to see this place," Bob Holley said, showing him a copy of the photograph of Rocco Fedeli in front of the little church.

Trimarchi took it.

He only had to give it a quick glance.

"It's the shrine of the Madonna of Aspromonte," he said.

"Yes," Bernardi said, "that's what Fedeli's niece told us."

"Where is it?" Bob Holley asked.

"In a deep valley, one of the wildest and most inaccessible areas in the region." It was a place surrounded by pines, beeches, oaks, chestnut trees and bracken, Trimarchi explained, where every year, by age-old tradition, people came as pilgrims: young and old, rich and poor, saints and sinners. Among the sinners, the 'Ndrangheta. It was there that they met, coming from all over, even from across the ocean, to review their recent activities and establish a common programme for the following year. It was their parliament, and also their courthouse.

"You can't go there, at least not now," Trimarchi said, by way of conclusion.

The Americans looked at each other.

Trimarchi stood up. "A new face would be spotted immediately."

Barcelona

They had talked in code.

Short sentences, hints, nothing spelled out.

But they had understood. They were to meet in Barcelona. As they had so often before.

Antonio Russo and Diego Lopez were friends and brothers.

Russo had arrived in Barcelona after a non-stop journey in the Mercedes in the company of two of his closest associates, who had taken turns at the wheel, just as they had on other occasions.

They proceeded to Senyor Parellada, a restaurant they favoured for its relaxing atmosphere. Antonio Russo liked everything about it: the little table lamps of red and white glass, the yellow, white and blue walls, the staircase with wooden banisters of the same colours.

A good meal of paella and sangria refreshed them after their journey. When they had finished eating, they went to their usual hotel, which was in a street off the Ramblas.

The receptionist greeted Russo as courteously as ever.

"Welcome to Barcelona, Señor Russo. We've reserved your suite."

"Thank you," replied Russo with a smile, handing him a hundred-dollar bill.

"Many thanks, señor. Would you like some company tonight?"

"Yes, the same girl, at midnight." He smiled again.

"Midnight?"

"Yes."

"Of course, señor."

They met at a flamenco *tablao* called El Cordobés, bang in the centre of town, conveniently close to the hotel.

When Antonio Russo entered, Diego Lopez was already sitting at a table, dressed in an elegant grey suit. He was always very punctual. He was about forty, of medium height, thin and dark-skinned, with jet-black hair, and he was the head of the Cali cartel, which exported cocaine to Europe. He was a very wealthy man. He had had some hair-raising experiences in his life, but had never given up, never retreated into himself, never questioned what he was doing. As soon as he saw his friend come in, he stood up and went to him, and the two men embraced and slapped each other on the back, as if they had not seen each other for a long time.

"Isn't Pedro here?" Antonio Russo asked.

Pedro was Diego's brother, a few years his junior. He had been present at their last meeting.

"No, 'Ntoni, I'm alone. Pedro stayed in Cali. He can't always come with me. Someone has to keep an eye on the boys." He smiled. "I'm sure you understand that!"

"Of course," Russo replied, also smiling.

He knew that Diego had what amounted to an army under him, with fast motor boats, arms . . . Who better than his own brother to stand in for him?

In the meantime a waiter approached them with two glasses of sherry.

The two men ordered tapas.

"House wine?" the waiter asked.

"Yes, thanks," they replied.

They knew it was of excellent quality.

"We've had a heavy loss," Antonio Russo began, without too much preamble. "Almost a hundred kilos got damp, but most was completely soaked. My backers don't want to pay what they agreed. And this is a great problem for me."

Diego's face abruptly clouded over. He had heard about the problem, but now it was a question of money. That was why they had arranged to meet.

"It was your people's fault, not ours," the Colombian replied after a moment's silence. He opened and closed his fists, and thumped the table. Antonio Russo had never seen him look so angry or heard his voice sound

183

so tense. It was clear he had no intention of taking responsibility for what had happened.

"No, it wasn't our fault, Diego."

"What are you talking about? You're completely wrong!"

"Diego, it seems the drugs weren't properly insulated before they were stored."

"That's not possible. My men are professionals. They don't make mistakes."

"But the drugs arrived wet. You have to believe me."

Suddenly they fell silent. They had seen the waiter approaching. They drank their sherry, looking at each other in silence.

When the waiter had walked away, they began talking again.

"It must have been your divers," said Diego. "They may not be as skilled as they should be."

Antonio Russo shook his head. "No."

"Let's eat, 'Ntoni," Diego said.

Silence fell again. The place was starting to fill with customers.

"I have a proposal," Diego resumed.

"What is it?"

"We'll send two of our chemists to Calabria to save the drugs. That's all I can do. You can't ask more of me than that."

It was his final offer.

Antonio Russo knew that. "How can they save them?" he asked.

"By treating them."

"How?"

"With microwave ovens, acetone filters . . . In practical terms, they turn the stuff back into base cocaine and then again into cocaine hydrochloride. They'll handle it, 'Ntoni. But you have to pay. There can't be any discounts. That's the one non-negotiable condition if you want to continue doing business with us." His tone had become even more determined.

'Ntoni seemed to reflect for a few moments. Then he said, "If the drugs can be saved, there won't be any problems about paying. But in future we'll have to be more careful."

"It's not me you should be saying that to, 'Ntoni."

"I'm saying it to both of us."

Russo gave him his assurance and declared himself in agreement.

"All right," Diego said at last.

Their relationship would continue. They were still friends, perhaps even closer friends than before. The next consignment would be even bigger than the previous ones.

"Have you brought the money for the new supplies?" Diego asked. "After what happened, my people want a good advance before they'll send it out. More than the other times. Otherwise they simply won't do it."

"Yes, of course I've brought it. That's what I'm here for, Diego."

"Where is it?"

"In my hotel room."

In the meantime, a flamenco show was starting. Two guitarists, a singer and a group of six female dancers, dressed in traditional costumes, had already appeared on the stage. Music filled the room with the sound of castanets. The dancers moved to the rhythm, their skirts, held in at the waist, swishing about as they leapt from side to side. It was a thrilling spectacle.

Both men were staring at the dancers, Russo winking insistently at them. After a while, he gave a deep sigh and said, "Diego, we have to go. It's getting late." He smiled. "I have an appointment."

"The usual?" asked Diego.

"Yes. Natalie."

The Colombian paid the bill and they left.

"All right, 'Ntoni. As always, you have kept your word. You've done a good job. Is there anything else?"

"That's all, for the moment. You'll receive the rest on delivery."

They were in Antonio Russo's suite at the hotel.

The briefcase, full of American dollars in hundred-dollar bills, was open on a little side table. They were sitting on two armchairs, facing each other. Diego slipped his hand inside his jacket, took out a gun and pointed it at Russo's chest.

"What are you doing, Diego?" Russo said, a look of genuine surprise on his face.

"I didn't think you were so naïve, 'Ntoni."

Antonio Russo made to stand up. "Don't move or you're a dead man," said Diego. His voice was firm and his eyes ice-cold. For a few moments Russo stared at the pistol. It had a silencer.

"Listen, my friend, I'm going to pay you. I brought the money. What's got into you?" He looked ever more astonished.

Diego moved the gun to his other hand and stood up. He went to the table, took the briefcase and sat down again. He was about to place it on the floor when Antonio Russo lunged at it with his hand and tried to grab it. With the gun only a few inches from Russo's chest, Diego slowly lowered his left eyelid and, with his finger poised on the cold metal of the trigger cried, "Stop! If you take it, I'll kill you. I'm not joking, 'Ntoni." He was in a towering rage.

Russo, who in the meantime had stood up, immediately withdrew his hand, slightly losing his balance as he did so. He was about to say, "We had an agreement . . ." when Diego kicked him in the groin, bringing him to his knees.

"Shut your fucking mouth, 'Ntoni. You've been fucking me about."

Antonio Russo tried to stay calm. He got to his feet and stood there, looking at Diego, who was still holding the gun firmly and pointing it at him. His voice as steady as he could make it, he asked, "Tell me, Diego, what exactly are you playing at?" There was no reply. He could feel his blood beating in his temples.

"You're making a big mistake, Diego," he said. "You fuck with me, you fuck with the whole organisation, and they won't like it, it's going to cause you a lot of trouble. Don't think you can escape. They'll track you down wherever you go."

Diego did not reply. His eyes were still ice-cold.

187

"Let's go back to what we agreed, Diego. You take the money, I take the drugs. I'll forget the gun, I'll forget all about this."

"Bullshit. I'm not falling for that!" His eyes still on the man who was now his enemy, he bent and again opened the case. He began taking out bundles of banknotes and checking them. He didn't trust Russo.

Russo quickly flung out his right leg and hit him in the testicles. Diego let out a groan and pressed the trigger. The shot made a slight, almost imperceptible hissing sound. In a split second, Russo leapt on him and pinned him down with his knees. He grabbed the gun with both hands and took it off him. Now it was his turn to hold the gun a few inches from his friend's face.

"I'll kill you, you moron," he cried. "Do you want to die?"

Diego was gasping with pain. Russo put his hand to his own arm to check if he was bleeding. Then he looked at his hand: it was clean. The shot had merely grazed the sleeve of his jacket. All the same, he yelled, "Get down on the floor. Go on! Down! I don't want to keep repeating myself!"

"What are you planning to do, 'Ntoni?" asked Diego, obeying.

Russo stood over him with his legs apart, then bent and pressed the barrel of the gun against the back of his neck.

"I'll kill you!" he cried again, cocking the gun. The metal click echoed in the air.

188

"What the fuck are you doing, 'Ntoni? Have you gone mad? Are you really going to kill me?"

"You started this. Now shut up! Don't move! I have something else in store for you." He took out his mobile phone and called his men.

"Take him to your suite," he said when they arrived. "We'll be leaving soon."

Head bowed, Diego was led out between the two bodyguards.

Now Antonio Russo just had time for a quick shower before Natalie arrived. She was only twenty, tall and slim with long dark hair and incredibly beautiful eyes that had apparently put a spell on him. Each time they met, he left her a thousand dollars, as well as a few hits of cocaine.

Even if they'd only spent a couple of hours together.

They wouldn't have any longer than that tonight.

PART THREE

ORANGE BLOSSOM

CHAPTER
NINETEEN

Wednesday, 12 November

The outlines of the mountains began to appear in the dim light of dawn.

The sky was covered in threatening black clouds. In addition, an icy north wind was blowing, howling in the dense foliage of the trees then occasionally subsiding into deep silence.

Captain Foti and three men from his team, wrapped in windbreakers and heavy woollen sweaters, advanced along paths that wound between tall trees. Weeds, thorns and shrubs were their only companions, apart from the music of the wind. They had set off several hours earlier. Helped through the most difficult areas by infra-red binoculars, they had made their way in the pitch dark, ears pricked for the slightest noise, the cold air freezing their faces and turning their eyes red and their lips white. Now they had almost reached the top of a hill. From here, they would be able to keep an eye on Antonio Russo's farmhouse, a few hundred yards away as the crow flies. From now on, they would be watching it day and night. Twenty-four hours a day. In a place like this, it was an intensely boring kind of stakeout, but they were used to it.

"How about some coffee?" Foti asked.

"Exactly what we need," the oldest of the officers replied.

The others nodded.

They poured the coffee, still steaming, from the camping thermos into plastic cups, and the white of the steam gradually wafted away into the air. The coffee was surprisingly tasty.

Foti put his empty cup in a plastic bag and went over the instructions.

"Any movement you see, any sign of life inside the farmhouse, write it down. Any cars that come, try to indicate the make, the model and the colour. And remember to take as many photographs as possible."

"We won't let anything get past us, Captain," one of the men replied. He sounded as if he meant business.

The wind was still howling, occasionally it seemed to be getting worse. It was a terrible autumn day.

"You'll be relieved when the time comes. Keep your eyes open, that's the main thing. Keep your eyes open."

"Yes, sir," they all replied.

"And remember to notify your colleagues should any emergency arise."

In the same area, though at a safe distance, another group of officers was sitting in an unmarked off-road vehicle. They were there to keep an eye on Antonio Russo's movements, following him if necessary.

"Yes, sir."

"Good," Foti said. "I'd best go now, before it starts to rain. The colonel's waiting for me." He set off back along the same path by which they had come.

Meanwhile, in the DIA's phone-tap monitoring room, the technicians had worked through the night, checking connections and making tests. Everything was in good working order. Now the officers were waiting while their computers downloaded the conversations already recorded in the monitoring room at the Prosecutor's Department.

As they waited, they talked about the previous night's dinner: grilled pork and porcini mushrooms, washed down with an excellent new wine. A great way to celebrate San Martino.

Meanwhile, officers of the *Squadra Mobile* were waiting for further orders in a hotel at Siderno, on the Ionian coast. They had moved there the previous evening, to avoid traffic on the Ionian Highway 106, the only road connecting Reggio Calabria and the area of their operation, which tended to become very congested during the day.

The officer in charge, Inspector Grassi, heard his mobile phone ringing. It was Chief Superintendent Bruni. "Stand by. Everything's in working order. Including the phones."

Operation Orange Blossom was under way.

New York

Dick Moore had gone back to his bachelor life.

Over the phone, Jenny had told him repeatedly that for the moment she preferred to be alone, that she needed time to think about their future, that the life they had been leading wasn't for her . . . Her clear resolve led him to suspect they were one step away from divorce. But he missed Jenny more than ever. He felt empty without her, as if he had lost a part of himself. And he missed Sam, too. The way he leapt for joy when Dick came home, the almost human look in his eyes, the cuddles, the walks in Central Park . . . Everything.

That morning, he found a report waiting on his desk: the results of the lab tests on the letter left at St Peter's Chapel. He read it. There was nothing significant in it except the confirmation that the letter had been written on a computer. As the mystery caller had said, there wasn't even the smallest of prints.

Neither lasers nor electrostatic detection apparatus had shown any indented impressions of handwriting on the paper.

The results were all negative. The sheet was as clean as if it had come straight from the factory.

There was no doubt in Dick Moore's mind: the mystery caller was a professional — and a son of a bitch!

As he was putting the report to one side, the phone rang.

He picked up.

It had been days since he'd heard from him, and he had given up hope of hearing from him again.

It was the switchboard operator at the other end.

"Director, there's a technician from the crime lab in Washington on the line."

"Put him on . . . Hello? Dick Moore here."

"My name's Bell, Assistant Director. I'm one of the —"

"Yes, yes, go on."

"I'm working on the finds from the site of the burned-out vehicle . . . The prints are from a size-ten-and-a-half shoe, and one of the soles has an interruption in one of the patterns."

"In other words?"

"The pattern seems to have been cut at that point by a sharp object. Perhaps a piece of metal or glass. We'd need to find out if there was any metal or glass at the site."

This sounded like an important detail, and Moore's mind went back to the crime scene. "I don't think so," he replied. "I'll certainly check, though I don't remember the Crime Scene Unit mentioning anything like that in their report."

"As a matter of fact," Bell said, "I have that report in front of me and there's no reference to it."

"If you could find out a little more, like the make of the shoe, the condition . . ."

"I'll do what I can."

"Keep me informed, please. Any time, day or night. I'll speak to you soon." He put down the phone.

He immediately called Special Agent Mary Cook. Seeing her enter his office with a smile on her face, he was briefly overcome with envy. He had always been against the idea of cohabiting, but now he was starting to have his doubts about marriage, and about the "wholesome" principles with which he had grown up. Perhaps he had been wrong in his attitude to his staff. Was he starting to look at Agent Cook in a different way?

"Please take a seat," he said, indicating the chair in front of the desk.

"Thank you, sir." Mary Cook sat down.

"Anything yet from the phones in Rocco Fedeli's restaurant and hotel?"

"Absolutely nothing relevant to the investigation, sir. Customers making reservations, staff phoning home, that kind of thing. I've been getting regular updates from the detective squad."

"And from our end?"

"Nothing there either. No comments from any of the people who recently had contact with Rocco Fedeli. It's as if nothing had happened. As if no one had ever known him."

"And yet we photographed them together."

"Obviously they don't want to talk about him," Mary Cook said.

"I see. Not looking too good. Carry on, all the same."

"Yes, sir."

He then told her what he had just learned from the technician named Bell.

"That's something at least," she said. "How about the tyre tracks?"

Dick Moore realised that he had forgotten all about them. "He didn't mention them," he replied diplomatically. "They can't have found anything yet. By the way, have you spoken to Bill?"

"Not today."

"Then phone him and tell him about these developments."

"I'll do that straight away, sir," she said, her eyes lighting up.

Dick Moore watched her as she left the room, again feeling a touch of envy.

That Wednesday evening, the Prestipinos had a heated argument, their only witness the silvery light of the moon shining through the windows.

They were in the house they had inherited from Angela's father, an outwardly modest dwelling built with the proceeds from the first kidnappings in the 1970s. Sitting opposite one another in the kitchen, they had been looking at each other for a while now, as if studying each other's faces. On the table were trays of food and sweets brought by relatives and neighbours, as was the local custom. Their thoughts, though, were elsewhere.

Their daughter was sleeping over at her maternal grandmother's house: she hadn't seen much of the old lady in her life; when she had, it was only for short periods. Angela felt bad about this, and would have liked to take her with her to America, even though she knew that it was not possible, given her mother's great age, her attachment to tradition and her boundless love for Calabria.

"Alfredo," Angela said at last, and it was like an opening round of rifle fire, "why did Don Ciccio stay out of things during the funeral? Why didn't he call in at our mother's house for a courtesy visit? Do you know?" These questions had been eating away at her. She knew the rules of the family, and something in Don Ciccio's behaviour wasn't right.

"How should I know, Angela? Don Ciccio's old, and he's not in good health. Did you see him? He walks with a stick!"

"No, Alfredo, don't give me that. This is me you're talking to. Even if he'd been at death's door, Don Ciccio should have come. It's a rule that's always observed. Respect is respect, and that's all there is to it!"

Her voice had become stronger and more resolute, and her eyes were full of anger. The expression on her face was one that her husband had never seen in all the years they had lived together.

"Times have changed, Angela."

"Don't give me that, Alfredo. Times change, yes, but Don Ciccio and people like him don't. They never change. They can't change. Not in a hundred years. You should know that. You grew up here. Like me. I can never change either, even though I live a long way away, I am and will always be a Fedeli. You should know that! Or maybe you don't?" There was a touch of scorn in her voice as she uttered these last words.

200

Unprepared for this reaction, he was silent for a moment or two, merely nodding his head slightly. Then he said, very calmly, "I know, Angela, I know, but please don't lose your temper. If you do, something may happen to you. You're damaging your health."

"Nothing's going to happen to me, damn it. They killed my three brothers, don't you understand? And besides, if you're so worried about my health, then tell me the truth! I'm sure you know it."

Alfredo looked at her questioningly.

"Tell me once and for all what Don Ciccio wanted with you."

"With me?"

"Yes, with you. You did go to his house on Saturday on the way back from the cemetery, didn't you?"

"Yes."

"So what did he want? And don't give me any bullshit, Alfredo. From you, of all people, I don't want to hear bullshit, do you understand?" Angela rose from her chair, went to her husband, and looked him straight in the eyes. Her own eyes were as sharp as knives. She hadn't been content with the answer Alfredo had given her when he got home on the day of the funeral itself. She had asked him then what Don Ciccio had wanted. Nothing, just to talk to me, he had replied. She had not insisted at the time, but she had not believed him, and by now she was really losing patience. She had to hear the truth from her husband's mouth, whatever it was. But he said nothing, just looked down at the table, as if he wanted to hide or even disappear.

"Look at me when I speak to you . . . Look at me! Look at me! Tonight I want to hear the truth!"

"He just wanted to talk to me!"

"But about what, Alfredo? What did he want to talk to you about? The mushroom harvest? Don't bullshit me, Alfredo!"

Her husband felt very small, like a midge about to be squashed. He had never seen her so angry or so determined. He had never heard her swear so much. No. This wasn't the woman he had married, the woman who had given him a daughter.

He summoned up his courage. "Nothing, Angela," he replied, barely raising his head. "The usual things. 'How are you, how's life in America?' Believe me. Don Ciccio's just upset about what happened."

"About Rocco?"

"About everyone. All your brothers and your cousin. They were all part of the family."

"That's it, Alfredo. Carry on talking crap. Carry on telling me lies. This is serious, don't you understand? I can't stand it! Tonight I want the truth. Only the truth . . ."

He shook his head, as if trying to dismiss the matter. He didn't like to talk about his encounters with Don Ciccio. Not even to his own wife.

"Don't be like that," he replied, and for the first time there was resentment in his voice. "I've always been honest with you. And with all your family. It's my family, too."

"So tell me what Don Ciccio wanted with you," she demanded.

Alfredo seemed to reflect for a few moments, with Angela's eyes still fixed on him. He realised he would have to tell her something. His mind was a whirl of dark thoughts, thoughts that might never leave him in peace.

"All right, Angela. As you wish . . ."

"*Tell me!*"

"He asked after my aunt, my uncle, my cousin. How they are, what they're doing, things like that. He hasn't seen them in ages and he was very close to my aunt's husband. They grew up together . . ."

"Is that it, Alfredo? How your relatives are? Is that what you're telling me? . . . If he asked you about your relatives, about your cousin, he must have said something *important* . . . I know these people . . ."

"You have to believe me. It may be he wants to tell me something else before we leave, because he asked me to come back and see him again . . . He has something to give me for them . . ."

"Like what?"

"He didn't say, and you know you can't ask questions of Don Ciccio."

"You're still not telling me the truth!" She went and sat down on the same chair as before, leaned her elbows on the table, and put her head in her hands. "I'm going to say one thing, Alfredo, and this is the last time I'll say it. Think about it tonight and tomorrow. I want to know everything, otherwise it's better that you leave. I don't want to see you again."

Her voice had become almost normal again. They stopped arguing. Alfredo stood up, went to her, and touched first her neck, then her cheek. She raised her head, looked at him in surprise, and got to her feet.

"What are you doing?"

He tried to pull her to him.

"Leave me alone. This isn't the time. You haven't understood a damn thing! You're an idiot. My brother Rocco was right when he told me that, but I didn't want to believe him."

With an almost violent movement, she wriggled out of his grasp. Alfredo walked away from her, towards the bedroom.

"You don't understand a thing, Alfredo!" she screamed, following him. "You have to tell me everything. I'm your wife, and you mustn't forget it. I've lost my brothers, and you know what they meant to all of us, not only to me. Believe me, I don't want to lose you, too, I don't want to be a widow so young, like all the widows in this village, alive on the outside but dead inside."

He stopped and turned. "You're wrong," he replied, in a resolute tone. "You won't be a widow, oh, no." And he closed the door.

Angela Fedeli's last thought before falling asleep was: *Before I leave, I want to go to the shrine of the Madonna of Aspromonte and pray to her that she protect me from harm and that those who killed my brothers come to a bad end.*

In New York it was 6p.m.

Lieutenant Reynolds had had an unusually busy day, with more than the usual number of robberies and muggings in his precinct. There had even been a grandmother who had come in with her eleven-year-old granddaughter to report that the latter had been sexually assaulted. It was the latest in a series of such assaults which had taken place recently. The assaults had become so frequent that many people believed there was more than one assailant. Reynolds, though, was sure there was only one man involved. The descriptions supplied by the victims matched perfectly: the same age, same physique, same height, above all the same completely bald, egg-shaped head. But in spite of his heavy caseload, Reynolds had continued to follow developments in the Madison homicide case: the interviews with Rocco Fedeli's closest associates, the continuing examinations of the confiscated documents, the investigation of Fedeli's business activities, the phone taps . . .

The file was getting thicker by the hour, but the investigation had hardly progressed. Nor had anything emerged from re-examination of the Susan George case. And the public was becoming increasingly impatient for answers.

Reynolds was just about to leave the office and go home, with all these thoughts buzzing around in his head, when he received a phone call from Rusty Sheridan.

"Can you come over?" Rusty asked, without preamble.

"Where?"

"Usual place. This is important, John. It'd be best if you could come this evening."

There was more than a touch of nervousness in his voice.

CHAPTER
TWENTY

Thursday, 13 November

"There he is!" the officer said, looking through the infra-red binoculars.

His colleague grabbed the binoculars and took a look.

It was almost two o'clock in the morning when the darkness that lay over the farmhouse was pierced by the headlights of a car.

The two officers exchanged whispers, convinced it was him. After hours and hours of pointless waiting in the cold, their patience was about to be rewarded. The car stopped outside the front door of the farmhouse. From the seat next to the driver, a man got out and entered the house. The car lights stayed on.

"He's coming out again, look!" one of the two officers whispered. "He has something in his hand . . . It could be a briefcase."

"Yes," the other said, "he's getting back in the car."

The car set off again, taking a secondary road that climbed up into the mountains. In the dark, they could not make out how many people were in the car. The officer who had first spotted it immediately got out his mobile phone and called Captain Foti. The other officer radioed his colleagues in the off-road vehicle, but they decided not to follow the car: given the late hour and the deserted roads, there was too great a risk that they'd be spotted.

After less than half an hour, the Mercedes came to a secluded spot, a kind of clearing. Here, the driver switched off the engine. In the valley below, the lights of several villages in the plain of Gioia Tauro could be seen. A few moments later, two men emerged from the woods and stopped a few yards away. Antonio Russo opened his case and asked Diego for his brother Pedro's telephone number. The Colombian supplied it immediately. He had been told that all he had to do was obey. Antonio Russo followed the usual procedure. When the phone was picked up at the other end, he said, "Pedro, I'm passing you Diego. Do what he tells you. You'll be seeing him soon." The phone call was brief and in Spanish. Then Diego was blindfolded by the man sitting next to him and made to get out of the car.

"Where are you taking me?" he asked.

No one answered.

"What are you going to do to me?" he cried.

Silence again.

He took a long, deep breath and let it out in a resigned sigh. The two men, who had hunting rifles over their shoulders, now approached, gestured to Russo and took delivery of Diego. They placed him between them, took him by the arms and set off into the woods along a climbing path, a *tratturu*, used by shepherds leading their flocks to pasture.

With a sneer on his face, Russo watched them go.

"There it is again!" the DIA officer whispered, seeing the car coming back.

Three people got out. The passenger who had been in the back seat and the driver shook hands with Antonio Russo, who entered the house. The two men got on a motorbike and drove off.

Russo did not leave the house again that night.

The officers noted everything down. The car had been away from the farmhouse for almost an hour and a half.

He felt exhausted, all his strength gone. As if he had walked all day without stopping.

But he hadn't.

He had only walked for a few hours, but over rough terrain, full of folds and stones and dips and climbs. Unable to see anything, but hearing the sounds of nature: the singing of the night birds, the shrilling of the cicadas, the chirping of the crickets . . . Supported by his two captors, he had gone round and round in circles without realising it, always coming back to the point of departure. It was a tried and tested method for disorienting kidnap victims and making them believe they were in a far more remote place than they really were. Then, at the end of a hard climb, followed by a brief descent, they had finally arrived at their destination.

"On the ground!" one of the two men ordered. It was the first time he had opened his mouth. The voice sounded fake to Diego, but he put his impression down to tiredness. He obeyed. They took his blindfold off. He looked around for a moment. He saw that he was in a kind of hut. The walls were of logs, the ceiling of corrugated iron. It was about six and a half feet by six and a half feet, and no higher than five feet. The outside was covered with a tarpaulin, like those used to cover trucks.

His whole body was shaking.

"Sit on that board!" the first man said, indicating a wooden plank on the left-hand side, with an iron chain next to it.

Diego did as he was told.

"Good. Now don't move." The man wrapped the chain around his ankles, put on a padlock, then wound it round his neck, fixed it to one of the logs, and put on another padlock.

The second guard had appeared in the doorway. "This is for your needs," he said, throwing down a metal bucket. "I'll come and empty it later. And this is drinking water." He placed a five-litre plastic can on the floor.

Diego looked at both objects. They turned his stomach.

This second voice, too, sounded fake. He took a good look at the two men. He saw that, as well as dark ski masks, they were wearing knee-length rubber boots. They were both short, but well built. He reached out his hand, picked up first the bucket and then the can, and put them on his left, in a corner.

"I'm cold," he said.

"You'll have to manage with the blanket."

He had not noticed that there was an old blanket in another corner. He reached out, grabbed it and threw it over his shoulders. "Can I have a cigarette?" he asked. The two men went out without replying. After a few minutes, one of them came back in. "Take this," he said, handing him a chunk of hard bread, a piece of pecorino cheese and a half-full bottle of red wine. "The wine'll warm you up a bit." Then he threw a windbreaker over him, accompanying the gesture with the words, "You can use this as a pillow." Diego said nothing. He felt drained. He shook his head and bit his lips, lost in thought.

He made an effort to keep calm. Panicking wouldn't help, he knew that. He took heart at the fact that his guards were wearing ski masks. That had to be a good sign. *They're not planning to kill me. 'Ntoni may be a bastard, but he's also a man of honour.* As he started thinking more rationally, his features grew less tense, and a little colour returned to his face.

The man stopped in the doorway. He looked at Diego and, with a rapid gesture, threw him a few cigarettes. "You can smoke these. But only these. Don't ask for any more."

"Thanks! How am I supposed to light them?"

"With these." The guard threw him some matches, then reached out his hand and gave him a stone. Then he lowered the tarpaulin and left.

With a trembling hand, Diego picked up a cigarette. He rubbed it between his fingers several times, as if petting it, before putting it in his mouth. He rubbed a match on the stone and lit it. The first drag made him cough violently. The second made his eyes water and gave him a strange sense of both exhaustion and dizziness. He took it out of his mouth and stubbed it out on the ground with what little strength he still had left.

He curled up in a ball on the wooden plank and closed his eyes.

"He's coming out, Demetrio. Look!"

The DIA officer was peering through the telephoto lens of the camera at the front door of the farmhouse. Antonio Russo had appeared and was now standing there, looking around.

"You're right, Ciccio. It's him. He's waiting for something. Ah, there it is, a car's coming, and a motorbike with two people on it."

They both began clicking away on their Nikons, taking one photograph after the other. The car and the motorcycle were parked on one side of the yard. Three men — the driver of the car and the two motorcyclists — walked up to Antonio Russo, shook hands with him and starting talking.

"If only we could hear what the sons of bitches were saying, Ciccio!"

"God knows what we're missing!"

The four men were now walking in the garden side by side. The man who had come by car was on Antonio

Russo's righthand side, and seemed to be nodding constantly in agreement. In the meantime, the two officers kept taking photographs.

"They're talking outside. In this cold!"

"Obviously. They're afraid of bugs in the house. They're always suspicious. They never change."

"You're right, it's in their nature . . . Look, they're saying goodbye."

"I see them, I see them . . . All three of them are getting in the car."

"It looks like a BMW to me, what do you think?"

"Could be . . . or a Mercedes . . . It's a four-door car . . . black . . . or dark blue . . ."

"Dark, anyway. God knows where the fuck they're going."

"Ciccio, you tell the others, I'll call the captain. They may be able to get the licence number."

In the meantime, the car was heading towards the gate. Antonio Russo had already gone back inside the farmhouse and closed the front door.

Ciccio immediately radioed his colleagues in the off-road vehicle. Then he wrote it all down in his notebook.

"Want some coffee, Demetrio?"

"I could really do with one. I can't seem to shake off this headache."

Demetrio was not yet thirty, but ever since he was a child he had suffered from frequent terrible migraines. He had been all over Italy, seeing specialists and undergoing tests. But nothing had worked.

212

New York

It was 8.30a.m. and John Reynolds was in his office, looking like someone who had not slept. And it was true: he hadn't managed a wink of sleep, unable to stop thinking about what his men were doing that night. When, at seven, he had finally received the call he had been waiting for, he had got up and rushed to the 17th precinct. The operation was over. His detectives had swooped on the members of a Brooklyn gang, all of them with priors including grand theft auto. Their names had been supplied by Rusty Sheridan the previous evening.

"It's possible they know something about the burned-out cab," his friend had said, giving him the names, a whole page of them. "They're on good terms with the Italians, and they do favours for each other. They've become the most dangerous gang in the whole fucking borough." He sounded as if he'd had enough of living there, an impression confirmed by his next words. "If I didn't have the gym, I'd be out of here tomorrow."

Reynolds had immediately set up the operation. He knew that even one small lead could blow a case wide open. All you needed were intuition and tenacity.

"We've pulled in a whole lot of them," Detective Steve Green said. Green was a young man, not much more than thirty. He looked a lot like Robert De Niro — a comparison that pleased him. He wore a pair of ripped jeans and a flower-patterned long-sleeved shirt. Being left-handed, he carried his gun on the left.

"Did you get everyone on the list?" Reynolds asked.

"No, Lieutenant. Some of them weren't in their usual haunts."

"Keep looking for them. Go back to their apartments until you find them. I want them all here. Don't leave anyone out. Anyhow, did we find anything?"

"One of them had a whole lot of stolen property in his apartment."

"What kind of stolen property?"

"Cellphones, stereos, camcorders, laptops. He couldn't tell us where he'd gotten them. Obviously, considering his priors, we're assuming they're stolen."

Reynolds nodded.

"We also found a badge."

Reynolds' curiosity was aroused. "What kind of badge?"

"FBI."

"Right. Anything else like that?"

"No."

"Uniforms?"

"No, sir. Just the badge."

"And how did he explain that away?"

"He says he found it."

Reynolds grimaced, as if to say, *I bet he knows a lot more than he's telling us.*

"Whose badge is it?" he asked

"We're checking that now. A team's already gone over to Federal Plaza."

"Let's hope they can tell us something . . . How about shoes with a cut on one of the soles?"

"No. But he takes an eight and a half, not a ten and a half."

"What kind of priors does he have?"

"Pretty much everything, starting from when he was a minor. He's worked his way up from vandalism, vagrancy and larceny up to drug dealing."

It was the typical pedigree of the petty criminal trying to make his way in the world.

"What's his name?"

"Harry Baker."

Reynolds leafed through his notebook until he found the name. Next to it, he had written *He's the leader*, underlining the word *leader* and adding two more words: *Highly dangerous*.

"I want to speak with this man Baker. Where is he?"

"In the holding cells."

"Bring him to the interview room."

"Right now?"

"Yes."

Detective Green practically ran out of the room.

Reynolds followed him after a few minutes.

The room was bare, apart from a table and two grey metal chairs screwed to the floor. The walls were mostly white, but with a dark green strip close to the floor. From the ceiling hung a phosphorescent light and a closed-circuit camera.

One of the walls had a two-way mirror.

A man in jeans and a black T-shirt, his arms covered in green and blue tattoos, was sitting on one of the chairs with an arrogant look on his face. He was handcuffed to an iron ring on the table. On his feet, he wore a pair of sneakers without laces. He was thirty-two years old, tall and well built, with reddish hair and a beard.

As soon as he saw the lieutenant come in, he looked up. His eyes were half closed, as if the sun was beating down on him. There was a kind of sneer on his face. He recognised Reynolds. He had seen him in the newspapers and on TV. He had even heard people around him talk about Reynolds as a particularly tough detective: some even called him "the Bulldog". Sooner or later someone would make him pay for it.

"I'm Lieutenant John Reynolds," he said, sitting down on the other side of the table, facing the prisoner. Then he nodded at Green, who took the handcuffs off Baker and remained standing next to him. Baker crossed his arms: the dragons and snakes tattooed on his biceps seemed to swell.

"I want my lawyer, Lieutenant," he said in a sleepy voice. "I'm not answering any of your questions."

"We'll call your lawyer in a few minutes," Reynolds replied. "But before we do, I want to give you a chance." His tone had become conciliatory, confidential, as if trying to establish a rapport with him. It was an old trick, and Harry Baker was wise to it.

"What kind of chance?" he asked irritably, looking at him with a questioning air. He had not taken his hands out of the pockets of his jeans.

"I'd like to talk to you about some homicides. Hear about the killings on Madison? I'd like to do something for you. It's an offer you can take or leave, because once

I walk out of this room I won't mention it again. And you won't get another chance. Drop your attitude now, and you can get out of here and save on lawyers' fees."

"I don't know anything, Lieutenant. You're wasting your time. But go on, if it makes you happy." A sarcastic half-smile played over Harry Baker's lips.

Reynolds was becoming impatient with Baker's arrogance.

"Listen to me," he said. "You're in deep shit. We found you in possession of a whole lot of things we think were stolen. At the very least, you'll be charged with receiving stolen property. But if you play your cards right, today could be your lucky day."

Baker looked at him with eyes full of hate, scorn and resentment.

Reynolds could feel the tension filling the room. With his usual calm, he went straight to the point. "I'd like you to explain how you came to be in possession of an FBI badge. This is my offer: if you tell us the truth, we can help you out over the charges of larceny and receiving. I'll plead your case myself, I give you my word, and I always keep my word."

"I already explained that last night, to the detective here," Baker replied impatiently, with a sarcastic smile. "Which part of it don't you understand?" He turned to look at Green, who glared at him in return.

"Explain it to me," Reynolds said.

"I found it."

"Where?"

"I don't remember."

"I get it. You don't want our help."

"I want my lawyer. I'm not saying a word."

"We'll call him in a while. In the meantime, you're under arrest for larceny and receiving stolen property. Don't forget you're also in unauthorised possession of an object that's the property of the Department of Justice, which is most likely a Federal offence. Now do you understand how much trouble you're in?"

Then Reynolds took a sheet of paper from a drawer in the table and read him his constitutional rights.

"I know my rights," Baker said. "That's why I want my lawyer."

"So, is that your last word? In that case, do you know what I have to say to you?"

"Go ahead, say it, don't be shy."

Reynolds had had enough of that smug, self-satisfied air. "Go to hell!" he yelled in Baker's face and left the room, slamming the door behind him. Green soon followed.

When Reynolds got back to his office he thumped the desk with his fist and muttered, "Son of a bitch!" Then he spotted a note that had been left there for him.

The badge belongs to FBI special agent MK. The agent reported the theft on 10 October, along with that of his identification card and a synthetic fibre FBI jacket, all stolen from his apartment.

He put the note down. Denis! The boy had said it. And they'd all made light of his testimony.

218

"Green," he said, "I want to know about all thefts from police officers in the last six months. And I need to know as soon as possible."

This might be the lead he was looking for. For the first time since the killings, he had the feeling he was finally on the right track.

CHAPTER
TWENTY-ONE

That afternoon, after having lunch with his sister-in-law and her family, Alfredo Prestipino went out alone and walked slowly towards the cemetery. The last part of the road was lined with cypresses, through which a few houses could be glimpsed. The cemetery gate was ajar, and yielded at the first push. He found himself outside a chapel standing beneath a wind-tossed cypress. Holding his hat with one hand to stop it from flying away, he made the sign of the cross with the other. He walked along the gravel path to his brother-in-law's grave. The flowers on it were still fresh, and their scent was intense. His eyes swept the cemetery. He was alone. He looked up at the sky and said a prayer. The clock of the main church was striking four thirty. He walked back to the exit. As he came out through the gate, he heard a voice behind him.

"Prestipino?"

He stopped and turned, momentarily confused. "Yes?" he replied in a thin voice, and a shiver went down his spine.

"There's someone who wants to talk to you."

"Who?" he asked, sure now that this was trouble.

"Just come with us. He's waiting for you. No problem, don't worry." The man had spoken in a reassuring tone. He was young, short and stocky, with jet-black hair. Next to him, another young man, taller, thick-set with dark hair, stood nodding his head. Both had their hands in the pockets of their padded coats and contemptuous looks on their faces. For a while, Prestipino looked at them, first one, then the other.

His gaze lingered for a moment on the two men's hands, still in their pockets. It was obvious they were lying. They weren't well intentioned, but all he could do was follow them.

"Walk to the car!" the stocky young man said, indicating a car parked by the side of the road a hundred yards further on. Alfredo started walking. The two young men walked behind him. With every step he took, his fear grew. He reached the car, a four-door BMW. Its engine was running, and a thread of white smoke came from the exhaust.

"Get in," the first young man said, opening the back door for him. The side windows and rear windscreen were blacked out. Alfredo Prestipino did not ask any questions. The only person in the car was the driver, who gave the others barely any time to get in before he set off at high speed. Prestipino folded his arms and dipped his head until it touched the window.

"Where the hell are they taking him, Salvo?" the officer from the *Squadra Mobile* said, more to himself than his colleague.

"We have to inform the others, Guido," the other officer replied. They had been tailing Alfredo Prestipino since the morning, and now they were concealed amid the bergamot plants near the cemetery, from where they had witnessed the whole scene.

"Salerno Milano 41 from 40, over."

"Go ahead."

"BMW, black, four doors, licence number AD315 . . . Subject on board, please follow."

"Received, over."

The call had been answered by an officer sitting in an unmarked police car parked just off the main road, a few miles from the village.

"Salerno Milano 40 from 41."

"Go ahead."

"They just passed me. What are your instructions?"

"Follow at a distance. We're calling Salerno Milano 1 now."

"Awaiting further instructions, over and out."

In the meantime, Guido had called Chief Superintendent Bruni on his mobile.

"The car mustn't be stopped, but we need to find out where it's going," Bruni ordered.

The instruction was immediately radioed to the men in the unmarked car.

By now, the BMW had reached the 106 Ionian state highway. Here, it could either turn right towards Reggio Calabria, or left towards Catanzaro. The BMW turned left, drove for a few miles, then took the clearway that led to the Tyrrhenian side. From here, it was only just over twenty minutes to the A3 Salerno — Reggio Calabria autostrada.

The officers in the unmarked car still had it in their sights.

New York

Dick Moore had insisted on being present.

It was noon. On the other side of the two-way mirror, in a room next to the small interview room, Denis was sitting between Moore and Reynolds. Behind them was the boy's father, Dr McGrey. They were there for the identification. Denis's father and a detective had come to fetch him from school earlier. He'd had to skip a lesson, which meant it must be something important. But the detective had not given him any explanation. On entering the 17th precinct, the boy's eyes had become alert and curious, peering into every corner.

"Here's our detective," Reynolds said, greeting him with a smile. "Welcome to the precinct! Now, I want you to look at someone. He's on the other side of this window. You just have to tell us if you recognise him."

"Do you mean I have to tell you if it's the police officer, the man I saw?" Denis asked, uncertainly.

"That's exactly it!"

"But I already said I didn't see him clearly."

"I know," Reynolds replied. "But let's just give it a try."

"Denis," the boy's father said, "they have to do their job." Denis nodded, although he did not seem very convinced.

Reynolds went to the window and opened two small wooden shutters. Harry Baker appeared on the other side. He was standing. Denis looked at him intently, going right up to the window, almost touching it with his nose. He shook his head. There was silence in the room. The boy turned to Reynolds and whispered, "I can't say if it's him. I'm not sure. What should I do? I only saw him for a couple of seconds."

"Is there any resemblance at all?" Moore asked.

"No. The man I saw was wearing a uniform and a cap. I didn't see his hair. This man has ginger hair. No. I don't know him."

Reynolds closed the two shutters. After a few minutes, Denis left the precinct house with his father.

Not long afterwards, Harry Baker would also leave it.

On his way to prison.

Of the reporters who had come to NYPD headquarters at One Police Plaza on Park Row that morning, David Powell of the *New York Times* seemed to be the most excited. He had heard that the detectives of the 17th precinct had made a large number of arrests, including the leader of a Brooklyn gang known as the Green Birds. It was rumoured that these arrests were somehow linked to the Madison investigation. Police Commissioner Ronald Jones, impeccable in his dark grey suit, had agreed to speak to the press.

"Please sit down," he said, indicating a long walnut table on one side of the room, where he usually conferred with his closest colleagues. "Now, what can I do for you gentlemen?" he asked. He sounded like someone who had no time to spare.

The four reporters quickly exchanged glances. Then David Powell spoke up: "We hear there've been developments in the Madison murder investigation. Apparently some members of the Green Birds have been arrested. The public have a right to be kept informed. People aren't feeling too safe right now, and they're looking to us to reassure them. I think that when there are important developments, it's in your own best interests to —"

Powell was interrupted by a uniformed police officer who appeared at the door to say, "There's a reporter out here with a TV camera."

"He can come in, but his camera stays outside," Ronald Jones replied with a grimace.

A few moments later, a tall, slim young woman in jeans and a sweatshirt entered.

"Please, sit down."

The young woman took a seat and pulled a notebook from her bag.

"This isn't a press conference," Jones immediately said. "What I say here is off the record."

The young woman put her notebook back in her bag. She did not look very happy.

"We were talking about developments," Jones said, looking at David Powell. "It seems you and your colleagues have heard about an operation mounted by the 17th precinct."

"That's right," said David Powell. "And we think the public should be informed."

"We have nothing concrete as yet," Jones cut in immediately. "My men are still at work. When the time is right, we'll inform you."

"But we know that objects belonging to the Department of Justice have been found, and that a witness saw a police officer in the doorman's booth . . . We also know that right this moment at the 17th precinct —"

Ronald Jones' face clouded over. "Write a single word of this," he said, "and you'll be prejudicing the investigation."

"Time's passing and the killers are still at large," Powell said curtly.

"Please be patient. When the time is right, as I said, you'll be informed by our press office."

With that, Jones rose to his feet, as if to say, *This is over, now go.* The reporters all got the message, and they left the room looking defeated.

But perhaps not yet resigned.

5.46p.m.

"Mother?"
    "What is it, Angela?"
    "Is Alfredo with you?"
    "No. Why?"
    "It's already dark and he's not home yet."

226

"Are you worried?"

"No."

"You know your husband! Maybe he met someone in the village and they got talking."

"That's possible, I suppose. But when he comes back I'll give him a piece of my mind."

"Don't you remember, Angela?"

"What?"

"When Rocco used to play with Alfredo outside the house?"

"They were always playing."

"And if I sent them on an errand, they'd never come back. You'd say to me, 'When are those two rascals coming back, Mother?' "

"Yes, I remember. All right, Mother, goodbye for now. I'll call again later."

7.40p.m.

"Mother, Alfredo still isn't back."

"Angela, you know a leopard never changes its spots. They get talking, the hours pass, and they forget to come home."

Angela really wanted to believe her mother was right. "As soon as he gets back, I swear, Mother, I'll kill him!"

"Please, Angela, don't be angry with him."

"Don't worry, Mother. Is Maria with you?"

"Yes. She's a great comfort."

"'Bye, Mother."

"Don't be angry with him."

The photographs were spread out across the table. All of them in colour, 7 × 5 prints, sharp quality.

They were passed around and carefully examined.

It was nine in the evening in Colonel Trimarchi's office.

"Foti, perhaps you'd take us through it," the colonel said.

Captain Foti told them about the meeting between Antonio Russo and the three men who had then driven off in the dark car.

"We know this is the same car — a BMW — that Alfredo Prestipino was seen getting into."

"Do we have any idea who the three men on the farm were?" Trimarchi asked.

"Yes, they're all known to us. Members of the Russo 'ndrina. One, the tallest, seen from the front here, and getting behind the wheel in this shot, is Russo's driver, one of his most trusted men, the son of a former estate manager of his."

There was a long silence. They were thinking.

Foti broke the silence. "At six twenty-five our men saw the BMW arriving at the farm. They'd been alerted by our colleagues in the *Squadra Mobile*, who'd followed it all the way from San Piero d'Aspromonte. There can't be any doubts. Our men in the off-road vehicle got the licence number this morning."

Everyone was listening even more attentively now. Foti went on to tell them that three men had got out of the car and entered the farmhouse, while the driver had left.

"Did they come out again?" the colonel asked.

228

"So far, only two. After about an hour. They set off on a motorcycle."

"Have we managed to find out who the third man was, the one who stayed inside?"

"No. It was too dark. But, logically, it must have been Alfredo Prestipino."

"Are we sure that Alfredo Prestipino went to Russo's house of his own free will?" Trimarchi asked.

"My men got the distinct impression that Alfredo Prestipino went reluctantly," Bruni said.

"You mean he was under duress?"

"Let's say there wasn't any overt violence, but from the way they were walking, and the way the BMW took off at such high speed, it certainly seemed he was taken under duress, yes."

"Then we may have a new element here," Trimarchi said. "Kidnapping."

They all looked at each other.

"Any other developments, Chief Superintendent Bruni?" the colonel asked.

Bruni explained that they were already in possession of the first batch of data concerning ships originating from the port of Turbo and carrying bananas. Almost all the ships in question had arrived at ports in Liguria. Now, with the support of the Customs and Excise Corps, they were focusing on those ships that had made the most journeys.

"Excellent, Chief Superintendent."

The last person to speak was the man in charge of the DIA's phone taps, Carabinieri Lieutenant Marco

Oliva, a tall, thin, young man with crewcut hair and a nose sprinkled with freckles.

"It's been mostly normal, everyday conversations," he said. "Except for those from the phone in the Fedeli house."

"Go on," Trimarchi said.

"The wife phoned her mother a couple of times. Both calls were short. The first one was at 5.46p.m., the second at 7.40p.m. On each occasion Angela Fedeli told her mother she was worried because her husband hadn't come home yet."

"Keep listening," Trimarchi ordered. "I repeat, we're dealing with a kidnapping. And considering the people involved, we can't rule out murder."

She was sitting in the kitchen. Still alone.

Angela couldn't stop wondering what had happened to her husband. She still hadn't heard from him. She had never known him to do anything like this before. It was as new to her as last night's quarrel. She could still hear the words spoken, the answers she'd managed to drag from him after a lot of beating around the bush. But it was his lies which had hurt her the most.

Now, staring down at an almost-empty cup of camomile tea, she was wondering about Alfredo's true nature. She knew perfectly well it was possible for a person to have a dark side to his character, which he tried to keep secret, even from his nearest and dearest. But the fact that she, of all people, hadn't noticed this in the many years they had been living together was what really tore her up inside. Maybe the way of life in

America, which was so different from here, had made it difficult for her to really know Alfredo. An old saying kept coming back to her: every cloud has a silver lining. Perhaps the misfortune that had befallen her, by bringing her back to her own country, her own world — to which she had always remained connected, like an unborn child connected to its mother by the umbilical cord — had opened her eyes. *Fortunately!* she said to herself, adding immediately afterwards, *Thank you, Madonna. Protect me always!*

Slowly, she grasped the handle of the cup, raised it to her lips and took a last sip of the tea, which was now lukewarm. Irritated, she thrust it away from her, to a corner of the table. Her face showed the first signs of exhaustion. But she did not stop thinking. In the end, she somehow convinced herself that it was only hurt pride on his part, and that he wouldn't be away much longer. Without her, she thought, shaking her head over and over, Alfredo would be helpless, without her he would lose everything. Then she sprang to her feet, and as she did so she murmured, almost as if she wanted to be heard by someone nearby, "As soon as he comes back with his tail between his legs, there'll be hell to pay, or my name isn't Angela Fedeli."

And with that, she went to bed.

It was going to be a long night.

CHAPTER
TWENTY-TWO

It was dark.

Diego could no longer hear a thing, not even those low whispers that had previously reached his ears from time to time. Thinking that his guards were asleep, he grabbed the now-empty wine bottle, inserted it between the floorboards and started to use it as a crowbar. After much effort, he finally managed to unscrew the big board that was holding the chain. He tried to get the chain off, but it was impossible, thanks to the padlock. What he could do, however, was move, with small, shuffling steps. He rolled up the chain and held it with one hand, while with the other he picked up his shoes and put them on. Then he lifted the tarpaulin, just enough to peer through. Everything was black. He shuffled out of the hut. Cold, damp air enveloped him. There was silence all around. He turned his head in all directions. He could see the moon peering out from behind the clouds. He stood there for a few moments, listening, then took a deep breath.

He remembered what one of his guards had told him: *The roads are watched, they'll kill you.* So he avoided them, and headed south, towards the valley, where he thought he might run into the herd of sheep that had been the one sign of life during the day, along with the whistling of the shepherds and the barking of the dogs. With one hand he held the chain, while with the other he supported himself on the bushes and the holm oaks. As he advanced, all he could hear was the sound of his own footsteps on the broken branches and his laboured breathing.

He slipped and fell, hurting his hands and tearing his trousers. But he did not lose heart. Ignoring the pain in his hands, he immediately got back on his feet. His one thought was to get as far as possible from his prison. To escape.

He seemed to have found a new, unexpected strength. And all at once, after almost an hour of walking amid weeds and bushes, he heard a deafening noise, made all the louder perhaps by the silence of the night, and stopped dead.

A few more minutes' walk, and he discovered the source of the noise: a swollen stream, more than six feet wide. He followed its course. After a while, he came to a kind of waterfall, and stopped. He thought for a few moments. Then he started to cross it. After a couple of steps, the water came up to above his knees. He stumbled, lost his balance, and fell in the water. It was freezing. He felt his skin wrinkle and his legs and back stiffen.

He looked into the woods. All he could see were long, dark shadows behind the trees.

He started shivering. At that moment, a flash of lightning lit up the sky. There was a rumble of thunder, then another, and another flash of lightning. It would soon be pouring with rain.

He finally managed to get moving again, edging up out of the water with those same small, shuffling steps. He was soaking wet and still shivering. Unsteadily, he started up the valley again, hoping to find a way out.

Instead, he found his way barred by brambles and thorn bushes. He felt as if he was in an impenetrable forest, something like the Amazon jungle. He tried to bypass these obstacles, and managed to get halfway up the hill, but after a while came to another stream — and another waterfall, even more swollen than the previous one. Here, he encountered the same difficulties as before. He changed direction. But it was no good. Every new place he came to seemed exactly like the place he had just left. There were no landmarks to help him orient himself. And in the meantime it was starting to rain. He came to a kind of cave. It was small, but big enough to shelter him. He entered and threw himself down on the ground, like a dead weight.

Friday, 14 November, New York

Lieutenant Reynolds was woken by the phone ringing on the night table.

He picked up at the sixth ring, almost knocking the phone to the floor, but grabbing it just in time.

At the other end, he heard Rusty Sheridan: "John, they've burned down my gym."

These were the only words his friend said, in a grief-stricken voice.

234

And they left him speechless.

It was as if his breath had failed him. He looked at the luminous dial of the alarm clock. It was 1.53a.m.

"I'll be right there," he replied.

But he was talking to himself.

His friend had already hung up. He hadn't even heard the click.

"They never leave you alone, even at this hour," Linda said, in a thin, sleepy voice. "I really hope this *is* your last case!" She turned on her other side, pulling the blanket over her. He did not reply. There was no point. He pretended not to have heard her. Nodding to himself, he got out of bed. Less than ten minutes later, he was in his car.

It was already day by the time Diego opened his eyes.

It had stopped raining. Light was starting to filter into the cave.

For a few moments, he was disoriented, and wondered where the hell he was.

Then he remembered. He realised that he had slept, perhaps for a long time.

He felt his body. It hurt all over. Slithering along the ground, he put his head out. The rays of the sun, filtering through the branches of the trees, illuminated his hair, which was full of earth and mud. All he could see was forest. But now, by day, the place didn't seem so bad.

Summoning up his courage, he left the cave and advanced along the ridge, panting with exertion. He was moving more easily now, his steps steadier, his hands better able to grip the trees, or at least the branches.

Soon, he began to see gorges, precipices, brambles, trees surrounded by thick undergrowth and, all around, a chain of mountains that seemed determined to keep him prisoner. There was no cultivated land in the area, only wild nature. He became even more afraid. The light of day was making him fully aware of the fact that the place he had been brought to was a natural prison. He wandered for a long time before he found a path.

He walked along it until he reached a wooden footbridge over a stream. For all he knew, it was the same stream in which he had slipped the previous night.

The footbridge swayed from side to side, and he had to stop several times to avoid losing his balance. At last, he reached the other bank. Here, a surprise awaited him. A short, fat man in a hood stood blocking his way, a gun in his right hand. As soon as Diego saw him, his heart began to hammer so forcefully in his chest that he thought he was about to burst. He stood there, motionless, trying to slow his breathing.

"Don't run away, or you're a dead man!" the man cried.

"Don't shoot me," Diego replied in a weak, dry-throated voice, lifting his hands in the air. It was almost a supplication.

"Good, that's the idea!" the man continued, approaching him and aiming his gun straight at Diego's chest. "Did you think you could play the hero? We still need you alive. Now move, you bastard! Turn round and walk!"

Silently, he obeyed, moving forward with unsteady steps. His face had turned as white as a sheet. Never in his life had he felt so threatened. All his self-assurance had suddenly evaporated. The hooded man followed him, the gun still pointed at his back. Several times, Diego had to ask the man to stop pushing him. They walked along the path until they reached the hut from which he had escaped. Here, Diego undressed and got under the blanket. He was shivering. He felt as if he had suddenly aged ten years.

After a few minutes, another man entered the hut, a ski mask covering his face. He was taller than the two men who had first brought him here.

"Where did you think you were going?" the man asked. His tone was mocking and his voice seemed, to Diego, as grating as nails on a blackboard.

Diego said nothing, merely lifted his head slightly.

"You have guts," the man continued. "I admire you. But you would never have got away. Our men are watching all the paths . . . We warned you they would kill you. You were lucky that it was us that took you. Besides which, even if you had reached the village, you would have found more of us there. Lots of us. I'm not saying the whole village, but pretty much. You would have been caught at a roadblock and handed back to us. Or else they would have killed you. No one gets out of these mountains alive! No one ever has! This is our territory!"

Diego said nothing. He was still shivering. He rested his head back down again. Then he began to cough so hard that he had to bend double and hold his stomach. Maybe it was flu, or maybe it was a way of venting his rage. The man approached and attached him to another floorboard. This time, though, with one more turn of the chain and with an even larger padlock.

"And don't try anything else stupid," he warned. "There's no one for miles around. Have you finally got that into your head?" And then he left the hut.

Diego silently cursed himself for getting into this situation.

The sun was shining in San Piero d'Aspromonte that morning.

The sky was an unreal blue, the air strangely warm and inviting. It was a beautiful day.

Angela decided to go for a drive with her daughter, perhaps to dispel the accumulated tension, or perhaps just to see again the places she loved. The two of them, alone together: an opportunity to talk woman to woman. Among other things, she wanted to discuss Alfredo's absence. Maria didn't know about that yet, but Angela couldn't hide it from her any longer. She was bound to find out, and it would be better sooner than later. And so they set off in an old Fiat 127, climbing into the mountains on a winding road with many hairpin bends. They came finally to the Stoccato plain, where the great wooden crucifix stood out impressively against the sky. They parked nearby. There was no one about. No prying eyes. They got out of the

238

car, and were engulfed in total silence. The chaos, noises, dust, roaring engines and smog of city life were a long way away. They could smell the fragrant scent of resin, wild flowers and herbs — nature uncontaminated.

"Come on, Maria, let's go!"

"Just a moment, Mother," Maria replied, looking up at the crucifix.

"Let's go!"

But Maria continued to look at the place on the chest where the crucifix had been retouched to cover the bullet holes.

"What happened here, Mother?"

"Nothing." She took her by the hand and pulled her away.

Their feet sank into a carpet of needles. They walked through the pine grove until they reached the ridge. From here, there was a breathtaking view: a lush valley, with the Ionian Sea on the horizon.

"Sit down, Maria, here, next to me."

The young woman obeyed. Then she pointed off to the right, towards a large rock shaped like a panettone. "How beautiful!" she cried. "It's like a sculpture!"

"That's Pietra Cappa, Maria. They tell lots of stories about it. Even today, they say the shepherds hear a strange noise coming from inside."

"Myths, I hope?"

Her mother nodded. "Oh, yes."

"Why hasn't Dad come with us?" Maria asked. "With him here, this place would have been even better." Her eyes had moved from Pietra Cappa to her mother's face.

For Angela, the moment to speak had come. "Maria," she said, "your father didn't come home last night."

"What? What are you talking about?" A sadness came into her eyes.

"The other evening we quarrelled and he left. But he'll be back, you'll see."

"What did you quarrel about?"

Angela hesitated, unsure how to reply.

"Tell me, Mother . . . Please!"

"He wouldn't tell me the truth."

"About what?"

That was an even more difficult question to answer.

"It would take too long to explain, Maria, and I'm not sure you'd understand. You grew up in another world. America is another world. All you need to know is that he wouldn't tell me the truth."

"No, Mother, you can't just leave it at that. I want to know where Dad is!"

"I don't know where he went."

"Then let's go to the Carabinieri. Something may have happened to him: he may have had an accident, he may have been taken ill. They'll find him." She began to sob.

Angela decided that the moment had come to explain a few things to her daughter. Things like the rules of the family, respect, loyalty, the law of silence, the way men of honour should behave. All this was new to her daughter, who listened wide-eyed.

"I don't like it here," she said when her mother had finished. "I just want Dad to come home. And then I want to go back to New York."

They returned to the car, walking side by side. Maria was still sobbing. She had a bewildered air about her, as if her mother's words had left her dazed. Angela thought it best to distract her and, once she had started the engine, she changed the subject. "This is the place where your uncles and I often came when we were little children. We liked it a lot, especially Rocco. He came here many times with his fiancée, Teresa, and I came with your father." For the first time, there was a hint of genuine nostalgia in her expression. But it was only for a moment. She reversed the car and set off back to the house. In silence.

"Who's Teresa?" Maria asked after a while.

"She was your uncle Rocco's fiancée. She lived near your grandmother's house. They broke up."

"You've never mentioned her before. Why did they break up?"

"Well, he would have liked to marry her, start a family with her, but she wasn't the right person for your uncle. She wasn't the right person at all."

And, saying this, she pressed her foot down on the accelerator.

It was the spring of 1986.

One night, a patrol car from the police station in Siderno had picked up Rocco Fedeli as he was running away from the furniture shop where he had just planted a bomb. The officers had arrested him for possessing

241

and carrying explosive material and attempted criminal damage. For the first time in his life, Rocco Fedeli had crossed the threshold of a prison. Returning home after six months on remand, he had been unpleasantly surprised to find his fiancée, Teresa, a tiny, very pretty eighteen-year-old, looking tense and anxious, so different from the way he had left her. She was hiding something, he knew. He had grilled her relentlessly, until finally she came clean and told him, weeping, how she had had to fend off constant advances from a friend of theirs named Pasquale.

"Pasquale tried to kiss me and put his hands on me. He said he wanted to make me a real woman. His face looked so different. He wasn't the friend we used to know."

"What about you?" Rocco had asked, looking into her swollen, tear-stained eyes.

"Me? What do you mean? What do you think I did? I wouldn't have anything to do with him. I told him that, if he kept on at me, I would tell my father."

Rocco had believed her. Ideas of revenge were already growing inside him.

He had been through a lot with Pasquale. He had loved him like a brother. But Pasquale had betrayed him in the worst possible way, taking advantage of his absence to make passes at Teresa. He must pay. And so, without hesitation, Rocco decided he would kill him. Pasquale's offence would be washed away with blood.

One morning, before dawn, he had taken up position near the sheepfold belonging to Pasquale's family. As soon as he saw him arrive and prop his black Vespa 50 against a tree, Rocco had come out from his hiding place and shot him five times with a sawn-off shotgun. The Carabinieri had linked the murder to the traffic in stolen livestock, which was very common at the time. The killer was never found.

A few months later, Rocco Fedeli had emigrated to the United States. Without Teresa. He'd discovered proof that she had lied to him: she was no longer a virgin.

"Hello."

"'Ntoni?" The voice was a man's.

"Speaking."

"You fix workers . . . And accountant to . . ."

"I understand!"

"You prepare workers . . . In two weeks . . .

" . . . "

"The . . . leaves tonight."

"How much?"

"About five hundred."

"Five hundred?"

"Five hundred!"

" . . . "

"Understood?"

"Yes."

"'Bye. Regards to Diego."

"'Bye."

It was 12.37 in the DIA's phone-tap room when the computer linked to Antonio Russo's phone line recorded this conversation. At last a sign of life. Russo had answered personally. A highly suspect call. As the duty officer listened to it, he felt a shiver of excitement run down his spine. He had immediately recognised the voice of Antonio Russo. The other voice, though, with its strong Spanish accent, was one he had never heard before. He listened to the conversation again. And then once more. However hard he concentrated, he could not make out the word before *leaves tonight*. He transcribed the conversation, indicating Antonio Russo with the letter R and the other man with an X. X for unknown. Presumably a drug supplier, he speculated, judging from both the cryptic nature of the conversation and its content. When he had finished, he handed the transcript to Lieutenant Oliva, who rushed straight to Trimarchi's office. There, the lieutenant waited for an interminable couple of minutes until the colonel put the phone down. Then he went in.

"Sir, we have a development." There was excitement written all over his face.

"Calm down. Take a seat."

Oliva sat down on the visitors' chair and handed him the transcript. As Trimarchi read it, he shook his head several times. Then he picked up the phone and summoned Captain Foti, Carracci and Bruni.

The call was indeed a development.

Little more than half an hour later, they were all there.

Lieutenant Oliva handed each of them a photocopy of the transcript.

"Five hundred!" Lorenzo Bruni said when he had finished reading. "It's true that Antonio Russo is involved in the construction business . . . He gets

244

subcontracted, for things like the endless modernisation of the Salerno — Reggio Calabria autostrada. Five hundred, though . . . Five hundred what? Did they have to be so damned cryptic?"

"And these five hundred whatever-they-are are coming in two weeks!" Carracci said. "From where? The man had a Spanish accent . . . It doesn't take much to put two and two together."

"It must be drugs, I agree," Bruno replied, staring at the transcript, apparently convinced. "Do we know where the call was made from?"

"Not yet," Oliva said. "But I've already contacted the phone company, and they're working on it."

"Let's hope we get an answer soon," Carracci said.

The lieutenant nodded.

"The something leaves tonight . . ." Bruni resumed, looking at Carracci. "What does that mean? From what my men have been able to ascertain, the average length of time it takes a ship to get here from Turbo is twelve to fourteen days. And then he says, 'Regards to Diego.' Who is this Diego?"

"There's no Diego we know of in the Russo 'ndrina," Foti said. "And it's not such a common name in these parts."

"It has to be drugs," Carracci said. "If we wait, we'll finally be able to put Antonio Russo in the frame. It'll give us time to carry out checks and put the teams in place."

"Correct, Chief Superintendent," Trimarchi replied, speaking for the first time. And, remembering Annunziato Spina's words, he thought to himself, As *long as one of his "contacts" doesn't tip him off.* "What about Alfredo Prestipino?" he asked.

"We can't wait two weeks," Foti said, guessing his chief's thoughts.

"Do we have anything new on Prestipino?" Carracci pressed.

"He still hasn't come out of the farmhouse," Foti replied.

"What about his wife's phone?" Trimarchi asked.

"Nothing new there," Oliva replied. "Not even to the mother." He looked down at the papers on the table.

"Nothing new at all?" Trimarchi insisted.

"Well, the only thing Angela mentioned when she called her mother was that she'd seen Don Ciccio Puglisi. Apparently he told her he didn't know anything, but said he would look into it right away. He even told her off for not telling him earlier. That's all."

For a while, nobody spoke.

Trimarchi broke the silence. It was imperative, he said, that they launch a raid on the farmhouse.

"What about the drugs?" Carracci objected. "If we do that, we risk losing them."

"What are you trying to say, Chief Superintendent?" Trimarchi cut in. "That a man's life is less important than a drug consignment?"

"No, no, I didn't . . . I didn't mean . . ." Carracci stammered, trying to defend himself.

Everyone immediately turned to look at him.

Trimarchi glared at him. He would have liked to tell Carracci where to get off. He was finding the man's contributions more and more obtuse.

"We'll still be able to grab the drugs when they arrive," he said, and everyone's eyes now turned to him. "As long as the port's in Italy. But, I repeat, the most urgent thing at the moment is to find out what's happened to Prestipino."

Silence fell over the room again. They were all weighing up how effective an immediate raid on the farmhouse might be.

Once again it was Colonel Trimarchi who spoke first. He was increasingly giving the impression of being the real person in charge of the task force.

"I think it's a good idea to report these developments to Prosecutor Francesco Romeo. Let him decide, if we can't."

They all nodded their approval. Having the prosecutor's consent would provide them with a safeguard on both professional and disciplinary levels.

"I'll go and see him straight away," Trimarchi said in conclusion. "Will you come with me, Chief Superintendent Carracci?"

"I prefer to wait here," Carracci replied, his eyes lowered, like a child who has been caught out in some mischief.

The Antonio Russo angle was proving to be a promising one.

CHAPTER
TWENTY-THREE

New York

It was all because of me . . . Yes, because of me . . .
Lieutenant Reynolds had been telling himself repeatedly over the past few hours.

Now he was in Dick Moore's office at 26 Federal
Plaza.

No sooner had he left Rusty Sheridan in Brooklyn
than he had decided he needed to talk to Moore. He
felt guilty about what had happened to his former
colleague.

The gym, Rusty's one true passion, his only purpose
in life, his great love, had been completely destroyed in
the fire, reduced to a pile of ashes. Nearby, in a
graffiti-covered dumpster, the police had found a gallon
can that still smelled of petrol. There was no doubt that
the fire had been started deliberately. And the reason
had to be the tip-off that had landed the leader and
some members of the Green Birds in prison. Now they
would have to act fast to avoid any further — and
perhaps even more serious — retaliatory action against
Rusty.

"It was Sheridan who tipped me off about the Green Birds," a grim-faced Reynolds began.

"Why did you swoop on them?" Moore asked, puzzled. "Was it because of the taxi?"

Reynolds took his time answering. He was in a difficult position. Up until now, he had only informed Moore of the thefts, saying nothing of the gang's likely involvement in the burning of the taxi. "Sheridan thought there was a connection," he said at last.

"Why?"

"Because the gang has contacts with criminal elements in the Italian community. He must have found something else as well, something he wanted to keep to himself."

Moore remembered what the anonymous caller had said about the people responsible for the homicides: *Italians, but not only Italians.* At the time, given Rocco Fedeli's known associations, he had thought of the Colombians.

It was only now that Dick Moore considered the possibility there might have been home-grown criminals involved. "What I don't understand," he objected, "is that, OK, you arrested the gang's leader, searched his apartment. But the guy'll be out on bail soon enough, maybe even today, tomorrow at the latest. Burning down a gym seems to me a little out of proportion."

Reynolds bowed his head. He saw again the images of the burned-down gym, smelled the nauseating odour of the still-smoking remains in his nostrils, remembered Rusty's tear-stained face.

"It's as if they wanted to send us a signal," Moore continued, stroking his cheek with his right hand.

Reynolds looked up. "A signal? Who to?"

"That's what we need to find out . . . Who to? Sheridan? Or to others, too?"

Reynolds curled his lips in a grimace.

"A signal to the gang that stole the uniforms, maybe," Moore said. "Because I believe that boy Denis. That's why the killers were able to work undisturbed: they were disguised as police officers. That's why the door of the apartment was opened to them. Everything fits!"

Reynolds looked at him, even more puzzled. Personally he had doubted the veracity of Denis's story, but maybe now he would have to think again.

"Yes, that's it, Lieutenant. And the reasoning is simple."

Reynolds continued looking at him. A little light had gone on in his memory. He nodded. "Explain it me."

If it had been the gang that had set fire to the gym, Moore explained, it would have made things more difficult for Harry Baker, their leader, who was still being detained. So it seemed more likely that the act was intended to do two things: to punish Sheridan and at the same time to intimidate those who were involved in the murders, the gang itself. To remind them of the law of silence. *Omertà*.

"But that would mean the gang's involvement wasn't limited to the burning of the taxi," Reynolds said.

"Precisely. In the meantime we have a badge, which we know was stolen. We need to find out if there have been other thefts from police officers and Federal agents. And we mustn't let any of the gang out of our sight. Any of them."

At this point, Moore's mind seemed to wander. Earlier, when he had stroked his cheek, he had realised that he had left home that morning without shaving. Now he thought of Jenny. She would certainly never have allowed him to go to work like that. How he missed her!

It was Reynolds who brought him back to the present. "We're already doing that," he replied, his face now a picture of certainty.

It was almost 4p.m. by the time Colonel Trimarchi got back to his office.

He had spoken at length, first to the chief prosecutor, and then to his deputy, who was in charge of the investigations, about Annunziato Spina's statements. Now he informed the others of the decision that had been taken: to raid Antonio Russo's farmhouse as soon as possible, that same night or by Saturday evening at the latest. The order had been imperative.

Carracci felt a trembling in his legs. It was a defeat, a bitter one. What should he tell Armando Guaschelli? That a decision had been made over his objections, even though technically he was in charge of the task force? He turned pale. But he swallowed his anger and said nothing, even though he was furious.

Later, when Trimarchi was alone in the office, he made a phone call — one he couldn't avoid — to Chief

Superintendent Ferrara's mobile. Ferrara picked up at the first ring.

"I'm sorry, Chief Superintendent," he said, after imparting his news, "but I thought you should know as soon as possible."

"You did the right thing, Colonel. If the prosecutor has agreed to a raid, then let's go ahead with it."

"We'll proceed as soon as we can. Tomorrow night, I think."

Under his desk, Trimarchi crossed his fingers.

New York

The records were housed at NYPD headquarters in a room half the size of a basketball field. There were steel shelves, stacked almost seven feet high and filled with files marked with tags of different colours. Lieutenant Reynolds had preferred not to delegate this task to anyone else. He alone would be able to overcome any possible resistance from the records clerks. One of them accompanied him now as he went to the section given over to crimes against police officers. From his jacket pocket, he took the sheet of paper Detective Green had left on his desk: a list of officers who had reported thefts over the last few months. He read the labels on the shelves and finally found the files he was looking for. None of them was particularly thick. The labels, protruding from the covers, indicated the kinds of theft. They were all different, but, compared with the number of thefts suffered by locals and tourists alike, they were a tiny minority, a small drop in a big ocean. The names of the victims were in alphabetical order. The lieutenant read out the names on the sheet, one at a time. There were thirty-six in all. It took the clerk less than ten minutes to find the files. He pulled them out, leaving tags to keep their places.

"Here you are, Lieutenant."

"I'd like photocopies of all the papers in each file."

"No problem, but it'll take time."

"I'll wait."

The 9.40 flight from Rome Fiumicino had just come through a patch of turbulence.

Ferrara closed his eyes and let his thoughts wander. He recalled his first years as a chief superintendent. All these memories coming back to the surface made him feel slightly anxious. There had been so many murders, so many deaths, it had been like living in a war zone. At times he had felt as though he was in Beirut . . .

He remembered particular areas of the city. He saw again the corpses, some of very young men, on the pavements, or in the middle of the road, or trapped in cars that had been riddled with bullets or even ripped apart by bazookas.

How could he forget the suffering he had seen on the faces of the victims? What he was feeling couldn't be anxiety, Ferrara told himself, No, what he was feeling was anger at the neglect prevalent in that wonderful land fragrant with the smell of the sea and the scent of orange blossom, in which the vast majority of the inhabitants were perfectly respectable people.

With a jolt, he opened his eyes, and the last faces vanished. His thoughts came back to reality — to the present, and the reason he was returning to Calabria. He looked out of the window and saw the runway lights. The plane, tearing through the darkness, was nearing the airport. When it landed and the pilot switched off the engine, Ferrara was among the first passengers to descend the steps. His legs had gone numb, and he stamped his feet on the ground. His muscles relaxed. The terminal was just the way he remembered it. On the way out, he had a pleasant surprise.

"How great to see you, Chief Superintendent, after all these years," the driver said, greeting him with a warm handshake.

"What are you doing here? Pietro, isn't it?" Pietro had been one of his men when he worked here.

"That's right. I came to pick you up to take you to your hotel. I'm working with the DIA now."

"Congratulations!"

In the car, Ferrara put a cigar in his mouth. He had a craving for the taste of it, even if he didn't light it.

"Same old cigar, eh, Chief Superintendent?"

"Oh, yes. My habits haven't changed."

"We're the ones who change."

A bitter smile played on Ferrara's lips. *He thinks I've aged, but he's not the young boy I knew either.*

"Are you married, Pietro?"

"Yes, sir, I have a daughter who's just started high school. She's a great girl. She wants to be a judge."

"I'm pleased. A good choice."

They were nearing the hotel.

"See what a nice seafront we have, sir? Do you remember? It wasn't like this in your time!" There was a touch of pride in his voice.

Ferrara looked out at the view. It was apparently the only thing that was new. During the ride, everything had seemed unchanged, even the streets with their patched-up tarmac. But the seafront had been completely refurbished and embellished with colourful flowerbeds and beautiful wooden benches. With its extraordinary view of the Straits of Messina and the Sicilian coast, it had become the ideal place to stroll on cool summer evenings. He thought of Petra, who would have appreciated all those flowers.

He caught a whiff of their scent. It was like the one emanating from his wife's greenhouse every time he peered in.

"They say it's the best promenade in Italy," Pietro said, a smug look on his face.

"I can believe that. It's really wonderful."

"Here we are."

Ferrara bade him farewell, got out of the car and entered the hotel.

Immediately after checking in, he pressed the lift button. As he waited for the lift to arrive, he looked around. He had the impression that a man was peering at him over the newspaper he held open with both hands.

When he got to his room, he attached the DO NOT DISTURB sign and closed the door behind him. He wasn't hungry. Even if he had been, he would not have been able to have dinner in the hotel restaurant. It was already closed. It was just after eleven o'clock, and his eyelids were drooping. The next day was going to be a heavy one, if Colonel Trimarchi's theories turned out to be correct.

Before he went to sleep, he made a last phone call to Petra. He knew how opposed she had been to this trip, so he tried to distract her attention by telling her about the wonderful flowers on the seafront.

But Petra was true to type. "Be careful!" she repeated several times.

"Don't worry, darling. Go to sleep now, it's late. When I get back, I'll take you to see *Carmen*." He sent her a kiss.

"I'll carry on reading a while longer. But you, *Schatzi*, be careful!"

With these words ringing in his ears, he closed his eyes and sank into sleep.

They were motionless under a clear sky sprinkled with stars.

And they were arguing.

Don Ciccio Puglisi had asked for a meeting.

An urgent one.

For that same night.

His emissary had been specific: "Midnight, on the dot . . . tomorrow could be too late."

Antonio Russo had understood that this was an appointment that couldn't be put off.

They were on the highest peak in the Aspromonte, Montalto, beneath the huge bronze statue of the

256

Redeemer. It was neutral territory for the two of them, which made it a perfect place to meet. It was also very safe, especially at this hour, when any light would be immediately seen, any noise heard, even a distant one. From here, on fine days, the view was breathtaking: the two seas — the Tirrhenian and the Ionian — Mount Etna and the island of Stromboli.

Tonight, there was an eerie silence, and the air was cold and sharp, but neither man minded. They were used to it.

"I don't want to hear any bullshit, 'Ntoni, your men were in San Piero . . ."

Don Ciccio's voice was even more hoarse than usual. He stood there, wrapped in a thick woollen jacket, looking fixedly at Russo.

"It's fine, Don Ciccio, it's a matter I need to deal with . . ."

"'Ntoni, you haven't respected your agreements, and you know what that means?"

"What agreements? Don Ciccio, you're thinking like the old days."

"Do you want war, then?"

"What do you mean, war? You can rest easy. Everything's the way it was. I just have to settle *my* business."

"'Ntoni, I'm giving you thirty-six hours. By midday Sunday, I want him back home, having lunch with his wife and daughter. That's my final word."

"Why are you so interested, Don Ciccio? After all —"

"That's my business. Remember, thirty-six hours . . . or you'll regret it."

"He'll be there, Don Ciccio, he'll be there."

And as true men of honour, they shook hands, looking in each other's eyes as they did so.

They returned to their respective cars, where their men were waiting, and got in.

The DIA officers, in position a couple of miles away, watched as Antonio Russo's Mercedes passed on its way to the farmhouse. It would have been too risky to follow as far as the Due Mari crossroads, so they had waited for him to come back.

New York

There wasn't much in the files.

Just reports. No clues as to suspects. All the thefts remained unsolved.

It was four in the afternoon, and Lieutenant Reynolds, having looked through the files, set aside just eight of them, to his right, one on top of the other. They related to thefts of uniforms, badges and other material allocated to officers. On top of the pile, he placed a sheet of paper noting the dates and the places. The thefts had been committed during the week ending 12 October, all eight of them in Brooklyn, the borough with the highest crime rate.

Something told him they were the work of the same criminals. The Green Birds?

He summoned Detective Green to his office.

"This is the list of thefts that interest us," he said, handing him the paper with the dates and places. "They're are all from the 81st precinct. We need to look at the files on the investigations. They may tell us something. Look particularly at the witness statements and the CSU findings. Maybe we'll have some luck . . ." He pushed the eight files across the desk to Green.

"I'll get right on it, Lieutenant. The 81st precinct is the same one where they're investigating the theft of the badge we found in Baker's apartment."

Reynolds nodded.

The coincidence hadn't escaped him.

Dick Moore was also beginning to take an interest in the Green Birds.

The FBI had been monitoring the gangs for some time. They were a threat to national security, second only to al-Qaeda. And some of them — including the Green Birds — had branches in several cities, several states.

Moore found a lot on their leader, Harry Baker, who had stamped his authority on the gang, often with exceptional violence. He was a real son of a bitch, with a record to match . . .

By the time he was seventeen, Baker had already been responsible for a number of muggings, car thefts, and breakins. Almost all committed in Brooklyn, where he was living with his parents at the time. Then he had gone on to more serious offences: assaults and rapes on a number of women, all very young, including the girlfriends of members of his gang: it was as if he were claiming some kind of *droit du seigneur*, by virtue of being the leader. Then he had switched to drug dealing and even arms trafficking. And not only in New York. The gang had spread its tentacles to other cities. Harry Baker was quite a character. Unfortunately, although he had often been a suspect, he'd never been convicted. There wasn't a shred of serious evidence against him.

And Dick Moore found something else in the course of his reading.

It seemed the FBI had shown an interest in Baker, too.

The reports were dated 1998, when the FBI had been keeping an eye on a pizzeria in Brooklyn, owned by a Sicilian, which was believed to be a distribution centre for drugs, according to the Feds. On several occasions, NYPD patrol cars cruising the area had picked up Baker as he was coming away from the place. Nothing had ever been found on him, but there was no doubt their suspicions had been founded. They were dealing with a very cunning criminal. Among the names that had cropped up in connection with the investigation of the pizzeria were not only Sicilians but also a few Calabrians, some of whom they'd caught in the act. But no one named Fedeli or Prestipino.

Unfortunately, thought Dick Moore.

The 81st precinct robbery files that Green had photocopied did not reveal very much.

Only one captured Reynolds' attention. At one of the crime scenes, some fragmentary fingerprints had been lifted — too fragmentary to be used in comparisons — and the print of a sneaker. He looked closely at the photograph of the sole. A shiver ran down his spine: there was a very strong resemblance between this print and the one found near the burned-out taxi.

"Send a photograph of this print to Dick Moore," he ordered Detective Green. "He can run it by his lab in Washington. And let's hope we have a bit of luck this time."

He picked up the phone and dialled Moore's number. Having told him that he would be sending the photograph of the shoe, he got on to the real purpose of his call.

"Harry Baker mustn't walk tomorrow. Not even on bail."

"I'll do what I can," Moore replied, after a moment's silence. "I'll have a word with the DA. The fact that Baker's also been charged with the theft of an FBI badge could bring him within our jurisdiction, like when FBI documents are stolen."

"In that case, I'll leave it with you. Let's speak tomorrow."

He hung up, relieved. In that moment, he'd have liked to shake Moore's hand.

CHAPTER
TWENTY-FOUR

Saturday, 15 November

It was night, and he was stuck in some kind of gully in the middle of the Aspromonte, surrounded by trees and thick undergrowth. He couldn't find a way out. He was lost. He could feel the breath of the 'Ndrangheta on him. They were hunting him down, eager for revenge. A vague figure suddenly appeared in front of him. Who could it be? It must be one of them. Then he heard a sarcastic voice. "Here he is! The Fox of the Aspromonte. Look what he's been reduced to. He thought he knew everything . . . ha, ha, ha!" He looked closer at the figure and saw that it was wearing a dark ski mask. But what most drew his attention was the object it was carrying: a sawn-off shotgun. And it was aimed at him. There was an explosion . . .

Chief Superintendent Ferrara woke with a start. He was in his hotel room, bathed in sweat. He lit the lamp on the bedside table and glanced in the mirror. His face was as white as wax. He closed his eyes. He opened them again. He closed them again and once again opened them. A nightmare! And what a nightmare! The ghosts had returned. His mouth was dry, and the room

262

was revolving around him. Slowly he got out of bed. He put his feet down on the floor and stood there.

From the mini-bar he took a bottle of water and drank it in one go. He immediately felt better. Unlike some people, he did not place much credence in dreams.

He opened the window and looked outside. It was dark, with just a few small lights on the sea from ships crossing the straits. The air he breathed in smelled strongly of sea salt. But the wind was cold, and he quickly closed the window. He got back into bed and Petra's last words came back to him: Schatzi, *be careful*.

At last he fell asleep.

Ferrara was in the foyer, waiting for his driver.

It was almost eight o'clock in the morning and the nightmare had by this time been completely dispelled. Petra had phoned him at six, dragging him from a deep sleep. She had wanted to wish him a good day at work and, above all, to advise him once again to be careful. Her concern for him made her more adorable than ever.

He had had breakfast with the other early risers among the guests in a little room on the ground floor, sitting at a small table for two near the window, with a view of the seafront. He turned frequently to look towards the coast of Sicily, feeling a strong sense of nostalgia. It had been quite a while since he had been back to his native Catania, even for a few days.

He had missed the tiny cream pastries and the soft brioches so much. A good cappuccino and a cup of espresso had invigorated him.

The only time he had been distracted during breakfast was when the howling of police sirens had broken the silence in the room, almost as if trying to emphasise that the State was still a presence, even here.

Colonel Trimarchi was sitting behind his desk, making call after call to finalise the operation.

Suddenly there was a knock on the open door and Foti entered, bright-eyed. He was holding a sheet of paper.

"Call me when everything's ready," Trimarchi said down the phone. He replaced the receiver and gave Foti an inquisitive look.

"I'm sorry, sir."

"What's happened, Foti?"

"I've just heard from the men on stakeout."

The colonel, as usual, sat back in his chair and motioned to him to sit down.

"Before seven this morning," Foti continued, taking his seat, "a car arrived at the farmhouse. A big car, our men said."

"The BMW?"

"It could well be. But what's new, Colonel, is that this is the first time there've been visitors so early."

"Do the men think it could be the same car that lifted Prestipino?"

"Yes, sir."

"How many people in the car?"

"Two. They went into the house, and still haven't come out."

"It could be they've come to take Prestipino away," Trimarchi said, shaking his head. "Tell the men to keep on the alert and inform us immediately. It's possible our plans will have to change."

"Of course, sir."

At that moment, Chief Superintendent Ferrara appeared. He was wearing a light grey suit and clutching a bundle of newspapers. In his mouth was a cigar, still unlit. As soon as he saw him, Colonel Trimarchi got up, went around the desk and shook his hand warmly.

"Welcome to Reggio, Chief Superintendent."

"It's good to be here."

"Did you have a good journey?"

"Excellent."

They sat down in the lounge, where the colonel filled him in on the latest developments.

Ferrara was silent for a moment, then asked, "Do we know whose car it is?"

"Unfortunately our men haven't been able to get the licence number. Because of the way it's parked, they can only see it from the side. But it's dark in colour, and the same make as the one that took Prestipino away. They're sure of that."

"And do we have the licence number of that one?"

"Oh yes. It's registered to a company run by a man who fronts for Russo, and is often used by his associates."

Ferrara nodded. "We must be ready. And we need to keep the prosecutor up to date."

The others nodded. Trimarchi picked up the phone and called the Prosecutor's Department. Immediately afterwards, Bill Hampton and Bob Holley arrived. Both greeted Ferrara and shook hands with him. Then Bob Holley handed the colonel a sheet of paper. "This list was sent by Assistant Director Moore. They're all Italians whose names came up in a Bureau operation, and they all have links to Harry Baker in one way or another."

"I'm sorry," Ferrara said. "Who's Harry Baker?"

"Forgive us, Chief Superintendent," Holley replied. "We forgot to inform you: Harry Baker is the head of a dangerous gang in New York, who's been arrested in connection with the case."

Colonel Trimarchi noticed that the list included the names of two men born in the area, one in Bovalino and the other in Gioiosa Ionica. "Good," he said. "The *Squadra Mobile* will need this list. They can take a look at these men's families. Foti, fax this to Chief Superintendent Bruni."

He looked at his watch: it was nine thirty.

New York

Judge Steven Goldstein of the Supreme Court of Brooklyn Kings County, was sitting on the bench between two flags, wrapped in his black robe. He was just over fifty, and had the reputation of being

266

conscientious and efficient. In front of his bench, at a little desk, sat a young stenographer.

The spacious courtroom was filled with defendants and lawyers. For almost an hour Goldstein had been hearing the charges against the arrested gang members. Now Harry Baker's turn had come.

Baker was standing on one side of the room, behind a glass partition. His lawyer, Robert Mills, who was nearly six feet tall with slicked-back dyed black hair, walked around the table and approached him.

"You-know-who says to say hello."

"Thanks," was all Baker said in reply, his lips curled in a grimace.

"You have to plead not guilty."

Harry Baker nodded. Mills turned to the judge and said in a loud voice that his client wished to plead not guilty.

Steven Goldstein hesitated for a moment.

There were four possibilities: to refuse bail, to release Baker subject to restrictions such as confiscating his passport, to release him on an already fixed and paid bail, or to release him with the condition that bail would have to be paid if he skipped town or failed to appear at the next hearing.

Robert Mills, who was hoping to get Baker released on a low bail, intoned professionally, "Your Honour, I ask that the evidence against my client be ruled inadmissible, on the grounds that it was obtained during an illegal search. My client is completely innocent of the charges against him, and there were no reasonable grounds to search him, let alone arrest him."

The judge looked down at the file, then slowly raised his head and looked at Mills, who was still standing there stiffly. "From what I've heard," he said, "I assume you have no intention of waiving the ten-day rule."

"That's correct, Your Honour. We don't want to waive it."

Goldstein looked at the diary on the bench in front of him and fixed the date of the hearing: precisely ten days away. Mills and the Assistant DA both noted it down. Then the judge leaned forward and asked if they had anything to say about the bail.

For the first time, Assistant DA Betty Fisher stood up. She was young and pretty and wore a sober grey suit.

She had had a long telephone conversation with Ted Morrison before the start of the hearing. He had told her how important it was to make sure that Baker was not released. She had replied that it might be worthwhile for the case to be put under Federal jurisdiction, but Morrison had disagreed. "We don't want to show our hand yet," he had said. "I'll do what I can," she had assured him.

"Yes, Your Honour, I have something to say. My office asks that bail should be set at sixty thousand dollars." She glanced across at Mills.

The judge looked up from the file in front of him and stared at her. Then, over his glasses, he squinted at Harry Baker. For the first time. And for a long time. As if, by studying him, he could understand the reason why such a high bail had been requested for the charges

268

of receiving stolen property and larceny. It was quite without precedent.

"I don't understand, Miss Fisher," he said. "From the papers in my possession I don't see anything that could justify such a request."

Turning a pen between her fingers, Betty Fisher replied, "Your Honour, my office believes that the accused may attempt to escape justice. He has refused to tell the police how he came into possession of the badge. In addition to which . . ."

She paused, put her pen down on the table and leafed through some papers. They were the notes of her conversation with Ted Morrison.

"In addition to which, there may be more serious charges against him," she continued in a resolute tone.

"What charges?" the judge asked, his curiosity aroused.

Betty Fisher seemed to hesitate. She knew that she could not go too far for the moment.

She looked down again at her notes. "I haven't yet received the information I'm waiting for," she admitted, "but the police are working on it."

Now it was the judge's turn to reflect. He adjusted his robe over his shoulders, looked down again at the file, and began writing.

"I'm going to be flexible in this case," he said, looking first at Mills and then once again, fleetingly, at Harry Baker. "I'm setting bail at forty thousand dollars. I'll reduce it if the police investigation hasn't come up with anything new in the next few hours." Then he closed the file, placed it on a pile of other papers on his right-hand side, and called the next case.

Looking defeated, Mills approached Harry Baker and murmured, "I'm sorry."

"Don't worry. So I'll be inside a few more days. It's no big deal. They won't find anything on me. And anyhow, you know they won't abandon me."

"Hold out a while longer," Mills said by way of farewell. "We'll get you out soon."

And with that Harry Baker was taken back to Riker's Island.

When Moore and Reynolds found out what had happened, they hoped he would stay there for ever.

There was no reason to change the plan.

The two men who had arrived that morning had not been seen leaving the farmhouse. Nor had Alfredo Prestipino.

Constantly updated by Colonel Trimarchi, Prosecutor Romeo had once again emphasised how important it was that the operation be carried out as soon as possible. It could not, and should not, be postponed. There had been no further conversations of interest on Antonio Russo's landline since the one recorded the previous day. The telephone company had confirmed that the call had come from a location in South America, which reinforced the theory that it had referred to a drug consignment.

During the meeting, Carracci, taking his courage in both hands, made one last attempt, this time in the presence of Ferrara, to put forward his view that they should wait until the drugs arrived.

"The *Squadra Mobile*," he said, with a scowl on his face, looking first at Trimarchi, then at Ferrara, "have ascertained that a ship with a cargo of bananas is due to arrive at the port of Savona on 29 November. The port of departure, as it turns out, is Turbo. It's clear that this is the ship we're interested in."

Trimarchi and Foti looked at each other, then both turned towards Ferrara, as if anxious to hear what he had to say.

His judgement was not long in coming. "I think we should inform the prosecutor about this, too. And then we'll do whatever he decides."

It was now clear that Carracci was the head of the task force in name only. The man who made the decisions was the prosecutor. And no one could do anything about that, not even Ferrara. To all intents and purposes, the minister's decree wasn't worth the paper it was written on.

Carracci remained silent. Being humiliated by Armando Guaschelli, head of the state police, was one thing, but by a colonel in the Carabinieri? No, that was too much to bear.

Trimarchi looked at his watch. It was 4.25p.m. "I'm going to see the prosecutor at his home. And this time I'd like Chief Superintendent Carracci to come with me."

Carracci shook his head. At last he spoke.

"No," he said curtly.

Diego had been feeling lousy all day.

He had been dogged by a cough and a terrible sore throat, as well as constant shivering. He must have a fever. Last night's attempted escape had left its mark on him. He felt like a limp rag. His body was burning. And he hadn't been able to eat anything. The hard bread and cheese which one of his guards had given him towards midday still lay on the floor. He had only been able to sip a little water from the plastic can. Towards nightfall one of the guards appeared, hooded as usual.

"We need you alive," he said, in the same fake voice as before. "Now pull yourself together and get dressed, we're going soon."

These words seemed to drag Diego from his torpor. The sense of emptiness that had dogged him dissipated a little. He put on the shirt, the sweater and then the windbreaker which they had given him as a pillow. It was quite big on him, at least two or three sizes too large. Then the guard took the chain off his ankles so he could put on his trousers, which were still damp, and his shoes. They, too, were soaked. Docilely, he let the guard place a cone-shaped hood on his head, with a little hole for the mouth. He found it difficult to breathe. For a moment, he felt as though he were about to faint. But he tried not to lose heart.

Then four strong arms lifted him under his armpits and dragged him outside. They set off along a path that climbed up into the mountains, until they reached a plateau. Here, the ground was softer. Diego could feel it. His feet sank into a carpet of grass. Then they began to descend. There were thick bushes and trees on the sides of the path. It was a brief descent, which did not last more than half an hour. Eventually, they came to a shack. They pushed him inside and took off his hood, at the same time putting on their own.

Diego was relieved to see that his new hiding place was larger than the hut they had abandoned. It was a solid construction about twelve feet by twelve feet, with drystone walls. It was also in a better state of repair, almost a suite compared with the previous shelter. There was a threadbare mattress on the floor, and a stove and an old cupboard stocked with food in the corner.

"You'll be better off here," his captor said. "We'll bring you some pasta later, and a little red wine. You'll soon be back on your feet."

"Thank you," Diego murmured.

"We need you alive," the other man replied. It was the second time he had said that to him in the space of a few hours. Then he added, "Keep using the bucket for your needs."

Diego picked it up and took a good look at it, examining it as if seeing it for the first time. It was made of iron like the previous one, but smaller in size.

Meanwhile, the DIA offices were buzzing with anticipation.

Prosecutor Romeo had again given the order, authorising the raid.

As far as the drugs went — provided Carracci's theory turned out to be correct — all they had to do was wait. And they already knew, in this case, who the consignment was for. They would get Antonio Russo in the end.

Carracci just had to resign himself.

The operation would begin in the middle of the night, but only if they were certain they would find Russo at home.

That had been the one condition the prosecutor had laid down before giving the go-ahead.

They were preparing to leave when Chief Superintendent Ferrara's mobile phone began ringing.

He recognised the number on the screen and immediately replied.

"Hello, Petra."

"Can you talk?"

"Actually, I'm in a meeting right now, but go on." He moved into a corner of the room.

"It's nothing, Michele, I just wanted to tell you that Anna's here from Florence."

"Good. Give her my regards."

"She's coming with me to the exhibition at the Capitoline Museum."

"What exhibition?"

"'The Fontana Sisters: fashion in history'."

"Oh, yes, now I remember."

"I have to write an article about it for the magazine."

"Good, I'm pleased."

"I'll call you again as soon as I get home."

"Yes, do that, Petra."

"Stay calm. Or rather, be careful . . . But when are you coming back?"

"Soon, I hope."

"It can't be too soon for me."

"Love you."

"Love you too."

New York

Before leaving the precinct house, Reynolds checked that the tap on Harry Baker's landline was active. He hadn't wanted to lose any more time. Even a call to a relative might turn out to be of interest.

Dick Moore, meanwhile, had ordered phone taps on the Sicilian pizzeria frequented by Baker and the Calabrians. He was still waiting for information about the latter from Italy.

The investigations in New York and Calabria were proceeding now in perfect harmony. And that was a hopeful sign.

It wasn't just Police Commissioner Jones who wanted the killers apprehended and brought to justice. Apparently the only thing that would make New Yorkers sleep peacefully in their beds was a successful conclusion to the case — that is, if the media were to be believed. That morning, the *New York Times* had published another leader on the subject:

MADISON HOMICIDE CASE AT A CROSSROADS?

The detectives of the 17th precinct seem at last to be on the right track. They are now focusing their attention on the gangs, arresting a number of gang members and even one of their leaders, who was found to be in possession of suspicious items. Police Commissioner Ronald Jones would not confirm these developments, but neither did he categorically deny them, and he was uncharacteristically nervous when questioned on the subject. It is to be hoped that the case can be resolved very soon and that the perpetrators of these terrible killings will at last be identified.

Though there was no by-line, Ronald Jones, when he read it, knew it had to be by that thorn in his flesh, David Powell.

It was just after 11 p.m. and everything was ready.

The DIA officers had assembled in the courtyard of the police station in Gioia Tauro, awaiting the arrival of a team from NOCS, the special forces unit, and another from Police Headquarters in Reggio Calabria. Over the top of their bulletproof vests they wore nylon jackets with the initials DIA in large white letters. In their hands, they held plastic cups filled to the brim with coffee. While waiting, they went over the operation, which had been planned down to the last detail.

"Follow the rules and wait before going in," Colonel Trimarchi ordered. "The NOCS team will go in first, after breaking down the front door. Those are the orders. And don't get carried away in the heat of the moment. Keep a cool head at all times."

The officers knew the farmhouse well from having taken turns watching it, and right now their colleagues were keeping them constantly updated. The Mercedes was parked in its usual place, under a lean-to in the garden, which meant that Antonio Russo must be at home. And with him were his guests, who had arrived in dribs and drabs over the last few hours. Everything seemed to suggest that a Mafia summit was in progress inside the house.

"What about the search warrant, Colonel?" Chief Superintendent Ferrara asked.

"Prosecutor Romeo issued it a couple of hours ago," Trimarchi replied proudly. "The information we provided, based on our phone taps and surveillance, was more than enough to convince him."

"We're ready then?" Ferrara asked.

"Yes, everything's in place."

In the course of the next half hour, the team from headquarters arrived, followed by the NOCS team in their trademark black tracksuits. They were in unmarked off-road vehicles packed with all the tools of their trade.

Last to arrive was Carracci, looking grim-faced. As soon as he saw him, Trimarchi said, "Good, now we're all here, let's go to the conference room."

Within a few minutes the room was full.

The officers sat in silence, like metro passengers during the rush hour. One officer was already sitting in the middle of the room next to a table with a projector on it. On the wall opposite was a white sheet. At a sign from Trimarchi, the officer switched on the machine.

The colonel introduced the Americans, then began to go through the operation in detail. Sharp images of the farmhouse began appearing on the screen: the garden, most of it given over to an orange grove, the high perimeter walls, the house itself with its wooden front door, the outbuildings.

"Are there any dogs?" the NOCS commander asked. He was a young deputy commissioner named Armando Greco.

"As far as we know, just one."

"Do we have to put it to sleep?"

"Yes, best not to take any chances."

Then Trimarchi allocated tasks to the teams.

The officers from Police Headquarters would surround the perimeter wall, the NOCS team would scale it first and smash down the front door, then the other teams would inspect the house and the other buildings.

"Please keep an eye on the outside of the house at all times. We don't want anyone escaping, or throwing anything out, like a weapon. And be careful, there could be a summit in progress. Remember that the nearest house is half a mile away and the village two miles." He ordered them to tune their portable radios to a private frequency.

"That's all. Any questions?"

"Are we planning on using helicopters?" someone asked from the back row.

"Yes. There are two NOCS helicopters ready to intervene. If necessary, they can reach us in a few minutes. They're in a sports field nearby, awaiting orders. Anything else?"

No one spoke.

They all filed out of the station. On their faces there was hesitation and anxiety, but also courage and concentration. The men from NOCS seemed the most excited. This was understandable, because they were rarely involved in such important operations or in arresting Mafiosi. They all got into their respective vehicles, depending on which team they were part of, put on their bulletproof vests, and picked up their M12 machine pistols or their pump rifles, as well as their Beretta 92/SB service pistols.

At last, the vehicles set off.

One at a time.

The sky was a little overcast.

CHAPTER
TWENTY-FIVE

Sunday, 16 November

They were nearing their target.

Colonel Trimarchi glanced at the clock on the car dashboard: it was after 1a.m. The night was at its blackest and everything looked shapeless. No smells. No sounds. He radioed the men on stakeout for an update. Apparently, Antonio Russo and his guests were still in the house, even though there were no lights on and no signs of life.

Reaching their destination, the drivers parked their vehicles by the side of the road and switched off all lights. The moon was covered by clouds and gave no illumination. In silence, the officers leapt out of their vehicles, closed the doors noiselessly, and set off along the dusty dirt road leading to the farm.

The excitement was tangible.

The NOCS team led the way, with sturdy rope ladders on their backs, to be used for climbing the perimeter wall. Behind them came the men from Police Headquarters with Chief Superintendent Bruni at their head. Ferrara and the Americans brought up the rear.

They all kept their movements to a minimum, advancing deftly and professionally.

Deputy Commissioner Armando Greco was first to climb the perimeter wall, looking about him through his night-vision viewfinder. Reaching the top, he lowered another ladder and, like a trapeze artist, landed on a soft damp carpet of grass. One by one, his men went over, followed by the rest.

They made straight for the furthest part of the farm, where they were sure they would be out of range of the security cameras. It was the only exposed area of the grounds, perhaps because it hung over a deep precipice. The house was about two hundred yards away.

Silence.

No sound except the chirping of insects. No barking of dogs.

Still silence.

Only shadows, darting about.

A marksman took up a position some distance from the front of the mastiff's kennel. The rifle, fitted with an infra-red sight, emitted a slight hiss. The dog did not wake up. It wouldn't wake up for at least a couple of hours.

In the meantime the house had been surrounded.

Antonio Russo's car was still parked in the same place. Beside it were two other cars, indicating that Russo's guests must still be inside. But there was no light in the windows, not even a dim one.

Suddenly there was a booming sound.

A dull one.

And a flash of light lit up part of the garden.

The heavy, iron-studded wooden front door shattered into pieces.

A matter of seconds.

Fractions of seconds.

And they were inside.

Each of the teams moved according to the orders they had been given.

The only sound was the crackling of portable radios. All the messages were the same: no one at home. Certainly they would not have expected to find Russo's wife and two children. A DIA officer had seen them go out that morning and they had not yet come back.

But why did the farmhouse seem uninhabited?

A thousand thoughts were going through Trimarchi's mind. He wasn't the only one. The stillness worried everybody.

"Keep looking," he ordered. "They must be somewhere."

Less than five minutes later, he heard Captain Foti's somewhat altered voice coming through his earpiece. "Sir, come downstairs."

"Where?"

"To the cellar."

Trimarchi rushed down the stairs with his pistol in his hand, followed by Carracci and Armando Greco and some of his men.

Captain Foti was standing in the doorway.

"There's something I think you should see, sir," he said immediately, in a voice tinged with excitement.

"What is it?"

"Follow me, I'll show you."

Trimarchi followed him.

They walked through the cellar. Large crates of wine and demijohns of olive oil stood against the rough stone walls. The air smelled damp and mildewed. Bulbs protected by metal cages hung from the ceiling. The floor was of beaten earth. They stopped in front of the furthest wall.

"Look!" With his right hand, Trimarchi pointed to racks of wine bottles and, next to them, an old cupboard pushed right up against the wall. "What's in this thing?"

"Tools, I'd guess." Foti opened one of the doors and pulled out a kind of briefcase. "Look, there's a home-made satellite phone, sir."

Trimarchi nodded. It was identical to the one they'd found in the quarry at Mazara del Vallo.

He remembered all too well the bunker where he had captured a dangerous Sicilian Mafioso a few years earlier.

"That's not all, look here!" Foti continued, approaching the wine racks.

"What is it?" Trimarchi asked, dubiously: he couldn't see anything unusual. "Is there wine in the bottles or something else?"

"It's not that, sir; I mean, it is wine, I think. But look!" He reached out his hand and started to push the wall. "See? It moves . . ."

The colonel peered at the wall. "It does seem strangely uneven," he said.

"It moves when you push it, as if it's about to turn," Foti murmured, still pressing. "You see?" The wall did, in fact, appear to be moving.

"Deputy Commissioner Greco," Trimarchi said, turning to the NOCS commander, "see if you and your men can do something. You may have to take the bottles away and demolish the wall. Use explosives if you have to." He stood aside to let them get on with it.

It proved unnecessary to use explosives. After several racks of bottles had been pulled clear, the wall yielded to stronger pressure and gradually opened to reveal a small tunnel, so low that you had to bend down to enter it.

"Police!" they cried. "Hands up! No one move!"

"Don't shoot!" an old-sounding voice replied.

A light came on: a bulb fixed to the ceiling with a loose wire. A grim-faced Antonio Russo was sitting on a bamboo stool. Next to him, around a small table laid with bottles and glasses, sat four men. Ropes, hides, reins, whips and saddles hung on the walls, and other riding apparatus from the ceiling.

A secret bunker.

To one side, a shower and two bunk beds.

A perfect shelter.

By now, Trimarchi, Foti and Carracci had entered, one after the other. The last one in was Carracci, his face as white as a corpse.

"The man to Russo's right is Peppino Ferrante!" Foti whispered in Trimarchi's ear, rolling his eyes.

"You're right, so it is!"

284

Peppino Ferrante was a boss, the head of the *'ndrina* named after him. He had been on the run for more than ten years, and his name was on the Interior Ministry's "thirty most wanted" list. There were multiple arrest warrants out for him, for homicide, criminal conspiracy and other offences. To all intents and purposes, he was the Scarlet Pimpernel of the region. Lately it had even been rumoured that he had died of a serious illness. He looked quite dishevelled, with several days' growth of beard, as white as his sparse hair. Seeing him in this place and these conditions, not much more than five feet tall, a thin old man in a pair of velvet trousers and a sweater, he looked inoffensive enough: he could have passed for a local farmer, back stooped with hard labour. But he wasn't. He was a highly dangerous member of the 'Ndrangheta, both feared and respected — and not only on his own territory.

The NOCS men handcuffed him. Both Peppino Ferrante and the man beside him had guns tucked in their waistbands, a Smith and Wesson .38 calibre special revolver and a Beretta 81 respectively, both with the serial numbers scratched out. Colonel Trimarchi radioed Ferrara and the Americans to join him. But the surprises weren't over yet.

A dull, almost rhythmic noise, reverberating about the walls, suddenly reached their ears. It seemed to be coming from the furthest corner.

Some of the NOCS officers approached cautiously, holding their breath. In the floor under the bunk beds, they found an old wooden trapdoor. It came up easily enough. A fetid stench of wool, meat and manure rose from the darkness, catching them by the throat. The noise had grown louder. There could be no doubt. It was coming from down below. It sounded as if someone was beating an object against a wall.

Two officers went down, one after the other, shining their torches in front of them. The floor of beaten earth sloped unevenly. The walls were of stone.

As they advanced, the stench became more pronounced. At the far end of the space, they saw a shadowy figure. A man was sitting on the ground with his back to them and his face against the wall, on which he was pressing both his hands. In his right hand he held a metal object.

"Who are you? Who are you?"

No reply.

Slowly they approached and saw that there was an iron chain wrapped around the unknown man's ankles and fixed to a large hook in the ground.

One of the two officers turned, walked back to the trapdoor and shouted up, "Fetch me a pair of wire cutters!" In the meantime, his colleague had taken off the hood covering the man's face and part of his neck and was now removing the strip of duct tape from his mouth.

Pale and terrified, the man gradually began to breathe more easily. Gingerly raising his hands, he rubbed his reddened eyes and dried the tears that were rolling down his cheeks. Then, with his fingertips, he pushed back the sparse hair that had fallen over his forehead. He seemed to be having difficulty speaking. All that emerged from his mouth were moans.

After a few minutes, another officer appeared with the wire cutters. They cut through the chain, took him under the arms, helped him to his feet, and lifted a flask full of water to his mouth.

"Drink it, that's it, drink some more," they encouraged him. And then, walking slowly, they carried him upstairs.

In the meantime, Ferrara and the Americans had arrived.

"But that's Alfredo Prestipino!" Detective Bernardi cried, astonished at how much older the man seemed compared with when he had met him in New York, only a few days earlier.

They all looked at Prestipino.

Only Antonio Russo was looking away. His eyes, as sharp as the blade of a sword, were fixed on Ferrara. Ferrara, in his turn, was studying Russo with mounting curiosity. For a moment he saw a flash of something in his eyes. It was not fear. It was something else, something he didn't like at all. Then he looked at the wall behind Russo and recognised the sacred image hanging there as the Madonna of Aspromonte, with a crown on her head and the Christ child in her arms.

Antonio Russo was as still as a statue. He seemed to have lost the power of speech.

"Take them to our offices in Reggio Calabria," Trimarchi ordered. "And you," he added, turning to some of his colleagues, "let forensics do their work, then conduct a thorough search. I want this place

287

turned inside out. And don't forget to look in all the other rooms."

The DIA men sprang into action.

"No, not Prestipino," Trimarchi said, as one of his men was about to take him away. "He stays here. He'll come with us."

Antonio Russo seemed to snap out of his trance. "You can't —"

"Here's the search warrant," Trimarchi said, taking it from his pocket and waving it in front of Russo's eyes. "It's signed by the chief prosecutor and one of his deputies."

Russo gave a dismissive toss of his head.

"In any case, we've caught you red-handed in the commission of a crime. Or rather, several crimes. Criminal conspiracy, kidnapping, aiding and abetting a fugitive, illegal possession of firearms, and that's not all . . . You'll also have to explain what you're doing with that gadget in the briefcase. Given such a long list of offences, we wouldn't even need a search warrant."

"I want my lawyer," Russo said.

"We can't wait for him. We'll inform him, but we'll start the search anyway. The operation is already under way. What's your lawyer's name?"

When Russo told Trimarchi the name, he smiled. He should have guessed it: she was a young woman from a nearby village, who, in spite of her youth, had been making a name for herself by defending important local Mafiosi.

"You're biting off more than you can chew!" Antonio Russo hissed threateningly. "You don't know what you're doing!"

"Oh, don't worry about me," Trimarchi replied, giving him an eloquent look that brooked no objection.

Russo fell silent. He was starting to feel like a lion in a cage. The colonel, Ferrara and the Americans left the bunker, while Carracci elected to stay with Bruni. He would follow the whole operation. When he was alone, he took possession of the briefcase. Perhaps it was only curiosity.

Out in the open air again, Ferrara took a deep breath. He had felt suffocated inside the bunker. Before getting into his car, he savoured the intense scent of bergamot in the air, a scent that reawakened old memories. The first phase of Operation Orange Blossom had been brought to a successful conclusion. He felt proud and even moved. That was something that had not happened to him since he had left the *Squadra Mobile* in Florence.

Some of the officers, walking the arrested men to the cars, were suddenly hit by a violent gust of wind. Their voices, whether thin or robust, were immediately wiped out, blown away like leaves, like talcum powder, like confetti.

They were in a hurry now to get back home.

PART FOUR

THE HEART OF ASPROMONTE

CHAPTER
TWENTY-SIX

The autostrada was almost deserted at this hour.

It was four o'clock on Sunday morning.

The police cars, speeding along through tunnels and over viaducts, reached the DIA centre in just over an hour. The arrested men were immediately led into separate rooms and each man was handcuffed by the wrist to a chair. A couple of officers remained in each room to guard them. Other officers began cataloguing the material confiscated so far and writing up their reports. They were all on a high; going home to rest was out of the question. In the meantime, in the monitoring room, other staff were waiting for the phones to ring, hoping they would catch a comment on the police operation in conversations between relatives of the arrested men. Colonel Trimarchi remembered that Prosecutor Romeo, when granting the search warrant, had asked that he be informed how things had gone, at whatever hour, so he had no qualms about phoning him now.

"I'll drop by and see you later," Romeo said, quite unfazed by the early-morning call. "And congratulations, Colonel! To you and your men! It was a fine operation. We've been looking for Ferrante for years. He has quite a few murders to answer for."

"We were lucky," Trimarchi replied.

"Sometimes we have to make our luck. As you did."

The colonel had just put down the phone when an officer burst into the room, his face beaming.

"Sir, Alfredo Prestipino wants to talk to you," the officer said, standing to attention in front of the desk.

"I'll see him as soon as I can. Has the police doctor checked him over?"

"Yes, sir."

"How did he find him?"

"In reasonable condition. His eyesight's a little affected, but that's understandable. The doctor's assured us he doesn't need to be hospitalised."

"It's better that way." The colonel exchanged knowing glances with Ferrara and the Americans, then said, "Tell him I'll be able to see him soon. In the meantime, don't leave him alone. Not even for a moment."

"Of course, sir. We've been with him all the time. Even when the doctor came."

"Good."

"He seems very down," the officer said. "For a moment I think I even saw tears in his eyes."

"Tell him we'll be calling him in a while," the colonel repeated.

He was about to turn to his American colleagues when the phone rang. He picked it up. It was Russo's lawyer. *Here it comes*, Trimarchi thought. He'd been expecting this call.

"I'd like to know if my client, Antonio Russo, is there with you. And if he is, I'd like to know the reason why."

"Yes, he's here," Trimarchi replied brusquely. "And he's under arrest."

"May I know the reason?"

"Criminal conspiracy, among other things."

"Other things? What other things?"

"I can't tell you that at the moment. The operation is still in progress."

"But my client is unwell. I'd like to see him to make sure that he's all right."

Trimarchi did not even wonder how the lawyer had found out about the arrest: he knew these people always found ways of sending messages.

"I'm afraid you can't see him now. But your client is well. If he needs to be taken care of, we'll see to it. Don't worry about that."

"Can I at least see him for a moment?"

"No. Any interviews need authorisation from the prosecutor. You know the law! I'll be in touch when the time comes." He slammed down the receiver angrily, then picked it up again and ordered the switchboard operator, "Please don't put through any more phone calls from lawyers. Tell them there's no one in the office."

He entered.

There was a sad, pained expression in his hollow eyes as they stared straight ahead, and deep furrows lined his cheeks. He was stooped, as if carrying the whole world on his shoulders, and so restless that he could

295

not stay still for one moment. He was even biting his lips.

"Do you feel ill, Signor Prestipino?" Trimarchi asked. "Don't worry about a thing. Please, just sit down."

Prestipino slowly lowered himself on to one of the two chairs facing the desk. He rested his hands in his lap and peered at the man sitting on the other chair.

Trimarchi introduced himself. "I'm the director of this operations centre. You already saw me at the farmhouse. And that gentleman sitting next to you is Chief Superintendent Michele Ferrara, who's come here from Rome. Now, you asked to speak to me?"

Prestipino looked at both of them in silence for a moment or two, moving his eyes from one to the other. Then he started drumming his fingers on his trouser legs. He appeared confused, unsure how to react to a difficult situation. He moved his head slightly, as if his mind was elsewhere.

"Yes, Colonel," he said at last, in a weak voice. He seemed to be trying to focus. Beneath his raised eyebrows, a gleam came into his eyes.

There was a moment's pause.

"We're listening," Trimarchi resumed. "Just go ahead."

"I recognised the detective from New York. He's from the 17th precinct in Manhattan."

"Yes, that's right."

Silence fell in the room.

"I've decided . . ." Prestipino said, but immediately broke off. He sat there motionless. In the strip lighting, his face appeared haggard and irresolute.

"Go on. What have you decided?"

"Is this interview being recorded?" he asked, controlling his voice with difficulty.

"No."

Another pause.

"The thing is, Colonel, I have something to tell you . . ."

"Go ahead then. We're listening . . ."

"First, though . . ." He broke off again, looked down at his legs and sneezed so hard that he bent double, almost touching his knees with his chest.

"Yes? First . . .? Come on now, Prestipino. Speak up!"

"First I'd like some assurances."

"What kind of assurances?"

Now he was looking Trimarchi straight in the eye. He opened his arms wide and said in a changed tone, "I want you to do something for me and my family, especially for my daughter."

"Do you think the information you have is so important?"

"Yes."

"That's just your opinion."

"Yes, it's my opinion, Colonel, but that's how it is. Anyway, I'm sure you'll be able to judge it for yourself. You have ways of checking. You saw the state I was in, and where they were keeping me, didn't you?" There was a mixture of pain and anger in his eyes.

Lips pursed, Trimarchi seemed to reflect for a moment. "What kind of assurances do you need?" he asked, and with a brief nod motioned him to continue.

Prestipino kept looking from Trimarchi to Ferrara and back again. After another pause, he said, "I'm in a lot of danger, and so are my wife and daughter. Anything can happen to me once I leave here, once I tell you what I'm going to tell you."

"Perhaps I haven't made myself clear," Trimarchi replied, somewhat irritably. "Before you can leave here, provided the prosecutor authorises it, you will have to be interviewed formally. You will have to explain what happened to you, why you were kidnapped. Because it was a kidnapping, wasn't it?"

"Yes, I was kidnapped," Prestipino replied in a thin voice, shaking his head slightly. "Are you planning to charge me?"

"If you don't tell us the truth, you may be liable to the charge of aiding and abetting a crime. And if that's the case, you could go to prison. Do you understand what I'm saying? It's an offence that carries a sentence of up to four years. And there are aggravating circumstances."

"No, not prison! I'd be in even more danger there. They'd kill me for sure. And what about my daughter? No, I don't even want to think about it."

He ran his hand through his sparse hair, which had turned greyer than before, and slowly rubbed his forehead. His eyes filled with tears. Genuine tears. They ran down his face.

"Come on, Prestipino, there's no need for that," Trimarchi said. "Just tell us what kind of information you have."

"It's about New York . . . My brother-in-law Rocco . . . But first you have to give me assurances."

"Listen, Prestipino," Ferrara said, intervening for the first time, "we may need to bring in Detective Bernardi. He's the police officer you recognised from the 17th precinct. What do you say to that?"

"That's OK by me, but I want assurances," he insisted. "I won't talk until I get them."

Ferrara left the room.

Lost in thought, Prestipino waited for Bernardi.

Ferrara returned after a few minutes, followed by Bernardi and Bob Holley. He had found them in another office, taking a closer look at the confiscated weapons, and had brought them up to date as they walked along the corridor.

Both men greeted Prestipino as they entered the room. He returned their greeting, and asked Bernardi if he remembered him.

"Of course I do. You're Rocco Fedeli's brother-in-law. We met that morning . . . on the nineteenth floor . . . and then later in the precinct house."

Prestipino nodded.

"Just tell us what you know," Bob Holley said, trying to be reassuring. "I may be able to talk to my superiors, including the Assistant Director of the FBI."

With a grave expression on his face, Prestipino weighed this up in silence, then said, "Thank you, but it's what happens afterwards that worries me. I'd like to talk to my wife and my daughter Maria."

"You can't do that now," Trimarchi said, his voice rising an octave. "You're in custody and, as I said, we may end up charging you. It depends on you." He glanced at Ferrara, who was listening impatiently.

"No, don't charge me, Colonel! That would be the end of me and my family!" With his hand, he wiped away the sweat that continued to pour down his forehead.

"There's only one other option," Trimarchi said. "We're being as open with you as we can."

"The colonel is referring to the witness protection programme," Ferrara said.

"I want to talk to my wife. I'd like to have a new life, I really would, but my wife needs to know. She hasn't had any news of me for days. And the evening before . . ." He broke off, his voice cracking. He felt a knot in his throat.

"What's the matter?" Ferrara asked.

"Nothing. I just need a glass of water."

There was a brief pause.

"What were you saying?" Ferrara asked when the interview resumed.

"Nothing, Chief Superintendent. The evening before they took me away, I quarrelled with my wife. That's all. The usual family quarrel. It may be that Angela thought I deliberately went away to do something stupid. You understand what I'm saying?"

"Of course!"

Prestipino threw a glance at Detective Bernardi, as if he expected him to intervene.

"We're in Italy now, Mr Prestipino," Holley said. "We have to abide by Italian law."

Prestipino put his right elbow on the armrest of his chair and moved his hand over his forehead. He seemed to be thinking hard.

"I'm sure, though, Mr Prestipino, that if your information is useful, Italian law could also help you, but first we have to know what it is."

"But I want to leave Italy and . . ."

"And?"

"And I don't want to go back to New York."

"Why?"

"Because I'd be in danger there, too."

Silence fell again in the room.

Ferrara and Trimarchi exchanged a series of glances with the Americans, but said nothing. Alfredo Prestipino had not moved. With a sigh, he said, "I'd like to trust you."

At that moment there was a knock at the door. Captain Foti put his head inside.

Trimarchi nodded, stood up and left the room.

In a quiet corner of the corridor, Foti walked right up to the colonel, almost touching him.

Anyone seeing them would have thought they were conspirators.

"What is it, Foti?" Trimarchi asked. "Has something happened?"

"Sir," the captain said gravely, "we left the briefcase with the cloned satellite phone in the farmhouse. I thought one of my men was going to bring it. But —"

"Don't tell me it's lost. I know the men were all keyed up."

"No, sir, I telephoned them. Carracci has the briefcase."

"Then what's the problem?"

"I spoke to Carracci and asked him to send it here with a driver."

"Well?" Trimarchi's face clouded over. He was getting impatient, and could not wait to get back to his office.

"Carracci wouldn't see reason, sir. He told me he has it and will bring it himself when the operation is over. You should have heard the way he spoke to me . . ."

"What do you mean?"

"It was as if it was his property. Something that's his by right. You see what I'm saying?"

"All right, Foti, let's wait for Carracci to get here. In the meantime I'll tell Ferrara."

"Can I be perfectly honest with you, sir?"

"Of course, go ahead!"

"I don't like this Carracci. I haven't liked him since the first time I met him. He's behaved as if he wanted to slow down the investigation. I don't know how to say this, sir, but . . ."

"Come on, out with it!"

"I just hope we find the memory on that phone intact. You know what I'm saying?"

"I know, Foti, but we must be patient. The police, especially the higher-ups, don't always think like us. Never mind. We're still loyal!"

Foti nodded. "That's why I'm in the Carabinieri, sir."

"Now go back to your men," Trimarchi said, patting him on the shoulder.

He stood there, puzzled, watching Foti as he walked away.

"Where should I start?" Prestipino asked. "With last night, or with New York?"

He seemed to have finally calmed down a little. Even his posture had changed, and he was no longer sitting with his shoulders stooped.

"Let's start with New York," Ferrara suggested, looking first at him, then at Bernardi, who nodded. "Tell us everything from the beginning. Take it slowly."

"It isn't easy for me, but I'll try . . . Anyway, I don't have any other options, I realise that now."

"It's a step you have to take. For you and for your family, and we know how much you care about them."

"Yes, I do. They're my whole life. Especially my daughter. She's a student, you know. She's studying law."

"Carry on."

"It was my cousin who had my brother-in-law Rocco killed."

These words, uttered without the slightest hesitation, created a kind of electricity in the room.

"Who is your cousin?" Ferrara asked.

"He lives in New York. He's the son of my father's sister."

His forehead was now drenched in sweat again, and he wiped it with his handkerchief.

"What's your cousin's name?" Trimarchi asked, breaking a silence that was becoming unbearable.

"His name is Luigi."

"Luigi what?"

"Luigi Cannizzaro."

"How old is he?"

"Older than me. There's more than five years between us."

"Where was he born?"

"New York. His parents have been living there since the fifties."

"Who's his father?"

"Rocco Cannizzaro."

"Where in New York do they live?"

"In Brooklyn."

Bernardi was taking notes in his ubiquitous notebook.

"Go on," Ferrara prompted.

Silence.

"Tell us why your brother-in-law was killed," Trimarchi said. He didn't want the interview, off the record as it was, to fizzle out.

This was the key question.

"He was killed because he betrayed the code," Prestipino replied without hesitation.

"What code?"

"The code of the 'Ndrangheta. A code these people — these Americans — don't know anything about. The same code I'm betraying now, though for other reasons. I'm betraying the ties of blood which bind us, which keep our families together."

304

The two Americans looked at Ferrara. It was the first time they had heard about the code of the 'Ndrangheta, or about a betrayal of the ties of blood in the Calabrian families, and they hadn't the slightest idea what the man was talking about. Ferrara shook his head slightly. He tried to urge him on, asking him what betrayal he was talking about. There was silence again. Then Ferrara and Trimarchi, speaking over each other, said "Tell us! We'll understand! Tell us everything."

"It isn't easy."

"We know, but now that you've started, you have to continue!"

"But these two wouldn't understand." He gestured towards the Americans. "To Americans, the 'Ndrangheta is a whole new world. They haven't discovered it yet. In the family, no betrayal can go unpunished. Sooner or later, they take their revenge."

At this point Prestipino lowered his eyes. He seemed to be thinking. He, too, was breaking rule number one, the law of silence. His own betrayal would not go unpunished. The 'Ndrangheta would make him pay. And, if they couldn't get to him, they would take their revenge by striking at his nearest and dearest, killing some family member or relative, maybe years later. From this time on, he would be a hunted man, with pursuers always at his heels.

Ferrara guessed what terrifying images were passing through Prestipino's mind. He tried to encourage him. "But this isn't a whole new world to us. We know it well. *I* know it well."

"I know that, Chief Superintendent," Prestipino said, looking Ferrara in the eye.

"Tell us, then!"

Prestipino drank a little water before continuing.

"My brother-in-law was a member . . ." He told them something about the life of Rocco Fedeli.

"And why were you at Russo's last night?" Ferrara asked. "Why were you being held like that?"

"Because Antonio Russo wanted some information from me."

"What information?"

"About what happened in New York and . . ."

"And what?"

". . . and what happened to the three million dollars."

Ferrara, Trimarchi and the Americans looked at each other. They had seen this figure quoted in the first memo they had received from Dick Moore. In the light of what they were now hearing, it seemed that Moore's informant was a reliable source. Prestipino's quoting of the same figure suggested that his testimony, too, was reliable, at least on this point.

"All right, Prestipino," Trimarchi said after a pause. "I'll inform the prosecutor and we'll see what we can do. Are you ready to repeat all this, and everything else, to him?"

Alfredo Prestipino nodded his head slightly.

"Say yes or no."

"Yes, if you give me the guarantees. Especially now that I've spoken. I'm done for in this place. I only hope

I can get understanding from my family, especially my daughter."

"All right. I'm going to have you taken into the other room. We'll resume as soon as possible." He called an officer.

By now it was almost eight in the morning.

When Diego woke up, the light of a new day was already filtering through the crevices in the stones.

He had slept all through the night. He looked around and saw that the wood stove in the corner of the shack was still lit. He felt better — he no longer had that awful cough from the day before — although his legs were aching from his misadventures in the mountains. At that moment, one of his kidnappers came in, hooded as usual, with an old wooden bowl in his hand, like those used by shepherds, and held it out.

"Here. Drink this. It's fresh goat's milk. It'll do you good."

Diego took the bowl and lifted it to his lips. He drank the milk in two long gulps, letting a few drops fall on the mattress.

"Thanks," he said.

"I'll bring you something to eat later."

"Thanks," he said again.

The kidnapper went out. In the brief time before the door closed again, Diego caught a fleeting glimpse of trees and vegetation. Then he began to hear noises which he had never heard in the other refuge. He realised he was in a different area. He heard car horns hooting, the rumble of engines, the cries of shepherds.

Then a man's voice saying through a megaphone, "Roll up, roll up, everyone roll up . . ." That was all, but the noises and the voice cheered him, and he felt a new energy coursing through his veins. A few minutes later, he even heard a church bell tolling, heard it loud and clear.

He adjusted the windbreaker he was using as a pillow. Being warm and snug made it easier to bear misfortune, he told himself.

He closed his eyes and went back to sleep.

CHAPTER
TWENTY-SEVEN

Corso Garibaldi has always been the heart of Reggio Calabria.

A semi-pedestrian zone, it livens up for a few hours in the afternoon when it becomes a meeting place where people — especially teenagers and pensioners — come to stroll and chat.

Here, in the central bar, Colonel Trimarchi and the Americans were sipping hot coffee, while Ferrara savoured a lemon *granita* and a soft brioche.

It had been a particularly long and exhausting night, and one full of surprises. Now they were taking advantage of the break to get some fresh air, have something to eat and drink, and compare notes.

"The thing is," Ferrara was saying to Bob Holley, "we're dealing with a world where no one talks, and anyone who does knows what's in store for him. A man of honour is someone who keeps quiet. You understand what I mean?"

"Yes, of course, but who's actually in charge?"

"Well, that would take a long time to explain. And it might be better somewhere else rather than here. The thing to remember is that the 'Ndrangheta is like a parallel society, with interests everywhere, but it rarely shows its face. That way, it stays a myth. And the thing they most appreciate is *not* asking questions." He looked around, hoping that no one had heard them.

As soon as they got back to the office, Trimarchi said, "It seems to me, gentlemen, that everything is coming together. I think we're soon going to see some concrete results."

They sat down in the lounge.

"I think Prestipino told the truth about the money," Ferrara said. "He also gave us his cousin's name."

Bernardi said he would inform Lieutenant Reynolds. Hampton echoed him with "And I'll inform Assistant Director Moore."

"I'd do that immediately, if I were you," Trimarchi said. "And from your end, maybe we could get something more about Luigi Cannizzaro and his parents."

"Of course," Bernardi and Hampton said in unison.

"Good. In the meantime, we'll see what we can find out about Alfredo Prestipino's father's family."

The others nodded, their heads tilted, their eyes half closed.

The wild-goose chase was now a distant memory.

New York

Almost simultaneously, phones rang in the homes of Dick Moore and John Reynolds.

Both were brought up to date on developments, down to the last detail.

310

Then they called each other and arranged to meet at FBI headquarters.

For the first time since they had begun investigating this case, they were galvanised. They could well be close to finding the crucial piece of the puzzle.

There was another reason why Reynolds was in seventh heaven. The previous evening, his daughter had told him that he was going to be a grandfather.

A grandfather! He smiled. He couldn't believe it.

The interview began at 10.30a.m.

Prosecutor Francesco Romeo, a short, plump, white-haired man close to retiring age, chose not to have Prestipino moved to the Prosecutor's Department, preferring instead to interview him in the DIA offices. It provided him with an opportunity to personally congratulate not only the colonel but all the men who had taken part on the success of the operation.

Now he was in the monitoring room, and sitting facing him on the other side of the desk was Alfredo Prestipino, who appeared suddenly rejuvenated.

"Is everything all right, Signor Prestipino?" Romeo asked with a forced smile, peering over the glasses resting on the bridge of his nose.

"Yes, I'm fine."

"I'm Prosecutor Francesco Romeo," he introduced himself.

"They told me you would come. Thank you."

"There's no need to thank me. I'm only doing my duty."

Then he turned to the technician sitting beside the desk and asked him if everything was set for the recording. Having received confirmation, he took a few sheets of blank paper from the printer, to use for making notes.

The interview began.

"So, Signor Prestipino, before anything else please bear in mind that you are being heard as a witness, not as a defendant. My office has no legal proceedings against you, and has been informed that you have information on the murder of your brother-in-law Rocco Fedeli and on the 'ndrina of San Piero d'Aspromonte. Is that correct?"

"Yes."

"Good. Let's start with the 'ndrina of San Piero, which is of more immediate concern to my office, being within our jurisdiction."

"You can ask me whatever you like."

"Was your brother-in-law a member?"

"Yes, he was a member of Don Ciccio Puglisi's 'ndrina."

"When did he become a member?"

"When he turned eighteen, he was baptised and became a foot soldier."

"I see. Can you explain what this baptism consisted of?"

"It happened during the feast of the Madonna of Aspromonte, you know . . . when all the 'Ndranghetistas meet. Rocco took an oath of loyalty and was baptised by the boss in person, Don Ciccio Puglisi . . . and from then on, he kept faith with that blood oath until . . ."

"Until what?"

"Until he violated the family's code of conduct."

"Could you please be more specific about that? *I* understand you, Signor Prestipino, but you must tell us more."

"My brother-in-law changed sides. He betrayed us . . . And he also took the money . . . To him, you see, money was everything in life. It was the only thing he cared about. Maybe it was the only thing he'd ever cared about."

"Can you explain about the betrayal and about the money?"

"I'd have to tell you about New York."

"Then tell us about New York."

There was a long pause.

"Would you like us to stop for a few minutes?"

"Thank you. I'd like a glass of water."

At this point Romeo turned to the technician and dictated,

"Let it be noted that at ten past eleven the interview was interrupted at the request of the witness and will be resumed in ten minutes."

The technician switched off the tape recorder.

"Signor Prestipino, I'm going to stretch my legs a little. In the meantime I'll have them bring you a bottle of water."

"Thank you."

"Would you like a coffee, too?"

"If possible . . . Thank you."

Romeo left the room.

He came back after ten minutes.

"Do you feel better now, Signor Prestipino?" he asked, sitting down behind the desk.

"Yes, thanks again." He gave a slight smile.

"Good. Then let's continue the recording." The technician nodded and pressed the *Play* button. "Let it be noted that it is now eleven twenty and the interview is resuming, in the presence of the same people . . . Now, tell us about New York."

"The real target was Rocco. My other in-laws and the other victims were killed because they were there, but also to send an even stronger message to all the members and avoid further betrayals."

"In what way had your brother-in-law betrayed the organisation, to be punished so harshly?"

"He had gone over to Antonio Russo. They were involved in the cocaine trade together. Rocco was using not only Russo's money, but his family's as well . . . All those dollars had gone to his head, Signor Romeo . . . America isn't like San Piero . . ." He shrugged his shoulders.

Romeo nodded, and gestured to him to continue.

"The next day, the morning of the New York marathon, Rocco was supposed to make a payment of three million dollars to a boss of the Cali cartel for a consignment of drugs, but the killers grabbed the money . . ." He lowered his eyes to his legs.

"Where did he keep the money?"

"In the safe in his den."

"How did the killers open it?"

Antonio Prestipino again looked down at his legs and crossed his hands nervously. He seemed hesitant, uncertain how to continue. Then, slowly raising his head, he let out a deep sigh and said, "It isn't easy to talk about certain things, Signor Romeo."

"Why?"

"I was the one who gave up the combination."

"Who to?"

"My cousin Luigi Cannizzaro, but I never imagined it would end up in . . . that kind of bloodbath."

He burst out crying.

Romeo made a gesture to reassure him, and dictated, "Let it be noted that the witness appears moved and has burst into tears . . . He can't continue." Then, to Prestipino, he said, "I realise it's a difficult situation for you to come to terms with, but my office needs to know every detail of what happened in New York. Please continue. So, it was you who supplied the combination of the safe?"

"Yes. Yes, it was me."

"Why?"

"I couldn't say no to my cousin."

"Why not?"

"He'd done me a favour, but that has nothing to do with this . . . and I don't want to talk about it."

"All right. Tell me how much money was in the safe."

"Three million."

"Three million dollars?"

"Yes. Three million dollars. And most of it was Antonio Russo's."

"Antonio Russo's? Is that why he had you kidnapped?"

"Yes, he wanted to know what had happened in New York, especially what had happened to his money."

"Did you tell him?"

"No. And if the police hadn't arrived when they did, I wouldn't be here. He'd have killed me."

"Where did Antonio Russo sell the cocaine?"

"That, I don't know. What I can tell you is that, according to Rocco, Antonio Russo controlled the whole cocaine trade not only in Italy, but also in other European countries ... He was a very powerful person ..."

"Did your brother-in-law tell you about any specific thing that Russo did?"

"No, but he told me once that Russo scared even him, and that he had a lot of connections — politicians, senior police officers ..."

"Signor Prestipino, you do realise these are serious allegations?"

"Yes, Signor Romeo, but I'm only telling you what Rocco told me. I don't know if it was true, or whether Russo was just bragging to make Rocco think he was even more powerful than he was."

"So you can't be any more specific. Is that what you're saying?"

"Yes."

"Did you recognise your kidnappers?"

"I was blindfolded. I just heard the voice of the one who questioned me. I assume it was Russo. I'd never heard him speaking before, I only knew him by name."

"I see. Can you tell me how they kidnapped you?"

"They tricked me into going with them after I left the cemetery. They said someone wanted to speak to me."

"Who were they?"

"Two young guys, real heavies."

He described the two young men and the driver of the BMW, even though he had only seen the latter from the back or in profile.

"Would you be able to help us put together an identikit?"

"Of the two young guys, yes. The driver, I'm not so sure."

"Good. It's now twelve thirty. This interview is concluded. The transcript will be signed by the witness and the interviewer."

The technician switched off the tape recorder.

"You're not going to prison, Signor Prestipino, but the DIA will keep you in custody until the Minister of the Interior has come to a decision. Today, I'll present the special commission with a request for urgent measures to be taken to protect yourself and your immediate family."

"Thank you, Signor Romeo, for my family, too . . . My daughter, you know, is studying law. She wants to be a judge in America."

"I'm pleased to hear that, Signor Prestipino."

Romeo signed the transcript, said goodbye and left the room.

A crucial piece had been added to the jigsaw.

New York

It was just after six in the morning, and for some time now Dick Moore and John Reynolds had been discussing the new information received from their colleagues in Calabria.

And something else, too.

The name Luigi Cannizzaro was in FBI records.

It was on the list of names that had come up during the investigation into the Sicilian-owned pizzeria in Brooklyn.

"We need to check him out right now," Dick Moore said, thumping the desk with his fist. "Tap his phones. Keep him under twenty-four-hour surveillance."

He felt jittery.

The man responsible for the murders was right here in New York. And if it hadn't been for the tip-off from Italy, they might never have identified him.

Reynolds lowered his head and rubbed his chin, as usual. "I agree," he said. "We have to find out everything there is to know, including his connections with the Sicilian pizzeria owner and Baker's gang."

They had a long day ahead of them.

Four men were sitting in a circle on large stones, talking.

One was older than the others, and seemed to be their chief.

Inside the shack, Diego, who had just opened his eyes, slowly rubbed them. All at once he had the impression he could hear a chorus of voices. He sat up on the mattress and listened carefully. He was right. There was more than one voice. They were arguing, sometimes heatedly.

He tried to concentrate. Fragments of what they were saying reached his ears.

". . . so much bacon . . ."

"Don Peppe . . . the pile . . . now they're at school . . ."

"Who breathed?"

What language were they speaking? He remembered 'Ntoni and his men talking like that during the long drive from Barcelona. It was the same. Even the rhythm, the tone, seemed identical. "A special language," 'Ntoni had said once. It was the way the 'Ndrangheta expressed themselves, in a jargon known only to them, rich in double meanings and metaphors, a mixture of Italian, Calabrian and Neapolitan dialect with a touch of Sicilian. It was full of allusions and symbols, as befitted a secret society whose rituals were handed down orally from father to son.

Bacon, yes, bacon means the police . . . he told me that.

He listened more carefully. He was starting to get worried. His heart began to pound. He caught another word: *breathed*.

The odd word here and there, difficult to put into context. Of one thing, though, he was certain: these voices weren't fake, unlike those of the kidnappers who had watched over him up until now.

Suddenly, the men fell silent. After a few moments, the door of the shack opened wide.

"What the fuck are you doing? Listening?"

It was one of his kidnappers. The man was really angry. Diego did not reply. But for the first time he tried to look him in the eyes. They were very black and gleamed through the holes in the ski mask. He was even more afraid.

"And don't look at me like that, you Colombian prick! My eyes are dark, just like yours."

Again, Diego did not reply. He felt his blood run cold. The man came to him, checked that the padlock on his ankles was secure, and fixed one side of the chain even more tightly to the hook on the wall to the right of the mattress. Then he went out, slamming the door.

After that, Diego did not hear any more voices.

Meanwhile, Captain Foti had arrived in San Piero d'Aspromonte.

He had already combed through the files in the local Carabinieri barracks to find out something about Rocco Cannizzaro. Now, together with the marshal from the barracks, he was knocking at the door of Angela's house. It was a two-storey building, with a balcony on the first floor just above the front door. The concrete facade was unfinished.

It was early afternoon.

He knocked several times, but there was no answer.

"She'll be at her mother's, Captain," the marshal said.

"Let's go then. Where does she live?"

"Just a few minutes' walk from here."

They set off.

It was a very old stone house surrounded by a small vegetable garden. The marshal rang the bell.

After a few moments, they heard a woman's voice. "Who is it?"

"Carabinieri! This is the marshal. I need to speak to Signora Angela Prestipino."

"Just a minute!"

Moments later, they heard a click and the wooden door opened. They went in.

Angela was waiting for them just inside the door. She was dressed all in black: her skirt, her blouse, her stockings, the woollen shawl over her shoulders. She gave them both a searching, inquisitive look, as if, from the way they were standing, the expressions on their faces, she might glean some idea of the reason for their visit, even before they started speaking.

"Signora," the marshal began, "this is Captain Foti. He's come here from Reggio Calabria. He's with the DIA and needs to speak to you. Can you spare us a few minutes?"

The woman looked at them a while longer, then her eyes narrowed and focused on Foti.

The captain approached and shook hands with her. She had an unusually strong grip for a woman.

"Come in, then," she said, reluctantly.

She led them down a short corridor lined with the odd piece of furniture, at the end of which she opened a door and admitted them to the living room. She motioned them to take a seat and they settled on the sofa, but she remained standing, her arms crossed over her chest. There were no paintings or photographs on the remarkably soulless walls. The only image in the whole room was a photograph displayed on a side table with a lighted candle in front of it, an unframed photograph showing the three brothers who had been killed.

"Who is it, Angela? Who is it?"

The shout had come from the back door that led out to the vegetable garden.

"Nothing, Mother. It's for me. Don't worry." She ran her hand through her hair. "So, Captain, you want a word with me? Is it about my husband?"

"Yes. There's something you need to know."

For a moment, Angela's impassive expression betrayed a touch of emotion. But only a very attentive observer would have noticed the shiver that ran down her spine. "What is it?"

"I've come to tell you that your husband is cooperating with us and with the State Prosecutor's Department."

"Cooperating? What does that mean?" She shrugged her shoulders, but at the same time raised her voice until she was almost shouting. There was a growing anger in her eyes. She stooped to pick up her shawl, which had fallen to the floor, and put it back around her shoulders.

"Last night, we set him free . . ." Foti said.

"Set him free?" she echoed incredulously.

"That's right. He'd been kidnapped. And he decided to cooperate. He's in a safe place. Don't worry. You and your daughter will be safe, too, together with him."

"No, no, no."

A tomblike silence pervaded the room.

For a few moments, the woman continued to stand there, with her arms folded, glaring at the captain, as if trying to burn him to a cinder. What she had feared had happened. The truth she had tried in vain to get from her husband had finally come out. A traitor, that was what her husband was! Her immediate instinct was one of revenge, but she kept it under control for the moment. Never in her worst nightmares could she have imagined that something so horrible could happen to her. To a *Fedeli*.

"Alfredo Prestipino is dead!" she cried.

The words hit the captain like a bullet.

"Signora, your husband is well, and is waiting for you in our offices."

"Captain, you haven't understood! Or are you just pretending not to understand? If what you tell me is true, then Alfredo Prestipino has gone mad. And I have no intention of living with a madman. Mad people should be in asylums, with other mad people. As far as I'm concerned, he's dead. He doesn't exist, not for me, not for my daughter." She had uttered this condemnation in a steady voice, stressing every word.

"But, signora, your husband isn't dead. He wants to make a new life . . . with you. He's made the right choice, believe me. Come with me . . ."

"Really, signora . . ." the marshal said, intervening to support the captain.

But the woman did not give him time to finish his sentence. The blood was boiling in her veins.

"You can go now," she said. "My daughter and I are not moving from here. Captain, tell Signor Prestipino that for us he no longer exists. We have wiped him out of our lives, as of today."

Her eyes had turned ice-cold. Foti tried to say something, but she immediately cut him off.

"I have nothing to add, Captain. Don't make me waste my time. And you shouldn't waste your time either, you must have more important things to do . . ."

"I'll pass on what you said. But I think you're making a mistake."

"It's not for you to judge, Captain. You just have to do your job. There's only one person who has made a mistake here, and it's him . . ." This time she did not even utter the name. Her husband had become *him*. "He no longer exists for us," she said again, with venom in her eyes.

The captain and the marshal looked at each other. Neither of them had expected this reaction. Not even the marshal who, as commander of the local barracks, was familiar with the mindset of the place.

Angela Fedeli saw them to the door.

Hurriedly.

Then the tomblike silence returned.

Angela was quick to react.

She threw on an old woollen jacket and went out.

Almost out of breath.

CHAPTER
TWENTY-EIGHT

She found him in front of the fireplace.

Pavarotti's voice singing "*Nessun dorma*" from *Turandot* filled the room:

> *Ma il mio mistero è chiuso in me,*
> *Il mio nome nessun saprà!*
> *[. . .]*
> *Dilegua, o notte! Tramontate, stelle!*
> *Tramontate, stelle! All'alba vincerò!*
> *Vincerò! Vincerò!*

She saw him take the heavy tongs with both hands and turn over the firewood, his head slightly thrown back to avoid the heat of the flames. All at once, the fire flared up again, spreading a bright glow.

Angela Fedeli remembered her childhood, when her father would hold her on his lap in front of the fire, and she would ask him to turn over the logs with the tongs, almost as a game. She heard again her father's words: *Angela, don't go too close, the fire is deceptive, it's a traitor.*

Don Ciccio Puglisi turned. "Sit down, Angela," he said, motioning to one of the two armchairs in front of

325

the fireplace. He switched off the radio and sat down in the other armchair.

"Don Ciccio . . ."

"Let's have coffee, Angela. It's already made."

"Thank you, Don Ciccio."

"Grazia, you can bring in the coffee now!" he called to his wife. "And bring an extra cup!"

A few minutes later, Grazia appeared from the kitchen. "Oh, look who's here! Angela, I didn't know you were coming at this hour."

"I'm sorry, Signora Grazia, I should have warned you."

"What are you talking about, Angela? Don't worry. This is your home."

"Thank you."

"Now have your coffee, the two of you . . ."

The coffee pot was steaming. For a while, the only sound in the living room was the noise of the spoons stirring the sugar in the cups.

Don Ciccio drank his coffee in one quick gulp, put his cup down on the table, and said, "To what do we owe this visit, Angela?"

Angela Fedeli gave a deep sigh and told him about the visit from the captain and the marshal.

"Don Ciccio, Alfredo Prestipino has turned out to be a rat, an unworthy person. I am in mourning for the second time in a matter of days." Her frame of mind could be read in the expression on her face: shame and scorn for someone who had betrayed the values in which she had always firmly believed. Yes, she, too, despite being a woman, had always had faith in the

326

rules of the family, although, unlike her brother Rocco, she had never taken any formal oath.

They were the laws of life, written in her DNA. They were stronger than any other human feeling, including what she had felt for her husband.

A hallmark of the women of the 'Ndrangheta.

She had always been very aware of the family's activities. She had even shared their plans, their ambitions. In silence. Without expressing herself in public. Not even to her dearest friends. She had grown up steeped in the law of silence, believing that this and the other laws were much more important than those of the State, because they were the privilege of a special society. A society composed of real men. Men of honour, like her father and her brother Rocco.

Don Ciccio glanced for a moment at the flames licking the logs like angry tongues of fire. Then he turned to her and looked her straight in the eye, perhaps trying to instil in her a sense that he would protect her. Finally, in a slightly hoarse but courteous voice, he said, "My child, you have nothing to do with this. You've acted correctly, in the only way a real woman should act. For me, too, Alfredo Prestipino is dead. He made his decision to die alone. In fact, I can tell you this: he no longer exists for anyone in the family. You're still young. You must think of your daughter and your mother, who are your true blood."

She nodded. She would have liked to ask him why he had not paid her a visit, but she didn't. This was not the moment. Now she had to think of the present and, above all, of the future.

"You're right, Don Ciccio. Now I have only my mother and daughter left. And my mother is suffering a great deal. I won't leave her alone. She's still a strong woman, but she can't cope with her grief. She thinks I don't notice, but I see the big tears running down her cheeks. There's no point trying to wipe them away with my handkerchief."

"You have my blessing, my child," Don Ciccio said in a thin voice. "And my esteem."

"I will bear this cross, Don Ciccio. But I am, and will always remain, a Fedeli. I want you to know that. I remember how much you respected my father and also how much he respected you. You were like chips off the same block . . ."

Don Ciccio nodded, a dreamy, faraway look in his eyes.

His expression did not escape her, but she would have found it hard to say whether it was one of sadness or simply nostalgia. She bent forward submissively, took his right hand and placed her lips on it. It was the first time in her life she had done that.

"You will always have my respect, Don Ciccio," she said in a low, tremulous voice, her heart pounding ever harder.

Supporting himself with his stick, Don Ciccio slowly rose from the chair. Angela also stood up. He put his arms around her and held her as tight as if she were his own daughter.

"Angela, you're a real woman," he whispered in her ear.

There was genuine respect in his voice. It made her feel proud.

"Thank you, Don Ciccio. I'll never forget these words of yours. You were like a father to my brother Rocco. A father who knows how to punish when it's right to punish . . ." She paused briefly and again looked the old man straight in the eyes. "And you'll be a father to me, too. In fact, that's how I've always thought of you."

"You can count on me, Angela. Always. As long as I'm alive, and even when I'm dead . . . The family will not abandon you. You should never forget that. Whatever you need, the family will be there. Even when I'm no longer around . . . Forget about the past. Do you understand? The past doesn't count. We are all sinners, but everything depends on how our sins are judged . . . and who they are judged by."

"No, Don Ciccio, don't say that. The Madonna of Aspromonte will continue to protect you, and you will live to be over a hundred. You haven't sinned. I'm a good judge . . . My heart is a good judge and it's never betrayed me."

The old man gave a slight smile, revealing his meagre, yellowed teeth, and walked her to the door. Angela Fedeli left, looking tired and nervous. The worst fate in the world had struck her, worse even than death: the fact that she had lived for so many years with a rat. Her anger was growing, and her hate, until all that was left was hate, hate pure and simple.

She knew that Don Ciccio was the only man with the power of life and death over not only his members, but also their families. Had she managed to convince him to spare her life and the lives of her mother and Maria? She kept asking herself that question all the way home. She simply did not know. The one thing she did know was that she would have liked to kill Alfredo Prestipino with her own bare hands.

In her mind's eye, she saw his body, riddled with knife wounds, exposed in the middle of the main square of San Piero.

Grazia had the reputation of being a good observer.

She had only had to read Angela's body language when she brought her coffee to know the real reason for her visit. She had left the door of the kitchen ajar, to hear if Angela let anything slip that would confirm her first impression. As soon as the door closed behind Angela, Grazia went to a corner of the kitchen.

Here, in a little niche, there was a statue of the Madonna of Aspromonte. On a shelf in front of it, a vase of fresh flowers. She had picked them from the garden that morning. Every day, after getting up, she went through the same ritual: taking out the old flowers, changing the water, putting fresh flowers in, praying for the health of herself and her husband, and for other things, too . . .

She knelt, crossed herself, and remained in that position for a long time, looking fixedly at the statue. It was so perfect that it seemed real. Then she started to pray.

"My husband always did everything he could for him, and this was the reward. We hope that you, Oh Madonna, will punish him." She crossed herself again.

Then she recited the *Mea culpa*.

He had come back to the fireplace.

As the fire began crackling again, Don Ciccio Puglisi collapsed into his chair.

He closed his eyes.

And the past came back.

The shrine of the Madonna of Aspromonte, September 1981. It was a special occasion — the centenary of the solemn coronation of the Madonna — which meant that even more pilgrims had come there than in previous years. They had come not only from every part of Calabria, but also from abroad, from across the seas: Australia, America.

The meeting was held around a large tree stump in a wood as dense and dark as night, just a few hundred yards from the shrine.

Meanwhile, the pilgrims were enjoying themselves, some in the makeshift taverns under the age-old chestnut trees, some dancing in the open air to the sound of reed pipes and tambourines, some singing hymns to the Blessed Virgin . . .

As they did every year.

Rocco Fedeli, who had just turned eighteen, was in the middle of a circle formed by six men.

"Above and beyond family, parents, brothers and sisters," Don Ciccio uttered in a solemn tone, "there is the honour of the society which will be your family. But if you betray that honour, you will be punished with death. Just as you will be loyal to the society, so the society will be loyal to you and will help you in case of need. The vow you are about to make can be broken only by death. Are you ready?"

"Yes."

"Then swear."

"I swear in front of the society to be loyal to my comrades and to renounce my father, my mother, my sisters and brothers and, if necessary, even my own blood. If I should ever betray this honour, my flesh will burn, as this image is burning . . ."

The image in flames was the sacred one of Saint Michael the archangel.

"Now you are part of the family. From this moment on, you must not look at the wives of our friends, you must not establish any kind of friendship or, worse still, kinship with the police, you must always be willing to help . . ."

"I'll never forget this, Don Ciccio." There was genuine emotion in his voice.

"Come to me!"

Don Ciccio took him in his arms and hugged him. He kissed him four times, twice on each cheek. Rocco, in turn, starting from his left, embraced the other men and kissed each one twice.

This was the final part of the ceremony.

Rocco Fedeli had become a foot soldier, the first step on the Mafia ladder. A man of honour. Like his father and grandfather before him. Respected and feared.

The ringing of the telephone brought him back to the present.

He saw that the flames in the fire were again dying. He stood up slowly, leaning on his stick and the armrest of his chair. He took a log from the basket, and put it on the fire with the tongs. Then he covered it with smaller logs and poked the embers.

The fire suddenly flared up again.

It was a difficult decision to make.

Angela Fedeli's reaction had caught them off guard.

There were two options: to inform Alfredo Prestipino immediately, or to wait. It was nine in the evening, and they were still discussing the matter in the colonel's office.

"Maybe we could try again," Trimarchi suggested, in a disheartened tone.

I'm not going back, Foti thought. *Only if I'm ordered to . . . I'm still a soldier . . .*

Ferrara agreed with Trimarchi.

"I'll go myself, first thing tomorrow morning," the colonel suggested.

"I really think it's worth trying again," Ferrara said.

Thank God for that, Foti thought, and his face relaxed. "But what are we going to tell the husband?" he asked.

"I'll speak to him," Ferrara replied. "I'll tell him we're waiting for the go-ahead from Rome and that the whole procedure takes time."

"He's sure to ask about his wife," Foti replied.

"I'll tell him one of us is going to see her tomorrow morning."

The others agreed.

"Good," Trimarchi said. "Now, Foti, tell us what you found out about Rocco Cannizzaro."

Foti, relieved that he would not have to go and see Angela Fedeli again, presented the information he had gathered.

Rocco Cannizzaro was born in Bovalino on 2 January 1921. According to the records, he had emigrated to the United States on 21 May 1955. In 1940 he had married Serafina Prestipino, and the following year they had had a daughter named Elisabetta, who had died when she was just four years old. Luigi, their only son, had been born in New York in 1956. Serafina Prestipino was one of the sisters of Alfredo Prestipino's father, Carmelo, who had died with his wife in a road accident. Before emigrating, Rocco Cannizzaro had been suspected of the murder of a cattle farmer — revenge after he had stolen two cows. There were many crimes connected with cattle rustling in the fifties, but in this case there had not been sufficient evidence to put Cannizzaro on trial.

"Good," Trimarchi said. "We'll send a copy to Assistant Director Moore in New York. It's corroboration for them, too."

Whether because they were busy trying to find a solution to the problem or simply because they were tired, no one took any notice of the fact that Stefano Carracci was absent. Carracci had got back to the DIA late in the afternoon, and was in another room,

334

watching as officers inventoried all the material confiscated from the farmhouse: diaries, accounts, company records, documents relating to competitive tenders — some in the public health sector — travel tickets, and so on.

There were dozens of boxes full of these things.

That evening, Alfredo Prestipino reacted to Ferrara's words with bewilderment.

The chief superintendent had gone to see him in the one-room apartment he had been assigned in the wing of the DIA building set aside for the temporary custody of those who had turned State's evidence. Meanwhile, the arrested men had been transferred to prison, some in Reggio Calabria and some in Palmi.

"If my wife and daughter don't come with me, Chief Superintendent," Prestipino said, his resolute tone belying the frightened look in his eyes, "then this is all over. I'll retract everything, and you can tell the prosecutor that right now."

"There's no need to do that. You'll see, it'll all be sorted soon. You just have to be patient."

But Alfredo Prestipino had stopped listening.

Diego did not get any more visits that day.

His kidnappers had not brought him anything since the goat's milk. And he had not heard any more voices. His only companion now was the occasional toot of a car horn, and, depending on the wind direction, the distant sound of little bells as the flock descended slowly towards the stream. Sometimes, he also heard the cries of a shepherd. He felt weak and his head hurt. But the idea was starting to grow in his mind that something serious had happened. The word *bacon* kept coming back to him.

He was starting to feel anxious again.

They've gone away and left me alone, here on these mountains . . . I'll never be found . . . I'll die here . . . Alone like a dog . . . Or worse . . . That fucking 'Ntoni. To hell with him and all his men . . . To hell with him.

It was an absurd situation and, the more he thought about it, the more he realised that there was only one way out.

He couldn't wait.

It was a question of survival. He had to get away from here, and soon.

Luigi Cannizzaro lived in Bensonhurst, Brooklyn, north of Coney Island.

It was a neighbourhood with a large Italian community, and there was a lively Italian feel to the delicatessens, restaurants and cafés on the main thoroughfare, 86th Street.

His apartment was on the first floor of a small building with a pink front. The entrance was on a corner, between an electrical appliance store and a restaurant called Il Giardino. In front of it, a small parking area. Cannizzaro lived there with his elderly parents.

The Feds patrolled the area several times — they knew its reputation as a hotbed for extortion, prostitution and drugs — then set up their surveillance. They parked a van with sliding doors and blacked-out windows between two cars. On both sides, in dark green paint, it bore the logo of an electrical equipment company. Inside, two agents kept their eyes peeled on the entrance and the sidewalks. Simultaneously, two vagrants settled down outside the front door, as if to beg for coins. They were wearing creased shirts under dirty jackets torn in several places. On their feet they wore very old shoes, open at the tips, and they carried plastic bags full of scraps and old newspapers. They were to keep a lookout for Luigi Cannizzaro. They had memorised his photograph, the one on his passport, which had been issued only a few months earlier.

The plan also provided for a couple of unmarked police cars to watch over the area. To communicate between themselves, they used portable radios on an encrypted channel.

Special Agent Mary Cook was coordinating the various teams.

Even before the beginning of the surveillance, they had started tapping the suspect's telephones, both landlines and cellphones. In the last of Luigi Cannizzaro's conversations recorded to date, he had called his mother to tell her that he would soon be home for dinner.

The vagrants were on the alert.

At FBI headquarters, Dick Moore and John Reynolds were again discussing the latest developments from Italy.

I knew there was something about her! Reynolds thought, remembering Angela Fedeli sitting opposite him during the interview on 2 November.

"We should inform the Assistant DA," Dick Moore suggested after a while.

"I agree," Reynolds replied. "As soon as possible, I'd say."

"Maybe it's time we put in an official request for the results of Operation Orange Blossom, especially a transcript of Alfredo Prestipino's statement."

"Sure, that could be very useful."

"And there's another reason we should involve the DA's office."

"What's that?"

"They could take steps to have Alfredo Prestipino sent back over here."

Reynolds nodded. "I think that would be a good idea."

He stood up and went out. He was in a hurry. He'd arranged to meet his wife at a restaurant called Salute on Madison Avenue.

Moore lifted the receiver and dialled Ted Morrison's cellphone number.

I have to do it! I have to . . .

Diego was trying to saw through a link in the chain.

He was rubbing it with the stone his kidnapper had left him for lighting matches, which was quite sharp at the sides. At first, he was not sure he would manage it, but then, as he went on, he realised that he had made some progress.

338

Yes, I have to do it. And I will do it . . .
He continued to rub determinedly.
I can't stop now . . . I'll do it . . . It's now or never!

CHAPTER
TWENTY-NINE

Monday, 17 November

GIUSEPPE FERRANTE, ON THE RUN
SINCE 1991, CAPTURED.
BOSS SURPRISED IN FARMHOUSE DURING
COMBINED OPERATION BY DIA AND FBI.

On the front page of Monday's edition of the daily paper *La Gazzetta del Sud*, a six-column headline announced the outcome of Operation Orange Blossom.

In the early hours of Sunday morning, DIA and FBI agents interrupted a summit meeting being held in a farmhouse belonging to the entrepreneur Antonio Russo. The biggest surprise awaiting them was the discovery of the Scarlet Pimpernel of Calabria, Giuseppe Ferrante, known as Don Peppino.

Don Peppino Ferrante had been sought since December 1991 after escaping a police raid which had decimated the higher echelons of the 'Ndrangheta in Reggio, an organisation held responsible for a long series of murders which had steeped the streets of the capital and several towns in the province in blood.

A curious aspect of this brilliant police operation was the participation of agents of the USA's Federal Bureau of Investigation.

The police commissioner of Reggio Calabria has declined to comment, other than to say that he was not aware of this participation.

Our own sources, however, have confirmed that FBI agents were indeed present during the operation. Apparently this collaboration between the FBI and the DIA is linked to several murders which took place in New York on 1 November . . .

The article went on to list the names of the victims and provide background detail on the New York killings.

In the dining room of his hotel, Chief Superintendent Ferrara closed the newspaper angrily. The bastards! There wasn't even a by-line. Who the hell had written this and who were their sources?

Ferrara took his mobile phone from the inside pocket of his jacket and dialled Colonel Trimarchi's number. It was unobtainable. He glanced at his watch: 7.50. His driver would be here soon.

There had been a leak. There was no doubt about it. Well, that was only to be expected. What was unexpected, and what worried him, was the reference to the presence of the FBI. That was sure to make the investigation more complicated.

He left the hotel and stood outside the main entrance, waiting for the driver. He did not want to waste time.

Just then, a young man drove by at high speed, his car radio blasting out the song "Vita spericolata" by Vasco Rossi. Ferrara's thoughts went back to the beginning of the 1980s, and the evenings he and Petra had spent at a discotheque in Taormina.

By the first light of dawn, Diego had finally managed to free himself.

He had sawn through the ring holding the chain, which now hung from the hook on the wall.

He was exhausted. It did not even occur to him to also saw through the padlock which kept his ankles chained together. That would have been asking too much of his strength. At least he could now move, if only with short, shuffling steps. He rolled up one side of the chain and put it in the right-hand pocket of his windbreaker. Then, almost crawling across the ground, he edged towards the door. Slowly, he opened it. There was no one about, and no voices to be heard. He looked around. No ray of sunlight. Only clouds. Straight ahead, he glimpsed a mountain road disappearing round a bend.

He started moving down a slope thick with bushes and holm oaks.

Within a few minutes, he was swallowed up by the vegetation.

By the time Ferrara reached the DIA centre, Colonel Trimarchi was already in his office.

He was reading the article.

"Good morning, Colonel," he said, brusquely.

"Good morning, Chief Superintendent. I'm reading —"

"I read it at the hotel and tried to call you. What do you think, Colonel?"

At that moment Stefano Carracci arrived. They had not seen him since they had left the farmhouse.

"Good morning!" he said.

Look who's here! Trimarchi thought. *Back from the dead!*

"Hello there, Chief Superintendent Carracci," he said. "Did you see the article?"

"What article?"

"This one!" He handed him the newspaper.

"So, Colonel, what do you think?" Ferrara asked again, his tone now commanding, while Carracci started to read, his curiosity aroused.

There was tension in the air.

"It's obvious there's been a leak," Trimarchi replied, and stopped for a moment, Ferrara's eyes still on him. "I rule out the possibility that the source is in my office."

"I don't want to accuse your office, Colonel, but it's clear that not many people knew about the presence of the Americans."

"But everyone saw them during the meeting at the police station," Trimarchi replied. "We introduced them . . ."

Ferrara nodded. "I know it'll be difficult, if not impossible, to trace the source . . ."

The colonel nodded.

"This leak," Ferrara continued, "doesn't only put us in a bad light with our American colleagues, it could also damage the progress of the investigation. Whoever leaked the information could cause more damage — possibly irreparable damage — if he also finds out that Alfredo Prestipino is willing to cooperate."

"No one outside the DIA knows he's cooperating," Trimarchi replied. "It's the fact that it hasn't appeared in the press that leads me to rule out my colleagues."

Ferrara nodded. The thought occurred to him that Angela Fedeli also knew. The damage might already have been done.

"I still think you should conduct an internal inquiry," he said.

"Of course. But right now I'm going to San Piero d'Aspromonte."

Carracci had still not taken his eyes off the newspaper.

New York

The telephone on the night table rang at 3.05a.m.

Luigi Cannizzaro picked up at the fourth ring. "Yes?" he said in a sleepy voice.

"Gigi, did I wake you?" someone asked at the other end, in Italian.

"It doesn't matter. Go on!"

He had recognised one of his relatives. He was phoning from Italy.

"They told me to tell you . . . You know who . . ."
"Yes."

"That your cousin . . . is singing like a canary to . . . you understand?"

"Ah!"

"And another thing."

"Go on."

"In today's *Gazzetta*, it says there are people over here from where you are."

"Who?"

"FB —"

"I get it."

"That's all. A lot have been drunk."

"I see."

"Watch out for the gates. 'Bye."

"'Bye."

Angrily, Luigi Cannizzaro put the phone down. He knew that *a lot have been drunk* meant that a lot of people had been arrested, and that *the gates* meant prison.

Cannizzaro got out of bed. He had to leave before it was too late.

There was no time to lose.

Uh-oh. The two-note cry of a bird rose in the air.

Diego opened his eyes. His lips were numb with cold. He was lying on a carpet of grass under an oak tree that had been split by a bolt of lightning some time in the past. He had slept for several hours. He was hungry and thirsty, and his head and stomach hurt. His pale fingers were as stiff as pieces of iron. He tried unsuccessfully to get to his feet. He looked up at the clear sky and saw an eagle owl hovering between the trees. It had finished its night's hunting and, with its big wings outspread, was returning to the nest. He rubbed his eyes and followed the owl until it was just a distant dot in the sky.

He was breathing more easily now. Slowly, he set off, still crawling along the ground. Clutching at roots, he managed to move from one bush to another, from one tree to another.

After a few minutes, he came to a stream. The water, swollen by the rains, coursed between rocks and stones, pounding against the banks and gurgling amid the branches. Careful not to let himself be carried away by the flow, he crouched and drank great gulps of water. Stooping like that, his back bent, he was like a panther. He collected the water in the hollow of his hands and threw it over his face. He repeated this several times until he felt better, then set off again.

From here, he would have to climb the ridge until he reached the point where he had glimpsed the road.

The road was his only hope of salvation.

He tried several times to climb, but couldn't manage it: too much mud. He slipped, got up again, slipped again, and finally gave up. Soaking wet, he kept trying to find a way through, but continued to stumble. After a few steps, he always ended up back where he had started.

The runway was close to the sea, and the sirocco blowing from the African desert had covered it with a layer of yellow sand.

The officers of the Flight Group had taken the Augusta Bell 212 helicopter from the hangar. By the time Colonel Trimarchi and Captain Foti arrived, the propellers were already turning, slowly at first, then more rapidly, and the pilot had finished the routine checks. Everything was ready.

We really could have done without this wind, Trimarchi thought as he got out of the service car and walked towards the helicopter, followed by Foti.

The young police inspector in charge stood to attention by the door of the helicopter.

They got on board and sat down in the first seats, just behind the pilot and the navigator.

"We'll fly along the coast," the inspector said into Trimarchi's headphones. "It'll take a few minutes longer, but it makes for a more comfortable journey."

"OK."

After a few minutes, they were two hundred feet over the Ionian Sea, and some six miles out from the coast. Half an hour later, the pilot veered inland.

At the most convenient point on the banks of the river, the commander of the barracks of San Piero d'Aspromonte was waiting for them with his men.

In the meantime, Chief Superintendent Ferrara had gone to see Alfredo Prestipino.

He looked drawn, and barely smiled at Ferrara. He had not slept a wink during the night.

"Chief Superintendent, something doesn't seem right," he said. "I've been thinking about it all night."

"What doesn't seem right?"

"In all this time, I haven't had any news of my wife or my daughter. I don't see why. There's something you people aren't telling me."

"But, Signor Prestipino, it hasn't even been twenty-four hours yet!" Ferrara replied. "These things take time, with all the bureaucracy . . ."

"I know all about bureaucracy, but . . . What's bureaucracy got to do with my wife?"

"Colonel Trimarchi has gone to talk to her. He's in San Piero right now. Don't worry."

Alfredo Prestipino's face appeared to relax. "Then let's wait for him to come back with my wife and daughter. I won't carry on with my story until they're here."

"Yes, let's wait, and don't worry."

On the way out, Ferrara advised the officers guarding Prestipino not to give him any newspapers.

Especially not the *Gazzetta del Sud*.

After about an hour, Diego had managed to climb to a point that was overgrown with weeds. He grasped at the roots and hauled himself further up.

At last, he reached the road. It was like a mirage.

He sat down on the low wall bordering the road, close to a bend.

He waited, hoping a car would come.

When he heard the roar of an engine approaching, he got abruptly to his feet.

He kept his eyes peeled on the bend. After a few moments, an Alfa Romeo appeared.

He waved his arms.

More and more conspicuously.

But the driver ignored him, passing without even slowing down, without even looking at him. It was as if he hadn't seen him at all.

"Fuck!" he yelled after the car. "What am I, a ghost?" Instinctively, he touched his chest, his legs, his head.

He sat down again on the same wall. During the following half hour, other cars passed. Their drivers also ignored him.

What kind of place is this? Don't they see I have a chain on my feet? Or maybe they're ignoring me because I have a chain?

In the end, he had to resign himself.

Slowly, he set off along the road, accompanied only by the noise of the chain dragging on the ground.

New York

"Here he is! Yes, it's him."

Mary Cook had the target in her sights through the blacked-out window.

Simultaneously, she heard the muted voice of one of the fake vagrants coming through her headphones, informing her that Luigi Cannizzaro had just come out of the pink building. She watched as he slowly looked right and left, like a cautious pedestrian, then crossed the street.

It was just before five in the morning.

She was not at all surprised to see him; in fact, she had been expecting him. Even though the phone conversation had not been in standard Italian, the interpreter had guessed that it had been about something unlawful.

Luigi Cannizzaro, a tall, athletic, distinguished-looking man, was dressed as he had been when they had seen him come home the previous evening. The same long overcoat. The same hat, tilted slightly to the right. Reaching the other side of the street, he walked to a black Ford Mustang GT with a decal of a boxer dog next to the rear licence plate. He opened the door, took another look around, and got in. He started the engine and pressed his foot down hard on the accelerator.

The Feds' portable radios started to crackle.

And their cars set off in pursuit on the almost deserted streets.

At about the same time, Colonel Trimarchi was talking to Chief Superintendent Ferrara on the phone from San Piero d'Aspromonte, updating him on the situation.

The only person he had found in Angela's house was her mother, and all she had said was that her daughter and granddaughter had left early that morning. The village, as always, was blind, deaf and dumb. There was no point asking if anyone had seen them.

"What shall we do?"

Ferrara did not reply immediately.

He was thinking.

Something told him the investigation was about to become more complicated. First that leak to the press, now the disappearance of Prestipino's wife and daughter. There was a real possibility that Prestipino would refuse to cooperate any further. And that would make them look really bad in the eyes of their American colleagues.

"Chief Superintendent?" he heard down the phone line.

"Yes, Colonel, I'm still here."

"What shall we do?" Trimarchi was becoming impatient.

"We need to know what's happened to Prestipino's wife," Ferrara said. "Let's keep an eye on her mother, have her tailed, see if she takes us to her. She must still be around. She didn't make any call that suggested she was leaving. But I'll have the passenger lists checked in case she caught a flight from Reggio Calabria or Lamezia Terme."

"Good idea, Chief Superintendent. I'm with you, I don't think she's left."

"Good. Stay there for a while, Colonel, and coordinate activities on the spot. I'll see to the rest."

"OK."

They hung up.

There was a feeling that the operation had ground to a halt.

Ferrara headed for the office where the Americans were. They seemed excited. Bill Hampton had just come off the phone to New York. Bob Holley smiled, and said, a touch smugly, "Things are moving on Luigi Cannizzaro. He got a call from Italy early this morning, and has just left home."

After an interminable walk, Diego had come within sight of a built-up area.

From a shoulder at the side of the road, he was now looking down at a small group of houses below him, a few hundred yards as the crow flies. He had made it. Not much further to go, and he'd find someone to help him.

After a while, his eyes fell on a sign. It was not only brown with the sun and rust, but also riddled with holes from bullets and shotgun pellets until it was little more than a sieve. He tried to read the name that must once have been written there. All he could make out were a few letters: AST . . . Z. The other letters had completely disappeared.

He set off again, gradually nearing the first houses. Rounding a bend, he saw a detached house surrounded by a courtyard. In front of it was a sign that jutted out into the street. On it was the word CARABINIERI. He came to an abrupt halt, his heart in his mouth.

He summoned up his courage and continued walking.

He saw a tall, thin young man in an impeccable dark uniform emerge from the house and walk quickly in his direction.

"Who are you?" he heard the young man say.

"Diego Lopez. I was kidnapped and I've escaped." His voice seemed suddenly to have regained its old strength.

The young officer looked at him in astonishment. He had only been stationed in this barracks for a few months. He had heard from his colleagues that hostages of the 'Ndrangheta sometimes escaped, but he really hadn't expected to see one standing right in front of him. He took him by the arm and said, "Come with me, I'll take you to see the marshal."

CHAPTER
THIRTY

New York

Somewhere nearby, a dog was barking fiercely.

Luigi Cannizzaro took the key from the pocket of his overcoat.

The Feds had followed him to an apparently disused warehouse in East Brooklyn. The building was surrounded by fenced-off parking lots and machine shops. The closest building, its windows all broken, stood a few hundred yards away on the other side of the street. This was one of the most dangerous neighbourhoods in the borough, even if you had a gun and a badge. It swarmed with junkies, dealers and prostitutes.

Luigi was about to insert the key in the lock when he heard footsteps behind him.

He turned.

He saw a man and a woman walking in his direction, arm in arm.

Carefully, he lifted the shutter, just as the couple, who had reduced the distance, passed behind him. He was about to enter when he felt two hands seize him by the shoulders and shove him inside, while someone else grabbed him by his trouser belt. He was pushed face down on the ground. His hat fell off, uncovering his grey, back-combed hair.

"FBI, don't move!" a woman's voice cried. He obeyed, and, as he lay in that position, hands gently frisked him all over.

He was unarmed.

"What are you doing?" he managed to say, his mouth still pressed to the floor.

"You can get up now," the same voice ordered him, as other agents entered the warehouse. He twisted round and sat up on the ground. He raised his big, dark eyes and recognised the couple he had seen a minute or two earlier.

"Show me your ID," he muttered, determinedly.

The woman took a document holder from the pocket of her jeans, opened it and held it a few inches from his face: the badge was golden, an eagle with its wings open above a shield with the words US.

"Special Agent Mary Cook," the woman said. "Now get up and sit here. We have to search this place. Come on, move!"

He got to his feet. Looking her straight in the eye, he asked her to show him the search warrant.

Mary Cook took a sheet of paper from a pocket of her leather jacket. "Here it is, read it." Her eyes came to rest on the gold Rolex the man was wearing on his wrist.

SEARCH WARRANT. It was the warrant Ted Morrison had issued to Dick Moore the day before.

Luigi Cannizzaro gave the impression of reading it, but in fact he was just skimming through it. He knew that in order to issue a search warrant they needed a probable cause, as required by the Fourth Amendment of the Constitution. He said nothing. For a moment he was disoriented.

Mary Cook summoned a tall, well-built agent and ordered him, "Don't move from here." He immediately took up position beside Luigi.

The warehouse was not very large.

It looked as if it had not been used for a long time. The air was stale. There were lots of objects strewn about: scraps of furniture, wooden crates, big cartons. In one corner was a room that must once have been an office. It contained a shabby wooden desk, a table, a few worn chairs, lots of cartons, and an old pool table covered in dust.

In groups of two, the Feds peered in every nook and cranny, while Luigi Cannizzaro, sitting on the chair, kept darting glances here, there and everywhere, as if trying to follow their every movement.

Men's and women's clothes spilled out of a ramshackle closet. Old clothes, long out of fashion. They checked each item, going through the pockets, examining the hems of pants, the sleeves of jackets. Nothing.

"They're my parents' clothes," Luigi Cannizzaro said in a thin voice. "They keep everything."

No one answered him.

In the meantime Dick Moore and Lieutenant Reynolds had arrived, accompanied by other FBI agents and some men from Reynolds' squad. As Moore passed in front of Cannizzaro, he glanced at him and saw that he was scared. He walked on, followed by Reynolds. They took up position in a far corner. After less than half an hour, voices could be heard from the office.

"Let's go take a look, Lieutenant," Moore said. They walked back in that direction.

The agents' faces were glowing with delight. Especially Mary Cook's. For a moment, she even winked at Moore. From a canvas bag, which had been placed on the old wooden table, she was taking bundles of banknotes. Lots of them, all hundred-dollar bills. There must have been a good few million there.

"Look at this, Assistant Director," Mary Cook said triumphantly.

Moore and Reynolds exchanged glances. Their eyes, too, were shining with a new light. They approached the table.

"Good, boys, carry on!" Moore said.

He walked to another part of the warehouse, where other agents had opened a wooden crate and were pulling out a couple of hunting rifles and a large number of single-bullet cartridges. The kind used for hunting wild boar — or for murder. Both rifles had had their serial numbers erased.

"Keep looking, boys!" Moore said, before joining Reynolds.

Luigi Cannizzaro, his head bowed over his legs, seemed lost in thought. Reynolds went up to him. "Mr Cannizzaro, you're under arrest." Then he read him his constitutional rights. Cannizzaro did not move, did not say a word.

"Do you want anyone to be informed of your arrest?" Reynolds asked. "Do you have a lawyer?"

No reply.

"I need to know, Mr Cannizzaro!" he insisted.

After an interminable silence, he said, barely looking up, "I want to inform my parents, and my lawyer, Robert Mills."

A shiver went down Dick Moore's spine. It was him, he was sure of it. Yes, it was him, the son of a bitch!

He shook his head slightly, looked him straight in the eye and said out loud, "Nothing in life goes the way we'd like it to."

Luigi Cannizzaro twisted his nose, cheeks and mouth into a grimace. He had been recognised. Then he lowered his gaze.

Moore did not add another word.

Reynolds had heard the sentence, and seen the expression of displeasure on Cannizzaro's face, but did not ask for an explanation. Nor would he do so. Just like the Feds! Something had been kept from him during the investigation, but it didn't matter now. He went to Cannizzaro and handcuffed him.

"Take him to my car," he ordered two of his detectives.

Dick Moore was already outside, talking into his cellphone.

Bill Hampton was on the other end. He was giving him the news.

"Bill, Mary was fantastic! She showed good judgement and a lot of courage. I'm going to recommend her for promotion, you can rest assured of that."

"If she carries on like this, she'll soon be in charge of me," Bill Hampton replied, accompanying these words with a sonorous laugh.

"You make a great couple, Bill!" Moore said, not even trying to conceal the envy in his voice. Then, before hanging up, he said, "See if you can find out from Prestipino who the hit men were."

The jigsaw was now almost complete. The crucial piece had been secured.

"Signor Prestipino, your cousin Luigi has just been arrested in New York. They found a large sum of money on him, millions of dollars . . . You told us the truth."

Alfredo Prestipino opened his eyes wide. "Yes, I told you the truth, Chief Superintendent. And now you know it."

Ferrara nodded.

They were sitting face to face on identical chairs in the one-room apartment.

"Now I'd like you to tell us something else."

"What?"

"Who carried out the murders?"

"That, I don't know."

Ferrara looked at him uncertainly.

"You must believe me, Chief Superintendent. I really don't know. My cousin had a lot of young guys working for him. They called him uncle. But I can tell you one thing . . ." He paused.

"Go on."

"I know for certain that on the day of the murders, my cousin waited for them in a yellow cab stolen by one of his most trusted men. Then they drove to Brooklyn . . ."

"Where?"

"I don't know where, but I can tell you they were killed and their bodies dumped in the ocean. You'll never find them."

"Who were they?"

"I didn't know them, but you can find out their names by looking into the disappearances of young men in Brooklyn in the days just after the murders, or even in the hours just after the murders."

"Are you absolutely sure of this?"

"One hundred per cent."

"I believe you."

"But you haven't kept your side of the bargain," Prestipino said.

"Why do you say that?"

"Because it's true. I'm still here and I haven't heard anything about my wife and daughter. Chief Superintendent Ferrara, I want to know the truth. What did my wife say?"

Ferrara was silent for a moment or two. Finally, he decided to put his cards on the table. There was no point in prevaricating, now that they'd had confirmation of Prestipino's statements. He told him about Captain Foti's conversation with his wife, and about the fact that they had no idea where his wife and daughter were.

"We're looking for them. We've informed the transport police, but their names aren't on any passenger list. Colonel Trimarchi has been in San Piero since this morning."

Prestipino had leapt to his feet with a wild look in his eyes. "Why didn't you tell me this before?"

"We were waiting, hoping we'd trace them. Please sit down, don't get too excited."

"No, Chief Superintendent. If my wife said no, it's no. I know her. She's like her brother Rocco. The same character. Strong. Proud. Determined."

"Do you have any idea where she may have gone?"

Alfredo Prestipino started pacing up and down the room, waving his hands, and muttering words Ferrara found incomprehensible. Then, suddenly, he calmed down and went back to his seat. "It's a long story, Chief Superintendent."

"Go on," Ferrara said, without taking his eyes off him. "We have time."

"No. Unfortunately we don't have any more time."

"What do you mean?"

"Don Ciccio Puglisi must have found out about my cooperating with you," he said, with anger in his eyes. "My wife and daughter are in danger. Or at least, my daughter is definitely in danger. We have to act quickly."

"Then tell me, Prestipino, and we *will* act quickly."

"The convent at the shrine of the Madonna of Aspromonte. That's where you have to go."

"Why there?" Ferrara asked, intrigued.

"Because that's where they must have gone, or rather, where they must have been taken."

"What makes you think that?"

"That's Don Ciccio's secret kingdom. It's where the 'Ndrangheta holds its councils. They must be deciding what to do next. Maybe they'll try to blackmail me by keeping my daughter as hostage. They could also kill her, if we don't hurry up . . . We have to go right now."

"Tell me one thing. Did Francesco Puglisi have anything to do with this business?"

"Don Ciccio was everything, Chief Superintendent. He was the one behind the murders. Nothing happens without his say-so. Now, let's go to the convent, before it's too late. Believe me, my daughter's in danger!" He leapt to his feet again.

"Calm down. Why didn't you tell us about Don Ciccio before?"

"I would have, once my wife and daughter were safe here with me. You have to understand. But let's not waste any more time now, let's go!"

"You can't come."

"Take me with you, I know the place, and we have to be quick!"

Now the picture was even clearer.

Every piece was fitting into place. At last!

The murders in Manhattan had been ordered by Don Ciccio Puglisi to punish Rocco Fedeli, who had betrayed the secret laws of the 'Ndrangheta.

But perhaps that wasn't the only motive.

Perhaps the old boss, the old patriarch, who still believed in tradition, had decided to kill two birds with one stone.

His executive arm, Luigi Cannizzaro, had done everything he could to point the investigators towards the 'ndrina of Antonio Russo, the up and coming man, who wasn't liked but had been tolerated for the sake of peace.

By doing what they'd done, they had hoped to put an end to the whole cocaine business, which had fucked everything up.

A double revenge by a master tactician!

An hour later, Ferrara was on board a police helicopter. Next to him, Alfredo Prestipino. Behind them, the NOCS commander and two of his officers.

Another helicopter, carrying Carracci, Bruni and officers from the *Squadra Mobile* had preceded them. They would meet up with Colonel Trimarchi and set off for the convent in off-road vehicles.

Him, too! Captain Foti thought when he saw Stefano Carracci emerge from the helicopter.

They were on the banks of the river, their point of rendezvous, where the helicopter deposited them after raising clouds of dust and stirring the nearby cane thicket.

Ferrara was talking to Trimarchi on his mobile phone. "Colonel, we'll stay on the opposite slope to avoid being seen and the noise of the helicopter being heard."

"OK," Trimarchi replied. "I'll let you know when we're about to surround the place, then you can come closer."

"Great! I'll wait to hear from you."

The off-road vehicles crossed the little bridge over the river in single file and proceeded along the uneven, potholed dirt road that wound up into the mountains. They did not pass any other vehicle, or any pedestrians. It seemed like no man's land, but the officers knew this was 'Ndrangheta territory.

They'll be watching us even though we can't see them, Foti thought, exchanging glances with the colonel.

Then, just as the road was starting to descend, winding ever more hazardously, Trimarchi heard Ferrara's voice in his headphones.

"Colonel?"

"I'm listening."

"We're in position."

"Good. We'll soon be in view of the target. From there, we'll go on foot."

"Fine. Let me know when you've surrounded it. We'll land nearby."

"OK. There's no wind and the sky's clear. There shouldn't be any problems."

Less than five minutes later, the off-road vehicles came to a halt and the officers got out. Among them was Carracci.

"From here on, we walk," Trimarchi said, "using the vegetation as camouflage." He turned to Foti. "Captain, I want you to take command."

At this point, Stefano Carracci stepped forward in his combat fatigues. "I'm coming, too. I'll take command."

They all turned to look at him.

He's crazy, Foti thought, glancing at the colonel. *It'll be suicide.*

"Are you sure, Chief Superintendent?" Trimarchi said. "This is difficult terrain."

"I'm trained, Colonel."

And he placed himself at the head of the group.

Trimarchi shook his head, then said, "I'll stay here with the vehicles. As soon as you radio that you're in position, we'll join you."

They got moving, and soon disappeared into the vegetation of a deep precipice.

In all, there were eighteen men.

Just over half an hour later, Carracci's breathless voice came over the colonel's headphones.

"We're here."

The colonel ordered the drivers to set off, then gave the go-ahead to the helicopters — there was another one now, with the Americans on board. Within a few minutes, they were hovering over the area around the convent, the heart of Aspromonte. The helicopter with the Americans stayed in the air, flying low to get a view through the trees, while the other slowly began to descend. It flew in a circle and touched down about a hundred yards from the target.

"Let's go," Ferrara said as soon as the door opened. He had been to this place many times in the 1980s. From a distance, it looked exactly the same as it had then, as if time had stood still. He felt a knot in his stomach. They got out and set off. The loud noise of the propellers accompanied them for a few more minutes. In the meantime, the other teams had surrounded the small group of houses in the old village and were keeping it under observation. Everything looked as if it had long been abandoned. There was no one about. When Ferrara and the others were twenty or thirty yards away, they heard a volley of rifle shots, followed immediately by a cry: "Police! Stop!"

"I'm the warden of the shrine!" another voice cried in reply.

They walked in the direction it had come from and saw a young man with his arms up in the air.

"I'm the warden!" the man was still yelling.

Alfredo Prestipino recognised him immediately. "He's a guard!" he said. "There must be others inside. My wife and daughter have to be here."

"Where should we go?"

"To the cellars of the convent. Right now."

"You wait here."

"Let me come with you."

"No, it may be risky," Ferrara said, and left a couple of police officers with him as protection. Then he got moving, followed by the NOCS men and the other officers, and entered the courtyard. Soon afterwards, he was joined by the colonel. Just then, they heard more rifle shots, followed by a burst of machine-gun fire.

A real shootout.

CHAPTER
THIRTY-ONE

The convent behind the shrine seemed to have been recently restored. Or rather, it looked as though work was still in progress.

It was on two floors. On each of them, an iron railing allowed visitors to look into the inner courtyard, at the centre of which was a stone well, its pulley now rusted. Rooms lined the high-ceilinged corridors. The officers crossed the courtyard and descended into the cellars. They did not have to break down any doors: all the doors lay on the ground in a corner.

"Police!" the NOCS commander cried. "Come out with your hands in the air!"

Ferrara joined him.

In a narrow room, sitting on small stools, four vague figures could be made out in the dim light. None of them reacted in any way. The officers shone their torches at them, revealing three men, all of a certain age, and a woman. The men, their faces furrowed with deep lines, could well be local shepherds. The woman, on the other hand, was well groomed and did not look at all local. She had a pair of knee-length rubber boots on her feet and a black woollen cloak round her shoulders. None of the figures moved.

"Who are you?" Ferrara asked, hand tight on his gun.

"We're friends." The answer had come from the man who looked the oldest. He was staring at Ferrara, thinking, *Look who's back, the Fox of Aspromonte!*

"Friends of who?"

"Just friends," the man replied, with a slight sneer on his face. "Four friends."

"Let's see your papers."

The other two men took their identity cards from their wallets and handed them over.

"What about you?" Ferrara asked the older man and the woman.

The man answered first. He had a battered face and an unkempt beard. "I left mine at home."

"Where do you live?"

"San Piero."

"What's your name?"

"Francesco Puglisi."

"What about you?" Ferrara asked, turning to the woman.

"I don't have any papers."

Her features were hard, her eyes weary, her attitude contemptuous.

At that moment they heard voices coming from the far end of the cellar. Ferrara walked in that direction, followed by a few officers. In a small room, the NOCS men had discovered a man and a girl. The girl was sitting at a small wooden table with a loaf of corn bread, a piece of Soprassata sausage and a few pieces of cheese on it. The man, who was very young, was standing next to her.

"Are you Alfredo Prestipino's daughter?" Ferrara asked.

She stared at him, a faraway look in her eyes. After a moment or two, she nodded.

Ferrara did not ask her any more questions.

He moved a couple of yards away, radioed the two officers who had stayed with Prestipino and gave them directions. "I'll expect you in a few minutes!"

Before long, he heard footsteps approaching.

It was Alfredo Prestipino, between the two officers. As soon as his daughter saw him she stood up and ran to his arms.

"Daddy!" she said, in tears, hugging him.

"Maria," he replied, in a cracked voice. There was a lump in his throat.

"Daddy, let's go back to New York. I don't want to stay here any more."

"Yes, Maria. We'll go soon." Two big tears began running down his cheeks.

Moved, Ferrara walked back to the other room.

"You're Alfredo Prestipino's wife," he said to the woman.

"I am Angela Fedeli."

"Your husband's through there. Come, signora."

She did not reply immediately, but stared at Ferrara. He in turn stood looking at her, as if studying her.

"Signora, your husband's here!" he repeated.

"He *was* my husband," she replied, without taking her eyes off him, almost as if in defiance. "He's not my husband any more. My name is Fedeli."

370

"What do you mean?"

"To me he's dead. I am a Fedeli. Now tell me, are you in charge here?"

"I'm one of the people in charge."

"Then let me go home. My daughter can do what she wants. She's already come of age. May the Madonna bless her."

"We have some formalities to get through first."

"Yes, Angela, they have to do their duty," Don Ciccio Puglisi interjected, his voice still hoarse.

"Then be quick about it," she replied, coldly and without hesitation.

The little group followed the police officers.

Angela Fedeli took Don Ciccio by the arm and walked beside him in silence.

She had made her choice: she would remain loyal to the secret code of the 'Ndrangheta. She had a duty to redeem the honour of her own family, the honour that her brother Rocco had offended. Her future would now be here, in San Piero d'Aspromonte, together with her mother and people who thought just like her.

Alfredo Prestipino walked to the helicopter, still hugging his daughter, the person who meant most to him in the world.

"Chief Superintendent Ferrara, come here!"

The head of the *Squadra Mobile*, Lorenzo Bruni, was waving his arms, urging him to join him at the edge of a thick wood just after the last houses in the village.

Ferrara walked quickly towards him. As he approached, he saw two men sitting on the ground, handcuffed. One of them had blood on the sleeve of his jacket. The police officers were holding two rifles.

"They fired at us with these," one of the officers said, showing the weapons. "The others escaped into the woods and something unfortunate happened."

Ferrara's expression changed. Bruni was still calling to him.

"Chief Superintendent, come here!"

"What is it, Bruni?" Ferrara asked as he came level.

"Follow me . . . Carracci . . ."

"What?"

"Carracci's been hit."

"Who did it?"

"I don't know. They shot at us as they were escaping into the wood."

"Have they been caught?"

"My men are chasing them."

They walked along the path through the wood for about a dozen yards.

Stefano Carracci was lying on the grass. Blood was gushing from the jacket of his fatigues, there was blood in his fair hair and little bubbles of blood emerged from his mouth. Ferrara bent over him and unbuttoned his jacket. His shirt was riddled with holes and covered in blood.

Stefano Carracci was already dead. He had been hit in the chest with lethal shotgun fire.

Ferrara closed the eyelids and made the sign of the cross.

His eyes fell on a piece of paper jutting out of one pocket. He took it and opened it. At the top of the page, in the middle, were the hastily scribbled words *Cloned satellite phone*. There followed a list of telephone numbers. Ferrara read it. Like a magnet, his eyes were drawn to the last number on the list. He knew it well. It was a number in Rome. A confidential number.

Was this Antonio Russo's "connection"? For a long while, Ferrara did not move. It was as if he was paralysed. This was a whole new element in the case, one he would never ever have imagined, and which he could certainly have done without.

New York

That evening, when Dick Moore returned home, he found a surprise waiting for him.

The door was not locked, as he had left it in the morning. The lights were on in the hall. Instinctively he put his hand on the grip of his 9mm Glock and slowly walked towards the living room, from which a dim light was filtering. He listened. There was no sound. He took his pistol from its holster and entered cautiously. His eyes met Jenny's. She was lying on the couch with a glass in her hand, looking in his direction. She'd been waiting for him for several hours. As soon as she saw him, she stood up, went to him and put her arms around his neck. It was a long, warm, patient embrace.

"I missed you so much," he whispered over and over in her ear as he hugged her.

"I missed you, too, Dick . . ." Her eyes were shining with a new light. "Do you still love me?"

He looked at her for what seemed an endless moment. Then he smiled. "I love you more than ever," he said.

"So do I. I'm sorry for what I've done."

"You don't have to apologise, Jenny. I understood. I understood and I promise I won't make the same mistakes again." He was about to take her by the hand when he heard an unmistakable whimper. Sam, who had run in from another room, was leaping about at their feet, trying to attract his master's attention.

That evening was a special evening for Lieutenant Reynolds, too. He and Linda went out to dinner to celebrate the long-awaited transfer, which had finally been confirmed a few hours earlier. He would change location and work more regular hours — a fact much appreciated by Linda, who had started smiling again.

Epilogue

Chief Superintendent Ferrara and his wife Petra had been in New York for a week. He had been invited by the FBI, and Petra, as promised, had taken a break from her work. At 26 Federal Plaza, a solemn ceremony was held in his honour and that of Colonel Trimarchi, who was also a guest of the FBI. Assistant Director Moore awarded both Italians medals. Then, in a brief speech, he thanked the Italian police forces for their cooperation, without which they would not have been able to solve the Madison homicides. That wasn't all. Without their help, they would not have been able to break up a dangerous 'Ndrangheta offshoot before it had had a chance to take root in New York. He summarised the results of the investigation and gave the names of the men who had actually carried out the murders: three members of Harry Baker's gang, who had disappeared on 2 November 2003. Their bodies would never be found. They were somewhere at the bottom of the ocean.

In conclusion, he underlined the importance of cooperation. "In a world in which even the Mafia has become globalised, the best weapon at our disposal in the battle against this terrible cancer is synergy between police forces around the world. We can only win this battle by working together, as we did in this case, where the crucial clues were identified and collected simultaneously at a distance of thousands and thousands of miles." Looking in turn at Ferrara and Trimarchi, he said, "Once again, thank you to the police forces of Italy."

As everyone was joining in the toast, Petra went up to Mrs Moore and Mrs Reynolds. Moved by the welcome she and Michele had received, she was determined to extract promises from them that they would come to Italy. "We're waiting for you in Florence." The two women smiled and said, "We'll be there!"

On leaving the building, the Italians were approached by a large group of reporters and photographers. One of the reporters managed to shake hands with Ferrara and murmur, "Thank you, thank you very much. *Grazie, Italia.*" It was David Powell of the *New York Times*.

At 8p.m. that evening, Chief Superintendent Ferrara and his wife Petra had dinner in the restaurant of the Hudson Hotel on West 58th Street, where the FBI had reserved a room for them. Before dinner, they had visited the delightful Sky Terrace on the fifteenth floor. The thirty-foot-high trees, ivy-covered walls and bright, fragrant flowers had impressed them so much that they had decided to spend a good part of their stay right there. What made the hotel even better was the fact that they were not far from the theatre district, Times Square, Columbus Circle and Central Park: to all intents and purposes, the heart of Manhattan, and its most beautiful area.

That evening Petra had put on a black dress and gathered her hair in a bun. She was wearing a pair of antique earrings inherited from her grandmother, which she put on only on special occasions. Such as now. And she had a single ring on her finger, a gold ring set with a ruby surrounded by diamonds, her husband's first gift to her.

They had ordered a bottle of Livio Felluga white wine, and now the waiter was pouring it. He saw them look into each other's eyes for a few silent moments. He smiled at them and walked away. They raised their glasses in a toast. Then she leaned across and gave him a passionate kiss.

"I'd really like to stay here, *Schatzi*," she whispered. She had the same radiant expression on her face she always used to have.

"So would I, darling," he replied, returning her smile. "But only for a week, no more."

She smiled again and drank another sip of wine. Then raising her glass, she asked, "What shall we toast to? Love?"

"Yes, darling, our love," he replied. They drained their glasses in one go, and then burst out laughing. When they had stopped, Ferrara said, "Now let's go. *The Phantom of the Opera* awaits us at the Majestic."

"Yes, let's go!"

And they left the hotel.

With their arms round each other, like young lovers.

Author's Note

Those readers tempted to start looking on maps for the villages of San Piero d'Aspromonte and Castellanza should be warned that they would only be wasting their time. These villages do not exist and are merely figments of my imagination. It may be that the inhabitants of villages of Aspromonte in the province of Reggio Calabria may see some resemblance to real places. But I want to assure them that I have used them in a purely fictional way, transposing episodes from my professional life.

The laws of the 'Ndrangheta, on the other hand, are all too real, as has been shown several times, thanks to the work and professionalism of the police forces, not only of Italy, but of other countries, too.

For those interested in going further into this matter, let me quote a few examples.

The first codes of rules were found in Nicastro in 1888 and Seminara in 1896.

During the 1920s, the Carabinieri confiscated a code from a member of the 'ndrina of San Luca, while in the 1960s, it was again the Carabinieri who discovered an example in the house of an 'Ndranghetista in San

Giorgio Morgeto. Two more were found by the police during operations in Gioia Tauro and Sant'Eufemia d'Aspromonte.

In Toronto in 1971, the Canadian police confiscated yet another from the house of a man from Siderno. It comprised twenty-seven pages, covered in almost incomprehensible handwriting.

The most recent finds date from the end of the 1980s and the beginning of the 1990s and were made in the houses of 'Ndranghetistas in Reggio Calabria, Rosarno and Lamezia Terme.

Other rules have been passed on to investigators by 'Ndranghetistas who have left the organisation and who, whether out of hatred for their enemies or for other reasons, have decided to spill the beans about its code.

Also available in ISIS Large Print:

Dark Country

Bronwyn Parry

For 18 years most people in the small town of Dungirri have considered Morgan "Gil" Gillespie a murderer, so he expects no welcome on his return. What he doesn't expect is the discovery of a woman's body in the boot of his car.

Wearied by too many deaths and doubting her own skills, local police sergeant Kris Matthews isn't sure whether Gil is a decent man, wronged by life, or a brutal criminal. But she does know that he is not guilty of this murder — because she is his alibi . . .

Between organised crime, police corruption, and the hatred of a town, Gil has nowhere to hide. He needs to work out who's behind the murder before his enemies realise that the one thing more punishing than putting him back in prison would be to harm the few people he cares about.

ISBN 978-0-7531-8728-9 (hb)
ISBN 978-0-7531-8729-6 (pb)

The Bricklayer

Noah Boyd

Steve Vail is a maverick: a trained killer and former agent who despises authority and who never met a rule he didn't break. These days he's working as a bricklayer. Now Deputy Director Kate Bannon of the FBI desperately wants his help.

Because someone is killing their operatives — in complex, subtle, twisted ways — and the body count is rising fast. Someone holds a fatal grudge against the agency: someone who knows how it works, and wants bloody revenge. And it might be an inside job.

To stem the tide of murders, Vail must re-enter a world he hoped he left behind long ago — his own past . . .

ISBN 978-0-7531-8726-5 (hb)
ISBN 978-0-7531-8727-2 (pb)

Accused

Mark Gimenez

"Scott, it's Rebecca. I need you." After years of silence, Texan lawyer Scott Fenney receives a devastating phonecall from his ex-wife. She has been accused of murdering her boyfriend, Trey — the man she left Scott for — and is being held in a police cell. Now she is begging Scott to defend her. Scott is used to high-stakes cases, but this one is bigger than anything he has handled before. If Rebecca is found guilty, under Texan law she will be sentenced to death. He will have her blood on his hands. As he prepares to take the stand in the most dramatic courtroom appearance of his life, Scott is forced to question everything he believes to get to the truth and to save the life of the ex-wife he still loves . . .

ISBN 978-0-7531-8670-1 (hb)
ISBN 978-0-7531-8671-8 (pb)

Nemesis of the Dead

Frances Lloyd

Ten holidaymakers are bound for Katastrophos, a tiny Greek island steeped in superstition and ancient myth. Ten people whose lives are about to change forever, because one of them is planning a ruthless murder. Detective Inspector Jack Dawes of the Murder Squad is working undercover to prevent it, and takes his wife, Corrie, to the island, ostensibly on a belated honeymoon.

Mayhem ensues when a storm destroys the island's primitive communications, cutting it off from civilisation. This, and a bizarre island ritual, provide the murderer with a perfect opportunity — but fate intervenes.

Finally, time runs out and a deadly battle of wits develops between policeman and killer. It is nemesis, dark-faced goddess of justice, who ends it with her powerful spirit of vengeance and retribution. Of the ten who arrive on Katastrophos, not all will return home . . .

ISBN 978-0-7531-8630-5 (hb)
ISBN 978-0-7531-8631-2 (pb)